BLOOD LUST!

Conan ducked with the same pantherish litheness
and speed he had exhibited before. And, still
crouching, he took a step towards his attacker.
Bending forward over that extended left leg, he
brought his own sword arcing over his head.

Conan's arm and blade did not, however, descend.
His fist brushed the top of his black-maned head
and his blade swept out horizontally from his
brow. The long sword slammed into the
Zamorian's mouth. A woman shrieked and the
ruby-wearing young noblewoman stared with eyes
gone bird-bright. Her bosom heaved and the tip
of her tongue came out to wet pink-tinted lips . . .

Also in the CONAN series published by Sphere Books:

CONAN THE ADVENTURER
CONAN THE WARRIOR
CONAN
CONAN THE CONQUEROR
CONAN THE FREEBOOTER
CONAN OF CIMMERIA
CONAN THE USURPER
CONAN THE WANDERER
CONAN THE AVENGER
CONAN THE BUCCANEER
CONAN OF THE ISLES
CONAN OF AQUILONIA
CONAN THE SWORDSMAN
CONAN THE LIBERATOR
CONAN: THE SWORD OF SKELOS
CONAN THE MERCENARY
CONAN THE BARBARIAN

Conan the Mercenary

ANDREW J. OFFUTT

incorporating
Conan and the Sorcerer

SPHERE BOOKS LIMITED
30-32 Gray's Inn Road, London WC1X 8JL

Conan the Mercenary
First published in Great Britain by Sphere Books Ltd, 1980
Copyright © Conan Properties, Inc. 1980
Reprinted 1981, 1982

Conan and the Sorcerer
First published in Great Britain by Sunridge Press, 1978
First published by Sphere Books Ltd, 1980
Copyright © Conan Properties Inc. 1978

TRADE
MARK

Set in Linotype Period

Printed in Great Britain by
William Collins Sons & Co. Ltd
Glasgow

CONTENTS

CHAPTER 1

The Plotters

Torches flared murkily on the revels in the Maul, where the thieves of the East held carnival by night. Elsewhere in Arenjun of Zamora, flames flickered almost daintily above fine lamps filled with scented oil. In the Maul, noise ruled, nor was it all of pleasant conversation.

Elsewhere in the City of Thieves, folk were more quiet spoken, and alleys that were less muddy were a little safer. The dancing golden light of fine oil lamps struck fire from the gems winking on the fingers of cool-eyed nobles with tilted chins. It brought soft gleams from the pearls sewn on the tunic-bosoms of merchants aspiring to their ranks. Lamp-glims coaxed green flashes from the emeralds about the fat neck of a lord's useless wife and blood-hued glints from her sneering daughter's rubies and garnets and carnelians. The whisper of good silk accompanied the movements of well-fed bodies.

In the low, greasy-beamed dens of the thief-clotted Maul, rascals gathered.

Here were cutpurses with ferretish faces, kidnappers with hooded, appraising eyes, swift-fingered thieves, restless doers of death, ever alert. Swaggering bravoes strutted their harlots with strident voices and unsubtle bushes of hair. Blue lace agates or badly-cut bits of rose quartz were their best gems, along with flashing mica and bits of glass. One bosomy Nemedian in the company of a balding Kothian mercenary – between employers – wore a piece of refulgent aventurine that covered her finger from knuckle to mid-joint. Supposedly of old Atlantis these stones, where the hexagonal pillar-mounted green crystals were said to have given the long-sunken land its power.

Not here; not in the Maul.

In the Maul of the Thieves' City of Arenjun of Zamora, power rested only in the sheaths and scabbards of the strong and swift.

7

Someone groaned from within the brooding dark maw of an alley. No one took note, or seemed to. Day's light would show whether the moan came from the dying or the bait of a trap.

One denizen of that dark clutch of muddy alleys and crumbling, pitted walls was missing this night, and was asked after in more than one rat-hole of a lowlife den. He was up-town this night, for his last three endeavours had brought him success.

The ruby-and-moonstone ear-rings plucked through an open window from a tabouret beside their sleeping owner's bed . . . these had bought him a good dagger a foot and a half in length, with its garnet-mounted sheath – and had paid his debts in two of the dives deep in the cess-pool called the Maul. While a councilman's spouse lay with her youthful lover in an alcove not ten paces away, her fine pearl-sewn collar, along with a goblet of solid gold (slightly mixed with tin, the fence had pointed out), had flitted out the window in a bronzed hand considerably larger than those of most burglars. These had brought the deft, cat-footed thief a good cloak worked with gold thread – sparsely worked, true – and a silken tunic whose blue caught the rather sullen glint of his eyes – as well as new credit in a third hole featuring thin ale and dreggy, watered wine. Two narrow bands of cloth-of-gold writhed about its neck and sleeves, which were tight over his heavy upper arms.

Strangely, his third success was a commission, and accomplished a good deed. For purloining a pair of carelessly-bestowed emerald studs and an indiscreet letter and returning them to their giver, he received no less than three pieces of gold and seventeen of silver. An odd number, admittedly. Offered two plus ten, he had demanded five plus five-and-twenty, and had settled with his employer in the time-honoured manner: in the middle. This last endeavour was enough to make a lad consider semi-honest employment. It was also enough to buy him a night out of the Maul, an occasion he hoped would lead to more and better things. Well cloaked and silk-tunicked, he strolled up-town.

Now the cloak was carefully folded and draped over the stool on which he sat before an intimately smallish trestle-board. A bit out of place, he nevertheless sat this night

8

among the noble and the wealthy – for they were not always the same. He plied an attractive young woman with more earnestness than expertise. Young she was indeed, at nineteen – and yet older than he, despite his hugeness of frame. His continued wearing of a sword had been questioned. 'Bodyguard,' he had said. 'My master will be along shortly. I'll just keep it.' And none had said him nay, even here in the Shadiz Inn where gathered none but the well-born or well-moneyed.

The attractive young woman said, 'They certainly grow men big, up in Symria.'

'Cimmeria,' he corrected.

He pressed forward towards her pretty face, leaning across the low round board in the up-town inn surrounded by unadmitted betters. When he nodded, his blue eyes flashed like sapphires.

'When I was a mere fifteen – oh, long ago,' he said, 'I was six feet in height and weighed twenty pounds less than two hundred. I was part of the howling horde of blood-mad northmen that swept down on Aquilonia's arrogant outpost of Venarium. We put those Aquilonians in their place – with sword and torch!'

Oh, 'long ago', is it, she thought; *and you not yet eighteen or I'm eighty!*

For she knew men and gazed cooly on him from knowledge, this girl of nineteen who had been a woman at fourteen and was plucked from the streets at sixteen by a fat merchant of eight-and-forty. She and her brass-dyed hair and gilded brass breastplates had slipped a bit since then, economically. At least her current lover was younger, with prospects, and with his virility still on him. Too bad, really, that he'd be along directly. This giant hill-lad with the square-cut black mop over his broad forehead and smouldering eyes like the blue lace agates dangling from her ears ... he was younger still, and he positively exuded virility.

Upper arms big as my thighs, only bulgy with muscle!

A boy though, and inexperienced, city-naïf, and surely a liar. And surely a thief, the street-wise woman thought. For how else in the City of Thieves could a foreigner with such an accent come by the silver he'd shown their aproned host?

9

Well . . . until her Kagul came, this northish youth provided good wine and amusement and constant tingly thrills, for he *was* virile. Though such things were behind and beneath her, Kiliya could not help contemplate, too, the separation of this boy from his coin . . . Within her, a match of wrestling took place.

'Fifteen! Oh, Conan! I am never sure whether you're serious or just trying to turn a poor girl's head with your lurid tales!'

He blinked, and dungeon questioners of the drunkard king could have drowned in the blue innocence of his eyes. 'I do not lie, Kiliya.'

They were youths together. 'Oh!' She gave him a round-eyed stare from twinkling brown eyes set in the pale flesh of Hybori ancestry mixed with the peoples they'd conquered. 'Never?'

'Hardly ever,' he said, and they laughed together. He moved his stool nearer hers. Under the board, his hand covered her thigh in every direction, and radiated heat.

She swallowed. 'What do you *do*, Conan, you big hillman? Oh – do you think we might have just a little more? Someone has sucked my cup all dry!' And she showed him her empty flagon.

Without taking his eyes off hers, he hoisted his arm straight up. He'd seen that wealthy importer signal thus, over there in the room's centre where he sat with a slimy-looking man and three women, one so hideous she must be the merchant's wife.

'More wine here, and none of that cheap Ghazan grape-juice!' the Cimmerian said loudly, without looking from his companion. In a lower voice he said, 'I'm . . . bodyguard, to a wealthy lord. He is grateful, as you can see.'

'Oh, yes. But . . . you mean you can really *use* that sword, with its positively ancient-looking handle?'

'Hilt.' He bent his left elbow in order to pat the sword girded on that same hip, a yard-long blade in a sheath of worn, nubby leather. 'Aye,' he told her. 'I can use it, Kiliya. I have. Its blade has been dyed nigh as red as those garnets there between your breasts.'

'Rubies,' she corrected.

He but smiled. It was a knowing grin, for they were

garnets, and she knew he knew it. Bodyguard indeed! The huge lad with his unlined face so tanned was a thief, sure. And her thigh sweated under his hand, and she didn't mind.

'Conan . . .'

'Yes.'

She was still working at the making of a decision: 'Every night some men of the City Watch come here. I think we shouldn't be here when they do – do you?'

His features arranged themselves into their version of an expression of sweet innocence, while he gestured with a huge bronzed hand. 'Why not? Are we not solid citizens of solid, upstanding Arenjun?'

'One of us,' Kiliya said, 'is not.'

He affected to look shocked, and bent forward. 'Kiliya! What is your evil secret? Surely you're not the one responsible for the fall of that big old Tower of the Elephant I've heard about?'

'I think my secret is that I am sipping wine and having my thigh fondled by a blue-eyed, huge-shouldered, sword-wearing, Symrian . . . thief.'

'Cimmerian,' he said equably. Then, 'I? A thief? Here? Hoho, my dear girl . . . thieves hide in the Maul, and there skulk like jackals.'

'I think,' she began, 'that some –'

'*Kiliya!* Whatever is my girl doing sitting with that *boy*? Ho sirrah – where is your other hand?'

Without removing the hand in question, from under the low board, Conan stiffened and turned to look over his shoulder. He gazed amid silence. Even in this section of Arenjun, an inn fell quiet when five men of the City Watch entered and their leader called out so – and particularly to a young sword-wearer who looked big enough to take on Hyperborean bears.

The Cimmerian remained silent, too. He but stared at the corseleted, helmeted man with the fancy dragon-headed hilt rising above his sword sheath and the swaggerish black moustachioes beneath his long nose. Conan was aware of his surroundings. He was not in the Maul, he was in the Shadiz Inn, up-town. He was surely in the presence of a sophisticated lady only pretending to be a bit less. Conan would not shout. He sat still, waiting, staring at the man who moved across the room towards him. All conversations had ceased; all gazes followed the progress among stools and boards of the Zamorian watch-sergeant, or were fixed on the big youth he approached.

Kiliya moved her leg; Conan's hand unerringly followed. Crom was his god; any who knew so many as one Cimmerian knew that Crom was surely another name for stubbornness.

Tall, lean, lithe, not ugly though blade-marked on one cheek, the watchman stood over the seated man in the gold-purfled blue tunic.

'I would not shout across the room to you, soldier,' Conan said quietly. 'It is my upbringing . . . I am no boy, and all three of us know where my hand is. I'd ask you to join us for a flagon, but we were just discussing leaving.'

'You will leave alone, you with your barbar accent, and that swiftly! If you would depart with both hands, put them in sight.'

No product of dissembling civilisation, the Cimmerian didn't bother affecting to look shocked. His eyes suddenly bore no resemblance to sapphires or pretty blue agates. They smouldered, like an impossible combination of ice and volcanic heat.

'I break no law, watchman. You are not hired to bully honest citizens.'

'I'm no watchman now, fellow. I went off duty a short candle ago. Just now I am an angry man standing over a boy whose paw is on the leg of *my* woman.'

The Shadiz had gone silent, and remained so. The wealthy and the noble sat very still, and stared. Such an encounter had no place in this inn, in their civilised lives. A Corinthian mercer in a floriated robe glanced over as if to measure his distance from the doorway. Four watchmen clogged it, watching their sergeant.

'Conan . . .'

At Kiliya's voice Conan turned back to face her. He said, 'Do tell this troublesome mouth that –'

He broke off at the feel of the man's hand on his shoulder. With an instinctive marking of the location of the thumb, Conan knew it was the left hand. Too, he knew what the right was doing. He heard the slither of metal against leather. The troublesome mouth was easing out his sword! Conan released Kiliya's leg while he pivoted on his stool. His folded cloak sliding easily under him, he swung on his hams while his legs swung up and out. At right angles to his torso they slammed into the watchman's left leg just above the greave-strap. There was more force than the Zamorian could have believed possible in that short swing – and more force than he could bear. With an inhalated 'Ah!' he went sidewise and down.

Stools scraped and a woman squeaked. A board slid and rattled on its trestle as a fat thigh moved swiftly. Someone muttered the name of holy Mitra. Conan meanwhile continued to pivot on his buttocks. His sandal-shod foot descended to slam on to the fallen guardsman's hip. The man groaned aloud.

'Kagul!' Kiliya cried out, pouncing up. 'You stupid barbarian *boy*! You've hurt Kagul!'

She hurried to kneel beside the fallen watch-sergeant. He had not completed his draw, having fallen on his sword-arm. Instead, he rubbed his thigh. Conan blinked and half-turned to stare at the young woman he had been plying with wine and strong looks and brags. But he'd thought . . .

His face went ugly. Then the gaze of the kneeling girl leapt up and past him, and he lunged sidewise. That way the sword in the fist of one of Kagul's men chopped into the tabletop, instead of the Cimmerian's shoulder. Wine flagons and sweetmeats danced. Voices rose all about and stools scraped; a blow had been struck in the Shadiz Inn! Too, but for the hardly believable pantherine swiftness with which the hillman moved his bulk, the sword would have removed most of his shoulder.

The surprised watchman took hold of his hilt with both hands to free his blade of the oaken board. He had every reason to believe that his intended victim was more surprised than he. He was wrong.

A bronzed fist came down like a sledge-hammer. The blow broke the Zamorian's forearm amid such pain that he swallowed his scream along with his tongue and had fainted before he hit the floor.

'Take him!' another of Kagul's men called.

13

More stools and trestle-legs scraped as other guests began making serious and assiduous efforts to be elsewhere. A *khilat*ed easterner stared. The Corinthian merchant departed the inn with such swiftness that his punk had to run to catch up.

'Damned barbarian,' a retired general grunted. 'Take him!'

'Take him!' Kagul snarled, rising with Kiliya's aid.

Kiliya, however, screeched: 'KILL him!'

That last did it. Rude watchmen and treacherous city-girls who turned out to be more bloodthirsty than the women of the Vanir were more than enough. The hill-lad's illusions ended. His brief flirtation with the well-born and the moneyed of Arenjun ended both in his mind and in physical fact. Better he'd courted that ruby-bedizened lord's daughter over there – who now forgot to wear her perpetual sneer while she stared, bright-eyed.

Conan lunged rightward, away from the two watchmen he'd downed, and he turned as he lunged. When he spun back, his long sheath of shagreen leather hung empty. His fist was full of hilt, and three feet of shining blade extended out and up before him.

A third watchman stepped forward and launched a stab with his sword. So the boy was big; who knew as much about sword-play as the trained policemen of a city half whose population was thief? True, one had only to train, and cultivate a swagger; sneak-thieves and cutpurses were wont to run, not stand and fight with uniformed men wearing good iron.

Conan did not seem to stand and fight either. He ducked with the same pantherish litheness and speed he had exhibited before. And, still crouching, he took a step towards his attacker. Bending forward over that extended left leg, he brought his own sword arcing over his head.

Such a high-elbowed, overhead stroke obviously meant a vicious downward slash, and the watchman protected his legs. He'd strike the chopping slash away with his own blade and chop open the barbarian's thick thigh on the backswing.

Conan's arm and blade did not, however, descend. His fist brushed the top of his black-maned head and his blade swept out horizontally from his brow. The long sword slammed into the Zamorian's mouth.

Blood splashed and the cry of horror and agony was only a burble. The man showed his inexperience by dropping his own glaive and turning his back to the Cimmerian. He lurched away with both hands to his ruined face. Conan spurned the fellow's back; his considerable experience in combat had taught him not to waste energy on a man already out of the fight. This arrogant watchman was out of it: for the first time he had found someone who fought back – and for the last time.

Conan was astonished to hear a cheering cry amid the screams and shouts of horror and outrage that filled the Shadiz Inn. Someone here had learned not to love the keepers of the law – was it that dark big-nosed man in the *khilat*? The retired general, one hand on his paunch, bellowed his desire for a sword, secure in the knowledge that he'd not be given one. A younger man, a soldier though here without uniform or arms, stared with narrowed eyes. He backed; the big hillman's cleverness and considerable experience had just been made manifest.

Kagul was up now, and looking mean, with a handful of hilt. Indeed, both hands; he also drew his dagger.

Conan faced three armed men, coming at him well separated.

He was quite cool now that he was at bay. 'Get back,' he said, and napes prickled at the animal-like snarl. 'If you value the lives of these curs, Kagul, call them off. Your experience is got from threatening shopkeepers and bullying little thieves and torturing harlots to make them talk. I have spent months in chains, back when I was but sixteen. I have blooded this sword in combat – do you understand? Combat. I'll not suffer these dogs to lay hands on me.'

The three blinked. Kagul's 'curs' looked nervously to their leader. He firmed his lip and showed Conan his right side, long dagger poised in his left hand, sword advanced in the right.

'*Take him,*' he said again, in a flat, inexorable tone. 'It is not necessary that he be alive.'

Conan crouched. 'Better come all at once,' he said quietly. 'First man dies.' Then he lifted up his voice: 'Up Bell' the

Cimmerian bawled, remembering the voice that had cheered his carving of a watchman. 'Up Bel! Name of Bel!'

Clamping his lips then he pounced, cutting at a watchman's eyes while holding the man's gaze with his own. The Zamorian fell back and stumbled against a table formed of boards on trestle. A woman shrieked and the ruby-wearing young noblewoman stared with eyes gone bird-bright. Her bosom heaved and the tip of her tongue came out to wet pink-tinted lips.

To the dodging man's left Kagul came in, stabbing low. On the backswing, Conan's blade met his with a loud clanging ring. Kagul was only just able to parry the Cimmerian's swift chop – a stroke that came far too swiftly. The hillman handled his blade as if it were of paper rather than of heavy old iron. And at once he was backing a pace, flicking his eyes leftward, ready to meet the third watchman. It was then that a new voice rose, surely elicited by Conan's loud invocation of Bel, patron deity of thieves.

'Best seek the window, hillman! I hear the tramp of more watchmen without.'

The rightward member of Arenjun's police whirled to confront the owner of the voice sympathetic to the outlaw. There was only time for his eyes to register sight of an Iranistani in striped shirt and leathern vest; then the blue-bearded man from the distant east drove a three-foot Ilbarsi knife into the Zamorian's belly.

That was all the aid he gave Conan, and surely enough. The stranger had after all removed an enemy and warned the Cimmerian of enemy reinforcements. He was over a stool and past a nervous, backing Zamorian noble and out the inn's open doorway in seconds.

Conan was alone, facing two antagonists, with more coming.

He did not wait for their attack.

The Cimmerian's alert eyes had already marked the location of a window opening on to an alley. He drove forward in a running stroke that Kagul elected to dodge rather than meet with his blade. The barbarian plunged on past, racing to the far wall – and, without pausing, he hurled his sword out the window. He followed, in a head-first dive.

Outside, the blade clanged off a wall less than six feet away; it skittered on the ground while Conan, doubling in midflight, struck the alley's hard-packed earth and rolled. He fetched up against that same wall, and came unwound without a groan.

To the Cimmerian, his movements were studied, methodical. To an observer had there been one, he'd have been a blurred series of movements. His tunic's hem tore. As he rose, he plucked up his sword in his left hand. Still rising, he transferred the long blade to his right. It slid into its sheath before he was fully vertical. He was not looking; his head was up and his gaze was challenging the darkness, scanning the inn's construction; the eaves, the shelf formed by a continuation of the ledges of upper windows. In the few seconds that had passed, Kagul and his remaining watchman had not yet reached the window. The five men of a reinforcing squad had not quite reached the inn's main door. Conan kept moving.

Inside: Hurling aside a watchman by means of momentum and well-fed bulk, the retired general reached the window. He caught just a glimpse of the flapping of a torn tunic-hem as the fugitive rounded the inn's rear corner.

'Outside and around! He's run into the back alley, heading west!'

'I'd have been out the window and on him, my lord General Stahir,' Kagul said, 'but you are blocking the window.'

The older man in the belly-strained tunic turned on the watch sergeant. Eyes stared, suddenly gone to ice in a slabby, purple-veined face.

'Enjoy the sound of your mouth, little man,' Stahir said. 'It is the second time tonight you have dog-yapped at a better. Once I report what your hot-headedness brought on this night, you'll be fortunate not to be talking to the torturer, much less retain a Watch command.' And Stahir swung away. More watchmen were boiling into the inn; it was not from a sergeant they'd receive their orders, but from a retired general.

When those watchmen raced around both sides of the Shadiz Inn to converge behind, they found nothing.

The moment he had rounded the inn's corner, on the

run, the Cimmerian used his momentum and his legs' power-ful muscles. He leaped; he caught a cornice; his biceps and the muscles of shoulders and back bunched as he pulled himself up. Like a great cat, he was acrouch on the window ledge. He moved along a pace, turned. He squinted into the dark, considering. All in seconds.

While Kagul was receiving unpleasant news concerning his future, Conan was leaping on to the roof of the one-storey building behind the Shadiz. By the time five watch-men reached the alley behind the inn, Conan was four buildings away, moving as only a Cimmerian could. He heard the seven watchmen calling to one another, spreading out, hurrying down dark alleyways. None thought to look upward; they sought a man, not a bear or mountain-cat.

Conan tore his tunic again, and only just forbore cursing. His fine new cloak lay on the stool of the Shadiz Inn, and not likely he'd be retrieving it! And now his fine new silken tunic was ruined. Could nothing good come of this night? Squatting, he moved along a roof's sloping lip to edge around an outthrusting, second-storey alcove. It housed a tiny window that, intelligently, would admit air but no thief or assassin.

Conan froze at the sound of voices. They emanated from that tiny window, which was of another inn. The Cim-merian frowned, paused, staring at the window as if to hear better.

'Why it is valuable to this Hisarr Zul I know not,' an accented male voice said. 'Certainly it is valuable to our lord!'

'And so we become thieves,' another voice said, also accented, and female.

Foreigners, Conan thought, and two of their words registered: *valuable . . . thieves*. Things were hard enough for thieves in Arenjun, he thought with misplaced chauvin-ism, without foreigners joining in! And they were discussing their plans, were they?

With a wolfish grin, Conan crouched close to the cornice, like a jungle beast in the dark. Most attentively he listened to the conversation inside the inn's second-floor room.

'For our lord, by Erlik!' the man had said.

'Aye,' the woman sighed. 'And by Erlik indeed . . . something called the "Eye of Erlik", and in the hands of one who fled Zamboula ten years agone. He is called a mage, this Hisarr Zul – do you know why, Karamek, such would want an amulet of our lord?'

'Our pay is good, and we've a third of it jingling in our purses. Cease questioning our good fortune, Isparana. We can live a year on what we'll receive for the return of the amulet to Zamboula – and live well! Enough that the Eye of Erlik belongs to our khan, and was stolen by an old enemy, and must be returned. You saw how nervous the khan was!'

'Karamek! Don't you even *know*?' the woman Isparana demanded, with incredulity ripe in her voice. 'Did you ask no questions at all?'

'Our job,' Karamek said with exaggerated patience, 'is to steal it back. We need know nothing more.'

'Well, listen then, my foolishly impulsive Karamek! The khan's Eye of Erlik is blessed for him, and peculiar to him through means sorcerous: by means of it he may be controlled or slain.'

'Erlik's beard! No wonder he wants it back!'

No wonder, mused the eavesdropper. *And wouldn't the Khan of Zamboula pay a pretty sum to see it safe in his own grasping hand again! Zamboula . . . methinks I have made Arenjun a bit warm for me, this night . . . One could do worse than to be favoured of Zamboula's ruler!*

'And think further, Karamek,' Isparana was saying, still with an exaggerated tone; the clever explaining to the impetuous boy. 'Were the khan controlled or slain, another would gain Zamboula's throne rather than his son, Jungir. That would be Balad! And –'

'Balad! By Yog Lord of the Empty Abodes! – that would be disaster!'

The only disaster, the Cimmerian mused, trying to settle comfortably, would be if a pair of Zamboulans were to aid Zamboula's ruler so – rather than a fine big expert thief from Cimmeria! And he listened closely whilst they laid out a plan. They spoke nervously of Hisarr Zul's awful guards, single-minded zombies who had no thought but to protect their master's domain and slay all interlopers. Karamek and Isparana presumed *other* defences too, shuddersome ones; it was for dark sorcery that the man Zul was driven from Zamboula these ten years past.

'Two night's hence, then, by Erlik's beard,' Isparana said, 'when the moon is gone and the sky dark as Hisarr Zul's heart!'

Conan, grinning wolfishly, already plotting, half-rose and crept off across the roof. He pounced to another and thence to the ground, so that by means of dark alleys he would soon vanish into the Maul.

Two nights hence, eh, he mused. *But on morrow's night there will be hardly any moon . . . and that's when I will steal this valuable amulet! Zamboula's nervous king should pay and pay well for his Eye of Erlik, to ensure his dear brat's ascension!*

As he crept away into the night, smiling, planning, he missed the rest of the Zamboulans' conversation.

'Two nights hence, eh?' Karamek said. 'Nay, nay, Isparana, you were best to stick to that which you know best, easy-girl! You forget that two nights from this is the Night of Ishtar, who is worshipped by the queen . . . *and* the Time of the Equilibration of Derketo, beloved of the king's mistress! The streets will be full of people bearing torches, and Hisarr Zul is sure to keep close to that palatial home of his. Nay – we will just take the amulet from his coffers on to-*morrow* night!'

CHAPTER 2

At the Keep of Hisarr Zul

Many peoples of several lands thronged the streets of
Arenjun. They flowed in a river of colour amid the temples
and darker domains of Zamora's myriad strange gods. Some
did or sought to do business, straightforward or no, legal
or otherwise. Some spied, for this or that priest or anxious
noblewoman, or foreign ruler or priest or hopeful little
baron. Some made assignations, for themselves or their
masters or mistresses. Many gossiped, so that the market
place of Arenjun gave off the sound of a great hive of bees.
Among the topics was Zamora's king: having formed the
habit of drunkenness during the rule of Yara the priest who
had died in the inexplicable toppling of his Elephant Tower,
my lord King seemed unable to break the habit. He drank
as much or more than ever. None was sure now who ruled
in Zamora, and who in Arenjun must not be crossed; at
least when all knew that Yara was the power, they knew
of whom to be wary!

Others in Arenjun walked about observing, asking casual
questions, pondering, reconnoitring. These were planning
thefts, and among them was Conan of Cimmeria.

Today he wore no fine cloak, and gone was his thrice-
torn tunic of blue silk. As they could be sewn on another
garment, the cloth-of-gold borders had brought him a
pittance. His casual questions and observances told him
little more about Hisarr Zul than he'd overheard last night.

The man was presumably a mage; a wizard at any rate.
He kept much to himself within a walled little estate at the
edge of Arenjun opposite that where lay the ruins of Yara's
once-bright tower.

There were low-voiced rumours of Hisarr Zul's guards, but
no specifics were available. The home of Hisarr Zul was
not robbed. No one knew anyone who knew the man, who

had indeed come here some ten years agone. From Zamboula? Perhaps; who knew? Who cared? Hmm . . . in point of fact, another man with an accent was asking about him today, too . . . You don't come from the capital do you, a king's spy in those ragtag mendicant's clothes? Here – have a cup of wine, big 'beggar' (one can never be too careful) . . .

Making his way through the city, the ragtag beggar with the smouldering blue eyes and square-clipped black mop discovered the sprawling domain of Hisarr Zul.

He saw no activity within the walls. He saw no one enter the gate and saw no one depart. He heard no animal-sounds from within the grounds and smelled no such odours, though he listened and sniffed, for he recalled the lions that had guarded the verdant grounds of Yara's keep.

Two things Conan had of the adventure of the Elephant Tower: the excellent rope of dead Taurus of Nemedia – and more caution. He spent hours at the reconnoitring of Hisarr's walled keep, though he seemed only to be wandering, begging. Within, the manse was impressive and strange. It was built of stone and corpse-pale marble, a pale sprawl, brooding and seemingly demon-haunted, with windows like flatly faceted amethysts.

'You're a big strapping lad, damn you!' a one-legged man snarled. 'Why do you interfere in the business of those who need alms? Do something! Go steal, damn you!'

That evening a cloak, worn but serviceable against night-chill, vanished from off a sleeping man just outside the Maul. The cloak was of red, faded by age and wear and weather to a rusty pallor. A bit later, a big man doffed that cloak and thrust it betwixt a skinny, gnarly tree and the base of Hisarr Zul's stone wall.

He stood in the darkness clad only in a loose, short, sleeveless tunic laced up the front and girt with a big sword-belt. From it depended a long dagger sheath on a thong; his old leather sheath was slung across his back so that his sword hilt stood up behind his left shoulder. Fastened inside the ill-got cloak was his pouch of coins, which he could not trust not to jingle during the coming venture in thievery. They were safer here in the shadows against Hisarr's avoided wall than anywhere in that thieves' den called the Maul!

His sandals he left, too, between wall and tree.

Also at his belt hung a pouch of tools and the excellent rope that had belonged to Taurus the Nemedian. Woven from the tresses of dead women taken by Taurus from their tombs at midnight, that older thief had told the Cimmerian, and steeped in the deadly wine of the upas tree to give it strength. Even bigger than Conan, Taurus had avowed that the rope would bear three times his weight.

Conan would not test it just now. The wall was only ten feet high.

First he looked carefully about, peering into the darkness. Hisarr's keep was set apart from contaminating neighbours. Conan saw nothing, heard no one. He moved away from the wall, at a crouch, still wary. His observations earlier had shown him no sunlit flashes from the wall's top; it was not imbedded with shards of steel or bits of glass, then.

Could it be true that eight or nine good thieves had quietly announced plans to rob this place, over the last few years, and that none was ever seen again?

Well, they weren't Cimmerians.

Ten feet away, Conan wheeled, ran, leaped, and slapped both hands atop the stone barrier. Bare feet helped him up mortared old rock, and in seconds he lay atop the wall, which was over a foot thick. He remained there for some time, alert and listening, striving to send forth his very eyes as rays of light to pierce the darkness. Though his hearing, like his other senses, was unusually keen, the battle-born Cimmerian saw, heard, smelled nothing menacing.

The moon, just now on the other side of Arenjun, was the merest crescent. He congratulated himself – as if he'd had a choice – on choosing well the time of his invasion; on the night of the morrow the streets would be full of religious revellers and their torches and eerie humming murmurs – punctuated by screams supposed to denote fervour.

He heard nothing, saw nothing. Silence lay over the brooding keep of Hisarr Zul like a black blanket. The double-winged, two-storey manse bulked silent, forty feet away, a pale place that might lair liches and drying mummies. Conan saw no light. He had noted one on the far side in the other wing, which was why he was where he was, amid dead shadows outside dark windows.

Forty feet of sod, grassy and beshrubbed with bushy evergreens, like shadow-sentinels rearing in the night. Near them might lie fallen needles to pierce and slow bare feet. He'd skirt them, then; it was dark enough that a man needn't seek tree-shadows. Forty feet. There might be dogs, traps, lions – unknown guardians. He considered. Creeping, skulking, he was as likely to arouse such guardians as on the run. In this darkness he was no less likely to spring traps. And skulking, he'd have less chance of escaping trap or sentinels, human or otherwise.

He dropped into Hisarr's grounds with hardly a sound.

Crouching, he was able to see less than he had from atop the wall. No matter. He'd marked every tree, and the house, and his path. He took a deep breath – and ran, as though a dozen demons pursued him.

Seconds later he was beside the house, and hardly winded. Nothing had happened. The only sound was his own breathing. Hisarr Zul either had no defences as had Yara, or – the Cimmerian, racing with such swift silence, had aroused none. Good! Beside the house, Conan looked up.

Would this conveniently-located window open?

No. Of course not. Nothing was *that* easy. He moved on. This one? No. He considered breaking it. No. Though the only light he'd seen was over in the other wing, he'd not risk the noise of shattering glass – which was nigh opaque, and amethystine in hue. The Cimmerian moved on beside the lich-pale wall. A shrub seemed to lean towards him and, superstitiously, his nape and armpits prickling, Conan avoided it in a wide semi-circuit. Was Hisarr a mage?

Another window, also purplish, also impenetrable to his glower, also secured from within.

Directly over his head loomed a small round balcony. Perhaps Hisarr stood there to watch the sunset. Perhaps its door . . .

Conan's pouch was stuffed with wrapped tools wedged with pieces of sponge, against noise. After removing it from his belt, he tied its thongs to one end of Taurus's rope.

24

Conan stepped back, and back, keeping close to the house. Panic threatened when he backed into the shrub he'd suspected of some impossible sentience. He was wrong. It was only a tall evergreen bush.

The balcony was more than ten feet above the ground. That second storey must have mighty thick floors, judging from the height of windows and balcony! An iron safety railing surrounded it. Conan squinted. The vertical bars of iron were thumb-thick, and spaced about eight inches apart. Conan aimed, tested and corrected his stance, wound up, aimed, and threw his tool-pouch. The rope streamed out behind it.

He muttered curses when the pouch struck one of the uprights and rebounded. He caught it without a clink.

'*Try* to hit one of those little rods and I'd miss nine in ten times!'

His second throw was more forceful, and only generally aimed. Trailing the ill-gained rope, the pouch rushed between two iron bars, across four feet of balcony, and plunged between two bars on the other side. Conan's grip of the rope stopped the pouch a foot short of the ground. He let it down, dropped his end of the rope. There was plenty of slack.

He secured the pouch-end of the rope to a low, skinny, deciduous shrub just out of its infancy. He knew it was dangerously weak. Taking a deep breath, he wiped his palms on his tunic at the thighs, spat into them, rubbed them together again. He backed away, on the side of the balcony opposite the tethered rope.

A running start and his leap enabled his left hand to catch the rope nine feet off the ground. A powerful yank and swing enabled him to slap his right hand on to the balcony's floor. He brought his left hand up beside it. He had moved swiftly enough to avoid tearing the little shrub out of the ground, though he'd felt it give.

Clever, Cimmerian, he mused. *Now there's a railing in the way of a swing-up!*

Precisely because he was a Cimmerian, and inordinately strong besides, he solved that problem: he gripped one iron upright at its base. Then another. He gripped the first one higher up. Not without grunts, he dragged himself up thus, by sheer strength of corded muscles.

On the balcony, he brought up the hair-rope and took it around two vertical bars. Laying hold of it with both hands, he braced himself, and pulled. He grunted, pulled . . . When he felt the little shrub's roots start to yield, he re-braced his feet before returning his strength to his task. That part of the plan worked; the young plant's roots tore free of the earth, and the cessation of resistance did not hurt the Cimmerian, whose backside was already touching the railing.

He reeled in his pouch of tools. The shrub came along. Detaching it, Conan wound up and threw with such strength that the root-heavy shrub fell to earth well beyond the wall he'd just come over.

Now, he thought while he methodically refastened the pouch and coiled the rope, *those perverse Zamorian gods will surely ensure that the balcony's door is securely locked, after all!*

This was an occasion on which being wrong did not make the barbarian unhappy. The narrow door that gave from house on to balcony was not locked. Conan entered the home of Hisarr Zul.

Despite his many cares, he was still the impetuous youth who'd have died under Yara's lions but for the Nemedian thief: he had no idea where in this house of two two-storeyed wings the Eye of Erlik might be – and he had no idea what the thing looked like.

He had made certain surmises. An amulet meant a smallish object, probably on a thong or chain. As its true owner was a king or rather satrap, surely it was a chain, not a thong, and likely a golden chain at that. Why was it called the Eye of Erlik? Well . . . most likely it was a figurine. Erlik, the Yellow God of Death, had yellow or greenish-yellow eyes. A little figurine then, on a gold chain, with topazes or pale emeralds for eyes. And surely it would be wrought of gold.

Having thus logically worked it out in his own mind, Conan assumed his conclusions to be true. Next: where would it be?

Not in plain sight, surely – but not in a treasure chest stored away, either. This room neither felt nor smelled

26

lived in. On the assumption that Hisarr would keep such a treasure somewhere near to hand, to gloat over, Conan found the door and departed the chamber.

Minutes later he was moving along a corridor lit dimly by a dragon-shaped oil lamp slung from the ceiling on a brazen chain. Impatient with himself and his lack of knowledge, he had decided to discover and mark Hisarr's whereabouts, in order to search elsewhere for the amulet.

Hearing that was almost preternaturally keen apprised him of the approach of stealthy footsteps. Two swift bare-foot paces carried Conan to a door; he pushed it open cautiously to reveal one more of too many rooms, all unlit. This one seemed bare but for a huge statue that appeared to be of jade, and a big black chest that probably contained the paraphernalia of this god's worship. From inside, with the door not quite closed, the Cimmerian watched the passage of a man he realized was familiar: the easterner from the inn last night! A thief, surely, as the fellow had responded to Conan's invocation of the thieves' god.

Staring, Conan remembered that he'd been told another foreigner had been asking questions this day, about Hisarr Zul. He had naturally assumed the man to be Karamek of Zamboula, despite a sponge-pedlar's remark that the man was surely from doubly distant Iranistan. Conan knew nothing of that land. Zamboula lay far south of Arenjun, with desert between. Iranistan was even farther south, wasn't it?

Wondering if his presence and that of the man in the sleeved, striped shirt and khilat were coincident or if the Iranistani was also on a mission concerning the amulet, Conan watched the other man pass. The corridor with its pink-tiled floor ran straight for twenty feet before it reached the manse's centre, and branched. The Cimmerian waited. When he was convinced that the other man should have turned, he peered out. The corridor was empty.

Conan was just about to slip out of his refuge when he heard more footsteps, coming from the same direction as had the Iranistani; the direction in which Conan had been headed.

Crom! The corridor was as busy as the market-place at noon-time! Conan eased back, eased the door to within an inch of closure.

This time he watched the approach of three men in martial livery: silent, grimly purposeful men. All wore spike-topped helmets, jerkins of silvery scale-mail over green-bordered white tunics, and greaves in the Corinthian manner. Each bore a sword naked in his fist and wore a sheathed dagger as well. They carried no bucklers. The watching barbarian stared.

These guardsmen of Hisarr Zul were . . . weird, horri-pilating. They plodded along without a word, as if brain-less, each with dull fixed eyes set in stupidity? – no, hopelessness! They looked like over-whipped dogs or refugees from some legion of lost souls. Yet . . . they were purposeful, too; single-minded in their quiet pacing. Why, their buskins were soled with the sponge brought so expen-sively across from the sea, for the lining of helmets!

They passed, following the Iranistani whether by chance or design. Again Conan set himself to wait. Those men did not look alert; indeed, they appeared drugged. He felt that with his stealth he could step forth and be on his way in the opposite direction without their ever turning to notice – but he was in no such hurry. He'd not risk it. He waited.

When he looked, the third of that eerie trio was vanishing along the leftward corridor. Conan heaved a sigh, wiped his palms, and left the room.

He had taken eight stealthy steps when the dinsome clamour arose, from behind him.

He wheeled to see nothing. The noise continued, emanat-ing from the leftward branch of the corridor: iron clangs, one of metal on metal and another of deflected blade raking wall. The Iranistani, Conan thought, may or may not have found what he sought. Of far more importance to him was that the zombie-like sentries had found him.

The sounds of battle continued. The Cimmerian could visualise it: the trousered foreigner at bay in the narrow hall, and – if he were good with that sword-long knife of his – holding the guardsmen back, for the corridors were not wide enough to allow them to attack other than close-bunched.

Not my business, Conan thought. *The Iranistani's only a rival thief. Too, I have much more freedom, with him keeping those three busy. Better I go and see whence Hisarr emerges to investigate the clamour – and I will search the room he's been in!*

The thought was intelligent, reasoned, and worthy of any thief with his mind on his business.

The Cimmerian, however, did not even turn back to resume his investigations. Last night the trousered foreigner in the leather vest had aided him. Maybe his shouted warning and blade-use had not been necessary. Nevertheless, the man had done it. Whether thieves had codes or no, the men of Cimmeria did.

Barefoot, Conan sprinted up the corridor towards the sounds of combat, and he reached up and back to draw his sword as he ran.

He turned the corner to see precisely what he'd visualised: the backs of three sentries. Beyond them the rather short, dark Iranistani held them at bay, though sore beset and surely fated to be struck down.

Conan struck as suddenly and murderously as a tiger lunging out of the dark, though as he charged he could not resist shouting, 'Up Bel!'

'Hoho! Up Bel indeed, big one! Ah! Whoever you are, Ajhindar of Ir-uh!-anistan has never had a boon so swiftly – huh! – returned!'

The battle was very short. Indeed, it proved no battle at all.

Two of the uniformed guards turned at Conan's voice, silent and blank-eyed and eerily purposeful. The third was just striking at Ajhindar the Iranistani. As he was to the Cimmerian's left, the latter kept the two now facing him at bay by slashing savagely at their face level so that one jerked back and the other squatted under the strike – which terminated with Conan's edge slamming into the side of the third man's neck. The blade bit through to sever bone, half-beheading the sentry.

'Nicely done!' Ajhindar called, and altered the direction

of his own stroke so as to take the middle man almost identically. And one foeman remained. Into his path fell the man Ajhindar had nigh-beheaded, and the slash at Conan's right side and back came to naught; 'nicely done' or no, the Cimmerian was having trouble extricating his blade from the bones of his prey's neck.

Ajhindar booted his victim out of the way; half-turning, Conan brought his blood-streaming blade out of his kill and back so viciously that it missed the chin of his fellow thief by inches. The guardsman ducked under that blurred sweep.

'Ho! Careful there, big one – don't really know your own strength, do you? Hooh!'

He'd caught hilt and knuckles in his left forearm, as the third man tried to strike in the crowded hall and Ajhindar stepped in too close to be sword-struck. Simultaneously then: the sentry's left arm swept around with his dagger aimed at Ajhindar's side; Ajhindar's trousered leg jerked up between the man's thighs; Conan struck off the hand holding the dagger so that it dangled by a few shreds of scarlet flesh. The severed artery continued to pump in long scarlet squirts that showered wall and floor.

'Fast, too,' Ajhindar grunted, stepping back as the sentry he'd crotch-kneed came bending helplessly forward, too agonised even to scream because of his severed hand. The Iranistani kicked him in the face, whirled aside, and sword-chopped the man in the back of the neck.

He had to wrench to extricate his long blade from the Ilbars Mountains.

'Well! With the exception of that stroke of yours to the wrist – for which thanks, big one – very neat! We seem to have left all three with half a neck apiece and no windpipe or jugular at all! I'm glad I helped you last night, friend. I've told you my name – yours?'

'I am Conan, a Cimmerian.'

'Ah, the black hair and blue eyes, yes. Cimmeria, eh? Grow them big up in those hills, don't they? Conan of Cimmeria: my thanks.'

'Merely a return favour for last night, Ajhindar of Iranistan.'

The two men grinned grimly at each other. At their feet,

corpses twitched and jerked and pink tiles went much darker. With his left hand, the loquacious Ajhindar checked within a tear in his trousers-leg. His fingers came away red.

'Uh! Bastard pinked me. A piece of his nice white tunic will bandage it nicely enough, if I can find any white left – wonder which one it was? Conan – why come you here this night?' Ajhindar was still smiling.

'For a certain *amulet*,' Conan told his new friend, happy to have one and of such prowess and good humour besides, 'dear to a certain desert-bound king. And yourself?'

'Ah gods, I feared you'd say that,' Ajhindar said softly, and struck.

Only the fact that the Iranistani's foot slipped in a sentry's blood saved Conan then, for he had not been caught so by surprise since he was thirteen. The foot did slip; the blood-dripping Ilbarsi knife did swing out wider than its owner intended; Conan was able to avoid it. The slash aimed for his neck missed him – almost. Instead of chopping into the base of the bullish neck, it carried away a ragged piece of russet tunic-sleeve and a smaller patch of skin, from a wound no deeper than the thickness of a fingernail.

Conan spun completely, so that when he again faced the Iranistani it was at a distance of three feet. Conan's left shoulder oozed blood; his sword was held low, angled up.

'Damn!' Ajhindar said, almost smiling.

'A friendship as swiftly broached as gained, *friend*,' Conan said, low and throaty. 'Why this?'

'You must know: I'm here on the same mission. My employer is my own king. Yours?'

'Me.'

'Damn again! Just a thief?'

Conan nodded. The man's easygoing manner and his treachery had hurt far more than the nick of his sword; Conan was bitterly disappointed.

'Join me then, friend Conan. My king will be grateful to my friend who aided me in bringing to him . . . the amulet.'

Conan considered only for seconds. 'After the treachery you just showed me? I'd be afraid to sleep, or turn my back, *friend*.'

Ajhindar sighed. 'And from what I've seen of you, just

now and last night, I suspect you're not ready to say, "Oh, sorry, Ajhy . . . you take the Eye whilst I go along home empty-handed." Am I right?'

'You are right, *friend*.'

'Ah, you're bitter. That's youth, of course. But look here, the place is full of valuables. All yours. I want only the amulet –'

'So do I.'

'Damn. And, from what I've seen of your prowess, I suspect too that my best chance against you is already taken – to remove you without chancing a fight.'

The Cimmerian said, 'Right again, former friend. Now – we have made noise, and surely someone's heard. I will stand away whilst you head for the nearest window, for I've no desire to slay you.'

The Iranistani still looked sad. He wagged his head. 'Out the nearest window . . . and go along home empty-handed, eh?'

'Right, friend. Empty-handed . . . but alive.'

Ajhindar heaved a sigh. He kept his gaze on the Cimmerian while he squatted and, by feel, armed his left hand with a dagger its owner was past using.

'Afraid I cannot do that, friend Conan. I'm on a royal mission, you see. And watched. Loyalty, fear of reprisals, and so on. Is it true you Cimmerians are barbarians?'

'So we're called.'

'Damn! And big too, and good. Well . . .' Ajhindar turned away slump-shouldered . . . and whirled to charge, long knife extended and dagger coming up to catch a man he knew was swift enough to duck.

Conan would not be caught twice by surprise, like some stupid Arenjuni watchman whose experience came solely from the practice field. Already he was embarrassed at nearly dying to Ajhindar's first trick. This time he struck away the other man's long knife with his own sword; dodged the dagger and twisted in so that Ajhindar's wrist struck his swordbelt – and kicked the Iranistani in the left leg, hard.

Ajhindar fought a moment for balance. With nothing but air to flail, he went down – hard – and his left elbow

32

struck the corridor wall, also hard. The dagger leaped from his hand in a nerve spasm, as if spring-mounted. Sitting on the floor with his back against the wall just beside a door with a ridiculously low-set lock, he gazed up at the Cimmerian.

Conan had not followed up. He still did not want to kill this man. He was a long way from the shark-like man he'd become.

'Damn,' Ajhindar said, looking mildly up at him. 'You are fast and good, big one. That dagger did me no more good than it did its original owner. I suggest you do not take it up as spoils. The thing's accursed.' He heaved a sigh. 'Well.'

'A *barbarian* offers you the chance to get up and go, Ajhindar; there is a bond between us. No, do not expect me to come within reach of your feet. I lost a fight once because I thought I had won, and was ankle-kicked. Never again.'

Ajhindar showed the Cimmerian a rueful grin and shook his head. He did not attempt to disguise his open admiration. 'How old were you, big one . . . ten?'

'Eleven.'

Ajhindar chuckled. 'I believe you!'

With another sigh, the Iranistani started to rise. His hilt slipped on the tiles, so that he tilted and fell sidewise against the low-mounted lock of the door beside him. Instantly, with a click and a little thunking sound, a panel dropped open in the door, like a drawer. It was at shin level, had Ajhindar been standing. As he was not, the two Kharami asps that emerged from their niche behind the panel bit the Iranistani on the face and neck, twice each within four seconds.

Jerking, groaning and looking horribly surprised rather than in pain, Ajhindar showed no terror. He let go his sword and grasped a yellow-banded viper in each hand. He hurled both serpents at Conan — who sidestepped and, very neatly, sliced both flying reptiles in twain without striking either wall or floor with his blade. Four sections of serpent struck the corridor wall opposite the Iranistani and dropped to writhe on the floor. The unshod Cimmerian

33

kept out of the way.

'You're the worst friend I ever made, Ajhindar of Iranistan.'

'Aye, I suppose. And dead, too. Damn! All because I slipped . . . Well, that's that. Friend Conan, you know I've minutes, only. Do give listen without question. My employer is Kobad Shah, king of Iranist – oh!'

Ajhindar shuddered and leaned back against the door of death. Conan saw that already the asps' particularly nasty venom, so potent it was milked for use on assassins' daggers and some arrowheads, was at work. The little trickle from a thumb-thick swelling that ran up Ajhindar's neck showed that one set of hollow teeth had sunk directly into his jugular.

Minutes? No, Conan thought. The man had seconds.

'Kobad Shah will pay much for what you seek, lad. *Much*. Don't be foolish enough to deal with a common Arenjuni fence. You know you have to – *uh!*' Again a shudder seized the stricken man. His face was darkening even as it swelled. His arms twitched. '– have to flee,' he said in a lower voice, and words were becoming harder for him to form and expel. 'Aren-j-junn . . . take the Eye . . . to – to Koobad . . . straight down this h-hall . . . the dainty little blade you s-sseeek is . . . in a case . . . in the gr-gre-e-eennn . . . rooommmmkh.'

Ajhindar of Iranistan slid down the door, purple-black of face, his tongue out, his dark eyes huge and staring. The hand he had tried to raise to his chest had never got there.

Conan gusted a sigh. 'Kobad Shah didn't give you much, friend. Just death far from home, by Morrigan! We will see who I deal with.' He glanced about. 'Meanwhile,' he muttered low, 'we've been about as soundless as a herd of horses!'

And barefoot, the Cimmerian stepped across and around blood and four human corpses, to seek out the amulet called Eye of Erlik. In his brain as a question lingered Ajhindar's phrase: '. . . the dainty little blade you seek . . .'? Meaningless. Whatever it might mean, and whatever form the Eye took, it would be his, and a dear price; it had cost the lives this night of one good man and three . . . others.

34

CHAPTER 3

In the Green Room

Following the path that had been Ajhindar's, Conan of Cimmeria reached the end of the corridor and faced a panelled door. This one had no low-set lock such as that which had resulted in the Iranistani's death, but the Cimmerian was wary nevertheless. He sword-prodded the door's handle and the panel around it ere he pulled up the brass handle and kicked the door open with the ball of his foot. His sword remained in his hand, unwiped.

The room he revealed was sprawling huge, floored with green tiles like leaves shaken from trees before their time. Dark tapestries clung to pale green walls. From a ceiling supported by columns of green-shot porphyry twinklingly alive with feldspar crystals, velvet drapes hung to the floor. They were the colour of cedar trees, save for one wine-red one in the corner.

Towards the centre of the room squatted a long low table and a longer, high one topped with a stone slab. On that slab clustered a seeming hodgepodge of formidable crucibles and rune-incused aludels formed of ochre earthenware; a thurible seemingly of gold and alembics foully coloured by the noxious-looking fluids they contained. A little square casket of crystal, braced with brass, had been broken into a thousand shards that gleamed and glittered in the light of a hanging triple lamp moulded in the form of genitalia.

Against the wall squatted an athanor, black and dull like a comminatory dwarf of iron. Conan saw that the room was cut by one window, covered by a heavy drape the colour of pine needles.

Round about loomed strange and horrific statues of night-black onyx and porphyry and mica-glittering basalt. Even those anthropomorphic ones were not quite representative of human subjects. They were kept company by a loathly mummy, umber with age and standing propped erect, gaunt and menacing of tetanic face and exanimate form. On the long table two purulent-looking tapers had been lit, and they burned with a stench as if their tallow came from the inhabitants of tombs.

Here was no adyton of gods; here was the inner domain and trove of a sorcerous wizard and his dark gods or otherworld demons.

Here too were two people.

They did not belong. Both were tawny of skin, black of hair and eyes. The man wore a dark red tunic over a long-sleeved shirt of black, and black leggings vanishing into soft black boots. The dull garb of a night-thief more cautious than the barbarian he stared at, and a nose like a hunting falcon.

The woman's shirt, too, was black, and her tunic a deep forest green. Its border was fretted with scarlet and she, like Conan, was barefoot. Huge wire circles swung silver from the tiny rings piercing her ears and her eyes were darkly kohled above a straight nose and lips red as cinnabar and liquid-looking as the strange metal it produced. Her brocaded belt was clasped with agate.

In her right hand she held a small hammer, its head cloth-wrapped. From her left, on a circle of gold chain, swung a tiny golden sword. A pendant – or an amulet.

The dainty little blade you seek . . .

'Erlik's beard!' she gasped. 'Is *that* one of his guardians? He's big enough to stalk bears with naught but a thorn as weapon!'

Conan hefted his sword. Their stares swerved to the red-smeared blade.

'It's a three-foot thorn, Isparana. I am not anxious to use it more this night. Crom, what a house full of rogues this is! Just throw that bauble over here, along the floor, and I'll stand still and watch you two leave. Best make tracks for Zamora this very night.' He could not resist showing off his knowledge. 'Tell your khan I have another offer for his amulet . . . and whilst I decide between it and his doubtless generous one, he'd best have Balad slain. Just in case.'

'You know very much, blue-eyes,' the man said. He drew his sword and his knees bent. 'Enough to know that we cannot *give* you the . . . "bauble".'

The Cimmerian sighed, a bit elaborately. 'I've no quarrel with you, Karamek. Is there to be no end of killing here, this night?'

The man looked thirty; the woman five or more years less. Her eyes were very wide. She was well constructed and a bit more than pretty.

'Erlik's name,' she whispered, 'you have slain *Hisarr Zul*?'

'No. Just three of his sentries . . . and another thief.'

'Bent on gaining the Eye?'

'That,' Conan said, 'is no concern of yours.'

Elbow crooked, sword up and ready, he paced into the room. He extended his left hand, though only a little, with his elbow at his side. Karamek's sword was after all drawn. 'Just toss the amulet.'

She clutched it the tighter. 'Karamek –'

'Hush, Ispa. *Back* to the door we used. Out, down, and away. If I'm not at the gate within an hour – ride!'

'Karamek –' she was unsure, though she'd started to back. The prize swung from her tight-clenched fist.

Conan started his charge.

Karamek pounced into his path, knees bent, face ugly. Conan had gained momentum; Karamek slashed. Only the Cimmerian's fair hurling himself aside saved him from that hard-swung, drawing stroke. Behind him, Isparana turned and ran. She passed through an open doorway in the room's far leftward corner. Conan, with a wild slash in Karamek's direction, followed at the run. He reached the door just as it slammed with a double thump. His only choices now were to whirl or be slain from behind.

He wheeled about just in time to parry Karamek's running slash.

The Zamboulan's racing momentum and the force of his blow carried him past. Slamming a hand against the wall for balance, Conan thrust a leg out. The Zamboulan tripped, crashed into the wall. A tapestry of blood-coloured velvet came loose in his hand and dropped over him. Conan stabbed into that moving lump of tapestry, three times, and his blade was newly smeared and again dripping.

The falling Karamek pulled the tapestry the rest of the

way down, atop his twitching, kicking body. A shinier red oozed out from beneath the wine-hued velvet.

The Cimmerian was already trying the slab of a door through which Isparana had fled. It was locked. With a snarled curse, he threw his shoulder against it. From the way it sprang back after yielding only a little, he knew the door was stoutly barred against him.

The word for excrement streamed from the Cimmerian's lips in three languages as he turned and ran across the green room towards its single narrow window. Thought she'd escape him by barring a door, did she? He would damned well –

A section of floor slipped away beneath his feet and, erect, he dropped three feet on to a surface below. The fact that the apparent thickness of the second-storey's floor had been explained was of no interest to the grunting Cimmerian. The trap door closed on his thighs – and held him fast.

Even while he struggled, Conan knew that Isparana had made good her escape, with the Eye. Nor did it seem likely that he'd be there in time to find her waiting at the city's gate. He could not free himself. His attempts to gain freedom by lunging, twisting, and at last prying at the resolutely closed panel succeeded only in bloodying his thighs – and costing him the last two inches of his sword's blade. That brought more curses.

He was caught in a superbly designed trap, set to catch anyone coming in the window by which the Cimmerian had sought to exit. Calling up the name of every god he could think of, Conan snarled a litany of curses and obscenities.

For what seemed hour upon tortoise-crawling hour, Conan remained trapped. The while, he cursed himself and Hisarr Zul and the two Zamboulans with equal zeal.

And then a man came into the room. He examined the tables, and came to stand staring at the Cimmerian.

'By Hanuman, see what I've caught – a bear-sized wolf in my little trap!'

Conan glowered in silence. *Swears by Hanuman the Accursed of Zamboula, does he? Well, come closer, old dog, and even pointless my sword will . . .*

But no, it would not. Slay this man and Conan might

never leave the place. The prospect of remaining here, the tiled iron of the flooring pinning his thighs, while he grew delirious with hunger and thirst and eventually died the black-tongued death . . . no. Conan would gladly pass his sword over hilt-first and take his chances weaponless but with his legs free.

Eyes stared down at him, eyes deep and dark as the interstellar gulfs that yawned black and infinite between the wan far stars.

A long tunic of ochre samite covered Hisarr Zul to the ankles. Its chest was bedight with fretted scrollwork of gold thread, set here and there with opals and some gleaming stones of a warm saffron. His strapless sandals were the colour of earth; his bracelet was multiply punctured gold; and five rings flashed from his fingers, four with stones of as many hues.

He was slender of shoulder and hip, was Hisarr Zul, and only the beginning of a paunch slightly rounded the drape of his body-formed, ungirt tunic. His eyes were large and dark and exigent, a bit protuberant and starey. Above a wide, high forehead hair like gleaming jet sprang back in grey-shot waves from a central point like an inverted spearhead.

Hands behind his back, Hisarr Zul paced about his trapped guest.

His skin was smooth in appearance, with an amber-like sheen, as if glazed. His age was indeterminate; he was above forty. A small, neat moustache seemed to spring directly from his nostrils and was side-trimmed so as to form a flattened triangle from upper lip to nose. His beard, too, was geometric though rounded; it formed a thick-hafted spear of black, aimed downward.

The slightly exophthalmic eyes stared at Conan. Behind, Hisarr Zul's hair showed an unruly curl or two, for all his back-sweeping of it. He was of average height and his voice was a sonorous baritone.

'So. You slew my guards *and* my pretty snakes, after they'd removed your partner.'

'I came alone. So did the Iranistani.'

'Ah, everyone came to visit Hisarr Zul tonight, eh? And where is the amulet?'

'On its way to Zamboula, in the hands of a woman.'

'A *third* thief!' Hisarr Zul's brows rose so that his dark eyes bulged the more. 'And it's she who succeeded, eh?'

'Four,' Conan corrected. 'There lies another – her partner.'

'Hanuman's . . . head,' the wizard breathed, on a descending note. He followed the direction of Conan's nod, and paced over to the velvet-draped corpse. On his face was an expression of considerable distaste, but he squatted to draw back the cloth until he had bared the pain-frozen face of Karamek of Zamboula.

'Of Zamboula?'

'Yes.'

'Hmm.' Hisarr rose and turned to gaze on Conan, one hand raised, toying with his little beard. 'You and the Iranistani slew the guards. Did you two fight?'

'Yes.'

'Ah. And you downed him. I wondered how the fool had got himself bitten in the face and neck. And so you account for his death, too. And for this one. Doubtless there would be another corpse outside, too, a woman's, had you not fallen afoul of my trap.'

Conan said nothing, but stared.

'Hmm. A young man, a youth, but big, and ruthless. A man of prowess, youth or no!'

They gazed in silence, each at the other. Measuring. Considering. One seemed infinitely patient; the other had to be.

'Northerner . . . you have cost me considerable, but the Zamboulan costs me more. You must be my agent, now. As such, and for certain compensations . . . beginning with my activating the mechanism that releases you . . . you will go after her, and return the Eye of Erlik to me.'

Conan would have promised anything to get out of this manse and not be turned over to the city watch. He said, 'Aye, Hisarr Zul. I am your man. I'll gladly chase down the Zamboulan wench, for a merciful and generous employer.'

'Umm,' Hisarr said, studying him thoughtfully. Then he walked around Conan, to the longer table. 'Of course every second we delay gives her a longer lead, doesn't it? Surely she has a fast horse or camel.'

'Surely, Lord Zul. We must hurry – and I'll need a faster

one.' *I may well have to ride a hundred or two leagues just to overtake her,* the Cimmerian thought. *After that, with the amulet and your fast horse, I may as well continue along that same route – to Zamboula, and a doubtless generous khan!*

Smiling, again pacing with his arms behind his back, Hisarr Zul returned to stand before Conan. Then, smiling, he bent forward, revealed that one hand held a thin copper tube, and set it to his lips. He blew a fine yellow dust into the Cimmerian's face. Hisarr then moved hurriedly away.

Conan collapsed in seconds, unable to breathe.

For once, Conan of Cimmeria awoke as civilised men did, drowsy and dull. Too, he felt strangely apprehensive, dolorous; *empty*. The fact that he seemed physically unimpaired did not allay his unease and sensation of malaise, of emptiness. He hardly noted that he no longer held his sword. An inexplicable and undeniable feeling of loss and sadness was on him.

'Tell me your name.'

Conan looked into the dark, starey eyes of Hisarr Zul. 'I am Conan,' he said low, 'a Cimmerian.'

'So, Conan of cold Cimmeria. You have just become acquainted with the powder of the black lotus, a delightful and useful blossom from the lost jungles of yellow Khitai.'

'I know of it. It is death. Why am I alive?'

'Paralysis is almost instantaneous, Conan of Cimmeria. Death comes in two minutes. I provided an antidote of my own making; to my knowledge, I alone know how to counteract the Yellow Death powder. You have but lain unconscious whiles the antidote aided your – very strong – system in throwing off the venom. Nevertheless, you do not feel . . . quite normal, do you?'

Conan would not answer.

Smiling, Hisarr set his foot at the edge of the panel that held Conan fast. He pressed down with his sandalled toes. The panel opened at once, as simply as that. Conan groaned with the tingling agony kindled in his legs by the return of full circulation. Blood had dried on his thighs in two horizontal lines.

'Get up out of there,' Hisarr said.

His face clenched in pain, Conan sat back, pressed with

both palms, and backed on his buttocks out of the trap. The wizard lifted his foot. The tile-bonded iron sprang back into place to conceal the trap. Not even the Cimmerian's eyes could see any difference in that section of the floor.

'You might want to rub your legs,' Hisarr said, pacing to the higher, longer table. 'You might also want to look into this.'

He returned to hold before the floor-seated Cimmerian a mirror no longer than Conan's hand, thickened by a small dome of glass or quartz. Conan stared.

'Why would I care about a . . . mir . . . ror . . .'

He stared into the reflective glass. First he'd seen his own face, as he had expected. Almost immediately, shifting patterns began to obscure it. The glass seemed to swirl, to liquesce, so that he blinked and could not look away. Then he was gazing upon a tiny man, trapped and fearful, seeking escape from the mirror, seemingly looking beseechingly at him from the other side of a pane of clear glass.

Conan stared. His armpits went prickly. He knew that face; he'd seen the face on that tiny man before . . . it was his own!

'That, Cimmerian, is your soul. It is mine, now. Do as I have said and I will return it to you on the return of my property to me – the amulet called Eye of Erlik. Try to betray me, and I will break that mirror. And –'

Hisarr Zul did no more than tap the mirror. Conan felt an inward wrench. He neither knew nor cared whether it was imagined or a result of those long fingers' tapping on the container of his . . . soul.

'Be still. If this is broken,' Hisarr said, 'your soul is lost forever. Nor can anyone but me remove it from this glass. Would you carry your own soul about with you forever like baggage, Conan of Cimmeria, ever fearful lest someone break the glass and . . .'

Conan shivered. Then revelation came. 'The guards! Blast you for a – your *guards*!'

Clearly identified now as a sorcerer, a thinly smiling Hisarr Zul straightened. Conan's eyes remained fixed on the fragile piece of glass in one of those long, thin, amber-sheened hands.

'Aye, Conan. Now you know their secret. My guards were soul-less. They too came here as thieves in the night, my dear thief of cold Cimmeria. I took their souls, and broke the mirrors that contained them! What was left served me better.' Hisarr went back to the table of his necromancy. Anxious blue eyes watched him set down the mirror, and Conan breathed a little easier. Only a little.

'Or so I thought,' Hisarr said, turning again to face the barbarian. 'Until one of your prowess came and defeated them. Who could foresee *two* thieves' making successful entry here, on the same night? Hanuman blast you – all *four* of you! Well. These soulless men, always together, totally purposeful though eternally hopeless, were enough to overpower any single thief within these walls. What must be done now requires more. You will be outside, without my direction. Hence . . . I would rather not break this mirror of your soul, Cimmerian. Knowing it is here, you will serve me better, than as a *thing*; a human homunculus that only obeys, without that spark of hope that makes us all ever seek freedom, and volition.'

The sensation of emptiness swelled within Conan. He knew what it meant.

He was soulless, damned and doomed, and he knew that he had discovered that which was worth fearing. Indeed he could not but fear, at prospect of losing forever his very soul, the *ka* and life-force that was he at base, that drove him, that made him unique as an individual, and that would live on after his death.

He knew that he would do precisely as this smiling monster directed. He knew that he would seek the stolen prize that might ease his life for years, if he kept it. He would not keep it. Like a lackey, an employee, a servant of this powerful, plotting mage, he would bring the amulet back here, to trade to Hisarr Zul of Arenjun for that which was worth far more.

Crom and Ymir and all the gods, he thought, nearly whelmed, *my* Soul!

'You agree of course. Now describe to me what you will be seeking.'

'A – a small sword, on a chain of gold.'

Hisarr gazed upon him, leaning comfortably back against

the long table, braced by his hands.

'Poor fool, you really know no more, do you? Well. Here is its precise likeness. A day more and it would have been *this* bauble that Zamboulan slut made off with! Look well, Conan. Know the Eye of Erlik, that can upset a kingdom . . . two! And as you know now, it is important enough to interest one in Iranistan, as well as this humble displaced Zamboulan of the Empire of Turan.'

With a smile that was pure nasty mockery, Hisarr placed a hand on his midsection and bowed. Straightening, he plucked up the amulet that hung on a thong around his neck, beneath his tunic. He removed it and brought it to the Cimmerian.

'A precise copy, Conan my dear devoted servant, of the Eye of Erlik.'

Conan looked at it, studied it. The Eye of Erlik was a sword-shaped pendant about the length of his least finger. The hilt was capped with a ruby pommel. Each end of the cross-bar guard was set with large yellow stones, barred each with a single black stripe.

Those stones, about an inch apart, seemed to be eyes that stared into his from either side of a long and pointed nose.

'Wear it,' Hisarr said, dropping it into the Cimmerian's palm. 'Perhaps you will find a use for it. Of course, it should be called the Sword of Erlik, or at least the *Eyes*, plural – but the world is not ruled by logic, my barbarian of Cimmeria. Now: once you are on the desert, the first oasis is two days' hard ride to the south. If you follow the clear trail, you will ride eastward from Arenjun for about an hour, and then turn due south and continue thus. The woman of Zamboula is on that course.'

'You – know this?' The Eye was a warm metallic presence against Conan's chest.

'I know it, Conan my dear servant. It is not for you to know *how* I am certain; I am Hisarr Zul, and I have my ways. Four hours have passed since I came to find you here. Do you merely follow that course. You are rested, and big and strong; you should gain on her by minutes every hour. Go.'

'My sword . . . I have no horse . . .'

'You are a thief, and have stolen coin secreted somewhere. I want nothing of the dead Iranistani; take his possessions. Obtain a horse. I would suggest, too, a khilat or kafiyeh. Your sword stands beside the rear door, with your belt. It is without a point, but serviceable. You are no thrust-fighter, with those arms!'

Conan looked down. For the first time he saw that his belt was missing, along with sheathed dagger and sword scabbard. That he had not noticed instantly bespoke the effect on him of the yellow powder and its antidote – and his horror at having lost his soul.

He hoped his pouch was where he had left it. He was not sure how long he'd been within Hisarr's manse; surely five hours, which was over four hours longer than he'd intended. Hisarr's slightly bulging eyes were staring; Hisarr's excellent voice was speaking, telling Conan how to reach the rear door of his mansion home. By that door he would leave . . . not as a guest, not even as a thief, but as a servant.

Conan glanced longingly at the mirror, and considered sudden violence.

'Only I can regain your soul from it, barbarian,' Hisarr said, stepping back. 'It will be safe with me for . . . let us say, one month.'

'Zamboula is farther than the journey of a single month!'

'See that you overtake her far sooner, then! Do you want conducting hence? Go, servant.'

Conan's glance followed the direction of Hisarr's gesture. Two more of the uniformed guardians had entered and stood by the door. Each held a naked sword. Each stared, empty-eyed; lost. A thousand ants seemed to creep up Conan's spine as he looked on those two dully purposeful men, once thieves. Once men.

Soulless, he thought, and hated Hisarr Zul for seeing his shudder.

Conan started for the door, trying to regain the wonted set of his broad shoulders, his lithe, confident swagger. 'I will tarry beside the Iranistani,' he said, and did so, a few seconds later.

The corpse was hideous and nauseous, a thing that had once been a man, now gone violently dark purple and

45

swollen like a dehiscent seed pod seconds from bursting.

'I'll not strip you, friend,' Conan muttered. 'You can help me a bit more, though.'

He pretended calm while he appropriated the Iranistani's weapon belt. From it were slung a sheath for dagger and sword-long Ilbarsi knife, and a pouch. Conan buckled on the belt, hoping that the pouch was coin-stuffed even while he doubted. Picking up the long blade from the Ilbars Mountain country, he sheathed it at his side.

'Show me the way out of this place.'

The two staring, silent guards did. His own weapons and belt were there at the door, with the coil of rope. Conan buckled his broad belt on over that of Ajhindar. One of the soulless men held the door wide for his departure into the night not yet lightened by pre-dawn.

'You have no soul,' the Cimmerian said, pausing in the doorway. 'Would you go on serving the man who stole it? Would you like the gift of death?'

For the first time then, Conan had speech of one of the guardians of Hisarr Zul.

'To live soul-less is to be dead while alive, Cimmerian. To die without a soul is worse.' And the once-man closed the door almost on Conan's heel.

Conan departed in horripilation. The voice that had pronounced those lost, awful words had been that of Hisarr Zul.

CHAPTER 4

At the Oasis of Death

In an oasis that was indeed a *long* two days' ride from
Arenjun, Conan lay on his back and stared unseeingly up
at a sky besprent with stars like a million scintillant jewels
– or a million staring eyes. Nearby his new horse rested.
A few yards away, a horse of one of the other visitors to
this oasis snorted.

Soulless, Conan thought, and hated Hisarr Zul for seeing
him shudder, for making him helpless.

Yet did it matter? Conan wished that he could be sure.
The grim Lord of the Mound who was Cimmeria's chief
god was savage and gloomy. He promised no life after this
one. At birth, he breathed power into the souls of men;
power to strive and slay. 'What else,' Conan's father had
said, 'should one ask of the gods?' Well, other men of
other lands asked much more, and believed much more. If
only Conan could be sure. If this life were all there was,
a soul meant nothing.

Yet . . . that feeling of *emptiness* remained in the Cimmerian, and he knew it would until he had regained from
Hisarr Zul the contents of that horrid little mirror. Let
someone else say that it was mere suggestion, and Hisarr's
eyes; Conan knew that he had been plagued by the sensation
at once upon awakening, before the mage showed him the
mirror and explained its portent.

After two days, Conan still cursed the wizard who had
become the most literal master of his soul.

From time to time he also cursed himself. He should
have behaved more sensibly in many ways, and the last was
that he should have stripped the corpse of Ajhindar of
Iranistan. It was a victorious combatant's due. The man's
sleeved shirt and loose trousers would have saved Conan
coins – which he could have spent on provisions.

He rode the best horse he could afford, wore the cheapest

protective clothing available, and had only his own pointless sword for defence.

His money, as well as the contents of Ajhindar's purse and his excellent Ilbarsi blade, had clothed Conan and bought scanty provisions; Ajhindar's belt and truly excellent dagger had to go to provide more food for a journey that might last days or a fortnight. (That it would last longer was inconceivable; Conan *had* to be back in Arenjun within a month.)

Thus had he left Arenjun, knowing that he was well mounted, indifferently armed, and poorly provisioned for day after sweltering day on the desert beneath a sun become deadly enemy.

During the afternoon of the second day, the horse — which Conan called 'Horse' – was complaining and showing impeded strength from lack of water. Confident of reaching the oasis, his new master had brought little. A man could endure much when he must, the Cimmerian knew; so could a horse. And then the oasis was in sight, and Horse smelled its sweet breath of water-scented air, and Conan had merely to sit his back. Horse knew where he was going.

Horse had brought him here to the oasis, and after that Conan had only to hold the beast back from swelling his belly with too much water too soon.

During those two days Conan had had much time to think. Thievery, he mused, was a precarious trade. So were many others, but thievery contained even more risks: law and the authorities, in addition to the angered objects of robbery. Now he knew, having met Isparana and Karamek and Ajhindar, that other thieves, good thieves as he was, had *patrons*. They stole for others, for this reason or that. They were paid – and presumably equipped, and afforded some protection or backing in the event they fell into the hands of the law. Now the Cimmerian knew that even kings hired thieves.

Certainly that was a better way for a man to further his chosen career!

A youthful hillman could dream of crowns and soft women, but it was not likely he'd ever wear that one or night with the other.

Once this revolting rewardless job was done and he had

his soul back of that scurvy Hisarr, he'd explore the possibilities of improving himself; try to bring himself to the attention of moneyed employers.

Meanwhile, he and Horse had their bellies full of water, at least, and on the morrow he'd leave here with more. Better to travel in the cool of the night, but Horse badly needed his rest.

Unexorcisable thoughts continued to crowd Conan's mind as he lay restlessly awaiting sleep in the officially nameless oasis some called Breath of Arenjun and others Sight of Kherdpur; the name depended upon the destination of the traveller. Over him lay the old cloak he had stolen three nights previous; nights on the desert were cool. Nearby Horse stood tethered, asleep.

On the far side of the pool of good water with its ring of hardy grass and shading palms were the men Conan had found here on his arrival. The three had exchanged few words.

Obviously the other two had been lying up, preparatory to travelling by night with their two camels and one handsome jasper-hued horse. No more anxious than they to hold converse, Conan forced his mount to the pool's southern bank before allowing him to drink.

The Cimmerian had slaked his thirst by lying prone beside his noisily sucking horse. Across the pool, one of the other two pilgrims watched, for lack of aught else to do, Conan assumed. He rose, tucked back into his tunic the false Eye of Erlik that had fallen forth, and commenced persuading Horse to leave off trying to suck the pool dry. The other man, dark and Hyrkanianly hawk-nosed under his white kafiyeh, looked away. He did not even glance over when Conan found it necessary to drag Horse physically back from the water. That the poorly-cloaked youngster was able to do so would doubtless have surprised the other traveller, had he been watching. Certainly his master's strength surprised the horse.

'We'll both fill our bellies again at daybreak, Water-hog,' Conan had told the animal, which now bore a name.

Now the horse slept while his penurious master strove to quell the tidal activity of his restless mind. He did wonder, idly, why the other two men had not yet departed.

49

Had the Cimmerian found sleep at once, he might never have wakened. The unnamed oasis called variously Sight of Kherdpur and Breath of Arenjun was about to become the Oasis of Death.

Though Conan did not know and would not have cared had he known, the two men with whom he shared the benefices of the oasis were from Samara, in the Misty Mountains to the south-east. They were entrepreneurs of a special sort. Presently they were journeying to Shadizar of Zamora to sell a motley assortment of goods, none of which had been gained through trade. Perhaps next time they'd be able to afford four or five camels . . .

One of them, Uskuda, had been to Zamboula more than once, along the caravan route from the Colchians. He had seen the amulet always worn by the satrap who ruled Zamboula for Turan. He assumed it to be valuable; it was a kinglet's. Just at sundown this night, he had seen that amulet again – or so he thought. Surely such a royal prize would nigh double his and his partner's profits, up in Shadizar the Wicked.

The newcomer was manifestly weary. Uskuda waited a long hour, and more.

Now, taking the end to bring him around opposite Conan's sleeping horse, Uskuda the Samaratan crept around the cabochon-shaped pool of water. His dagger was not yet drawn. Crouching, he drew it only when he was no more than two body-lengths from the supine, cloak-covered northerner.

Dagger in hand, Uskuda straightened in a rustle of trousers under desert robes and rushed those few intervening feet to fall dagger-foremost on the other man.

That rustle was not the first knowledge Conan had that the man was creeping upon him. He was unable to imagine himself the object of robbery, but was ever as untrusting and expectant of baseness as he was alert. He had devoted several minutes to letting his right hand creep out to the hilt of his sword, and easing it back under the cloak atop him. His left hand, meanwhile, had eased across his chest to the far rightward top of that faded russet mantle.

Though few indeed were the human ears that could have distinguished the whisper of Uskuda's dagger leaving its sheath, Conan heard. Now he heard the rustle of cloth, and the first two of the other man's rushing footsteps.

Conan's left hand whipped away the cloak while his right brought up the sword. At the same time, his stomach muscles tensed into stony hardness and his upper body came up from the ground.

His extended sword met the attacker between navel and crotch.

The force of his assailant's charge knocked Conan back to the ground. It also sent every wisp of breath gushing from Uskuda's lungs. He was not, however, spitted on a pointless sword. Perhaps he was cut a little, through his bulky clothing, and perhaps not; it did not matter. The attempt at murder – it would have been his eleventh, in point of fact – failed.

The iron muscles of Conan's right arm strained and bulged. He not only kept the other man from falling on him, but indeed hurled him aside, to his right. Only then did the Cimmerian remember that he had sought to transpierce a man with a sword no longer suited for such work.

Within three seconds more Conan was on his feet. His assailant rolled away, gasping. Though fighting noisily for breath and hurting low in his gut, Uskuda also got to his feet. As he came up, so did his sword. He had dropped his dagger.

The Cimmerian drove in and struck hard, full of righteous anger. Uskuda dodged away, the while slashing at Conan's thighs. Both blades sheared the air only and Conan knew this was an inexperienced blade-fighter. From new directions, the two crouching men again faced each other with bared teeth and slightly moving swords.

Uskuda feinted a short thrust. Conan twisted aside and, turning completely around, directed a whistling slash at the other's neck. Uskuda squatted under that killer sweep and chopped at Conan's legs. Bounding high, Conan alit and rushed on past Uskuda, who turned crouching. He knew now that he faced a deadly foe.

'I give it up,' the man from Samara said. 'I thought you were someone else!'

And while the Cimmerian paused to consider that offer of peace, Uskuda risked all in a long lunge that should have covered the barbarian's genitals with blood from his riven intestines.

It did not; with a clang that was like the striking of a great gong in the stillness of desert night, he struck the stabbing blade away. So forceful was that stroke that Uskuda's right arm was carried far out to his right, almost horizontal from the shoulder.

Not only had Conan's stroke been slowed by its clangorous impact with the other man's blade, the Cimmerian was both faster and stronger. Thus he recovered first. His backslash chopped deeply into Uskuda's right thigh, just at the knee. From the would-be assassin's lips burst a ghastly sound, neither a moan nor a cry and yet both.

Even as his leg buckled, Uskuda tried to strike with his sword. The leg collapsed faster than the arm could move.

Conan's arm had barely slowed. His sword blurred, catching the moonlight in a silvery flash. When he yanked the blade free of the other's leg, it trailed blood that rode the air in scarlet streaks and droplets. He added momentum and force by spinning completely around again, and this time chopped nearly through Uskuda's left arm, immediately below the shoulder.

Uskuda fell. He bore two deep, blood-gushing wounds and had but one hand to grab himself with. He clutched at neither wound. Now that he felt death more imminent than the dawn, he thought only of vengeance, if he thought at all. Twisting on the sandy ground, he struck at Conan's shins. The blow was weak; Conan was leaping upward; the sword's edge skinned the sole of his right sandal. Then Conan's foot came down on a wrist. Bones crackled and the sword leaped from nerveless fingers and Conan's sword chopped into Uskuda's chin and neck.

The Cimmerian twisted his unpointed sword to get it free of one who had less than a minute remaining in this world. Turanian Erlik's arms were outstretched for another guest in his domain of death.

For a few instants the Cimmerian stood looking down at his attacker, reflecting on the difference between honest thieves such as he and idiots like this who sought to slay first and seek what might be there in booty after. Then Conan's ears gave him reason to spin around.

'You—you killed Uskuda!'

'True, in a few seconds,' Conan said equably. 'Your partner tried to stab me as I slept. I was not sleeping.'

The second man failed to perceive the illogic of seeking vengeance for a partner who'd got precisely what he deserved. He charged. Conan struck hard at his curved sword and kicked so hard that the man staggered several paces backward and fell into the pool. He dropped his sword to fight the water.

Letting go his own weapon, Conan waded in. First fetching the flailing, spluttering man out so as not to spoil the water, the Cimmerian slit his throat.

The night was again still but for the nervous whickering of horses. Wiser camels remained hunkered down in their kneeling postures of rest, and merely stared with mild interest. They had never stopped chewing.

Conan stood victorious; to him went the spoils.

CHAPTER 5

The Dragon Hills

Before dawn Conan rode south on the well-rested horse of those who had sought to slay him. Behind him plodded Water-hog, at the end of a long tether made of the hair of dead women. His newer beast Conan called Horse.

The Cimmerian now wore a handsome vest of tooled leather, a much better cloak, and a kafiyeh with a chrysoberyl in its double band of woven black horsehair, and a pair of boots into which, fortunately, their former owner's blood had not spilled. A curved eastern sword hung at his left hip, and two daggers; his own truncated sword was slung in its shagreen scabbard from the pommel of his saddle.

He was well fed and of good cheer.

More food swelled one of the packs borne by the horse behind him; Water-hog had become temporary sumpteranimal, though in a few hours Horse would take his turn. Water-hog also bore three water-sacks and a pack containing some of the wealth-hopes of Uskuda and his late associate.

The camels had proved recalcitrant, and the Cimmerian no drover. After both kicking and cursing them soundly, he left the supercilious beasts – still chewing – and vowed to take possession of them on his way back to Arenjun. Of course that was naïve, but Conan, like all sensible men, hoped and dreamed.

All day he rode hard, due south. At dusk he rested for an hour, and changed horses, replacing saddle with packs.

He rode on into the night, letting Water-hog pace himself as he wished. The northerner hardly noted his crossing of the Road of Kings, on which some day he'd be a conquering rider. A caravan he met directed him to a well, where he and his horses tarried to drink. First refilling the leather-covered pottery jug by which water was drawn up,

Conan rode on for another hour. Only then did he halt his weary beasts.

Reeling with weariness himself, Conan nevertheless remembered to tether both animals. All three slept, disregarding the dawning sun and an inhospitable bed of rock and sand.

A few minutes after he awoke hours later, the Cimmerian was again on his way.

Two horses and full packs and belly cheered him, as did the words of the caravanseer he'd talked with; yes, they had met another lone traveller, headed south. A woman? Well, that pilgrim *had* been a spindly sort though chesty – by all the gods! So that was why! Aye – a woman! And the caravanseer cursed. Clever of a woman, uncleverly travelling alone, to disguise herself with loose clothing and a jallaba with sand-hood!

Now Conan was reasonably sure that he followed Isparana of Zamboula.

The terrain roughened and was all rocky and rolling, and for three hours Conan approached what appeared to be a great grey dragon sprawling across his path. No longer could he push his horses so rapidly. They profited little from that; the going was not easy.

At last he reached the 'dragon', a long range of interwoven hills that would have been called mountains by those not of Cimmeria.

Conan sat and stared glumly at the slumbrous dragon of stone, bare of vegetation save for a scraggly cedar rising out of rock here and there to perch precariously. Now he saw that he must cross a series of east-west hills, sprawling one behind the other in parallel lines. And every hill's crest looked like the back of a rooting hog. He'd be hours and hours getting through and over this multiple barrier.

Nor was that all. At the very top of the farthest humpback hill, perhaps a mile and a half distant but many hours' difficult ride, Conan saw another traveller. That rider was just reaching the rocky hill's summit. Mounted on a camel, the other pilgrim led another, which Conan saw was well laden with packs of provisions. The camels' high plump humps bespoke their lack of need for water.

The rider bore no hump. Indeed, even in flowing white

desert garb and dun-coloured jallaba, the rider was small, narrow of shoulder.

Conan knew it was a woman. He assumed that it was Isparana.

It was maddening! She was in sight – and perhaps a day away! With his horses again weary and soon to be in pressing need of water, the Cimmerian knew that he was at least a day behind her. He sat and cursed by Crom and by Lir, by Badb and Nemain the Venomous, and by Macha and Mannanan. Far off in the hills of Cimmeria, they paid him no mind.

Then, from behind a huge boulder little smaller than Hisarr Zul's manse, another rider emerged.

This one must have met Isparana along the mass of rocky hillsides; now he was no more than fifty feet from her pursuer. As he paced his horse forward he raised his hand in a gesture of peaceful greeting. Conan was glad enough to return it. He and his horses were too tired to fight or run, and sweat ran from under his hair.

Besides, behind the first man came another, and another. And still another. And a fifth.

All wore arms, and cloaks of the same colour, and spiked helmets with pendent camails; helms and cloaks were alike: uniforms. Their features were Hyrkanian, and Conan knew that he was braced by five tall, dark-faced Turanian soldiers. From Zamboula? He thought fast.

'Hot enough for you?' the first asked, pacing forward.

Conan hated the phrase, which must have been a cliché ere Atlantis sank. Yet the words, like the dark-skinned man's voice and mien, were encouraging; they were friendly.

'Becoming so,' Conan said. 'You're as strange a caravan as I.'

The Hyrkanian grinned. 'We're – Tarim's name! Where are you from, with those *blue eyes*?'

'Cimmeria,' Conan said easily. The man was a provincial who'd never seen eyes coloured other than brown! Encouraged, Conan lied glibly. 'More recently I left Shadizar. Surely you haven't come all the way up from Zamboula.'

'Cimmeria!' the man was shaking his head. 'I've never seen such eyes! No, we're out of Samara, and ours is the worst job loyal soldiers can be handed by a callous commander. We follow two men – we hope. Have you seen –'

'Thieves?'

'How did you know?'

While the other four Turanians reined in before him, Conan gestured. 'Several days back, at an oasis –' He broke off then, realizing he'd never see those camels again. Damn! These southern and eastern gods did conspire against a man!

The Turanian leader looked a bit stern. 'Yes?'

Conan jerked his head and gave the man a rueful look. 'Oh, I'd hoped to go back and get those camels, but they're lost to me anyhow – there's a long caravan ahead of you. Yes, I've seen them, if you follow thieves. They were at an oasis where I stopped. My horses and I needed both water and sleep. The two there before me had camels. I supposed they were waiting to travel by night. It was dusk. I went to sleep, across the water-hole from them.'

'Hm. And?'

'And one of them tried to kill me while I slept. Fortunately, the fool stumbled. I kicked him into the pool, dragged him out, and saw his companion coming at the run. I cut the first one's throat.'

'Nice of you not to foul the water.'

'So I thought. His partner was running at me then, with a sword. We fought. I was better than he.'

'They took you by surprise and you killed them both?'

'Only one took me by surprise.' Conan sat up in his saddle, to remind the frowning Hyrkanian of his size. 'I'd have brought their camels, but I couldn't make them follow me. As I am in haste, I left their packs.' He grinned. 'I couldn't even make one of them get on to his feet!'

All five soldiers laughed, but not in scorn; they knew camels.

'You don't know camels,' their leader said.

'I don't. I think I don't want to.'

'Camels like to think they're accompanying you, not being driven or led,' a soldier said.

'You seem to have one sword too many,' another observed.

'Only a half,' Conan said, and carefully, using his left hand, he drew his own blade from its saddle-slung sheath.

'I broke this in the fight. It was a good sword, too.'

'Looks it. Also old; gone brittle, perhaps. And the one you wear belongs – belonged to one of the men we follow.'

Conan nodded. 'I hope you aren't employed by a lord who'd see an honest man disarmed.' *Try and do it*, he thought, while more than hoping they would not.

The leader shrugged. 'No, no; keep it. I do fear we are employed by a lord so niggardly that we must search the packs of your sumpter-animal, though.'

Conan affected a great sigh. 'Ah, and I am passing anxious to catch up to the rider you five just met, too.'

'That woman? I can't imagine why. Unfriendly bitch!'

'Indeed!' Conan said, nodding and grinning; a man among men, talking about a woman. 'She is indeed! Her former lord, back in Shadizar, is not all that unhappy to see her go. He does want back a few little trifles she took with her, though. You noted a well-laden sumpter camel?'

'Aye. So. She lied to us, and both you and we follow thieves! Well, I regret the necessity of searching your pack, uh – where did you say you come from?'

'Shadizar – oh. Cimmeria.'

'Cimmeria. Up north somewhere?'

Conan nodded. 'The weather is a bit chill – though I admit I'd welcome it right now. I came down to warmer climes to seek my fortune, and found employment as bodyguard to a moneyed sort in Shadizar. If I don't catch up to Isparana, I may as well keep on going.'

'Check the packs,' the Turanian leader directed, and two of his men went to do so. He looked Conan appraisingly up and down. 'A man who is employed as bodyguard and kills two men who surprised him in sleep would be welcome in Samara – if he chooses to wear one of these.' He touched his helmet.

'A northerner with my accent and these eyes, employed in Turan?'

The man gestured. 'Of course. We're not bigots. Men who are good with weapons can find employment anywhere. Or death, if they choose not to be on the side of the Empire and its laws. Kambur here is from Iranistan.'

'I will remember,' Conan said, and twice asked the man's name, and committed it to memory. Arsil, of Samara.

Fifteen minutes later the Cimmerian was advised that this necklace and this chalice and these matched pearls would have to go with the soldiers. Oh, and this dagger with the jewel-crusted hilt.

'These have been specifically listed as missing, and by a man of wealth and power,' he was told. 'We have no listing of these other things, and you don't look like a thief. They must be yours.' And Asril of Samara winked.

'In truth,' Conan said, 'I believe one each of those gold coins belongs to your men. You must have dropped them.'

'Hmm. Since they are Samaratan, you must be right. One each, men, It has been our pleasure, Cimmerian.'

'I admit it hasn't been mine. My pack is lighter. And I am farther behind Isparana. Is there no way around these hills, or a way through them faster than the route she took; the way you came?'

The Turanian frowned darkly and shook his head. 'Conan: there it is. One winds one's way up, starting behind that grandfather of boulders. You don't want to know about it, or take it.'

Conan continued staring questioningly at him until Arsil spoke on, with reluctance. He gestured.

'From the top of the first hogback a man can see a gorge; a ravine that slices through the rest of the hills. It was the pass through the Dragon Hills for hundreds of years. It still looks tempting. In the face of crossing so much hard terrain, many have been tempted and have succumbed. The gorge is haunted or peopled by . . . something. Over the course of the past ten years, when the haunting began, exactly two of those who entered the gorge – seeking a short cut through the hills – have emerged. Both were inexplicably abraded, and both were mad; driven mad by the demon in that gulch! One babbled about a lich, a sand-lich, and now the ravine is called the Gorge of the Sand-lich. The bones of all others who have ridden into that deadly pass lie within . . . though their animals nearly always emerge. Take the fortune doled out by wise gods, Conan of Cimmeria, good and bad; cross the hills despite the time, and avoid that demon-haunted gorge, for it is only a pass and a short-cut to Hell.'

'No one has invaded in force? You know nothing more?'

'Tarim's beard! Is that not enough?'

'Aye . . . my thanks, Arsil of Samara. I must ride. I'll be a day crossing those accursed hills!'

'Very nearly,' the Turanian assured him, nodding. 'Less than two days' ride beyond, though, lies a fine sprawling oasis. Rest there, and count your blessings for having met us, and avoided that beckoning passage to Hell! Good fortune, in catching your woman!'

'Not my woman.'

'Make her so then, man – if only temporarily!' And reining about, Arsil joined his men, to lead them northward.

Thus the one and the five parted, with the Turanians riding on to attempt retrieval of the rest of the loot stolen in Samara. Conan had seen no reason to tell them that he'd paced one hundred steps eastward from the oasis of death, and there buried the very best contents of those recalcitrant camels' packs.

His horses slipped and slid and complained as they made their way up that first rocky hill, and Conan found it expedient to dismount and make his way on foot. Descending the other side was no easier, and by the time he reached the narrow valley that separated the first and second hills he knew what he was going to do.

Mounting, he rode a short distance westward and entered the long, rather broad gorge he had seen from the hillside. Certainly he believed in demons and hauntings; he also believed implicitly in himself. And he was in a hurry.

CHAPTER 6

The Sand-lich

The deep slice along which Conan rode was nearly straight
enough to have been chopped here by a single blow of the
sword of a giant, provided the blade had been curved, and
a bit wavy. Long ages ago roaring foaming water or resist-
less ice must have torn out this ravine that forged between
hill after hill. No valley this, but a cleft through the land
that would accommodate no more than three mounted men
riding abreast. Granitic rocks in greys and browns, shot
with occasional splotches or veins of red and ochre, rose
thrice the height of a mounted man. The forbidding rock
faces seemed to glower down on the lone rider with his
two horses. Conan kept to his left, availing himself of a
bit of shade.

The horses were restless, nervous. The very sand seemed
to shimmer and shift, gem-sparkling, under their gingerly
pacing hooves. Conan told himself that the intermittent low
moaning sounds emanated from a breeze blowing down the
gaping cleft between looming cliffs.

There was no wind. There was not so much as a breeze.

The sun was a palpable force, shade or no, and Conan's
head seemed to fulminate. At least he saw no corpses, no
bones. His mount paced deeper into the gently bending
gorge. The very air was menacing, oppressive.

Keeping a tight rein lest the beast try to make good on
his threats to bolt, Conan never ceased turning his head.
Eyes hard as blue agate burned this way and that, seeking
to project a gaze to pierce the very stone that hemmed him.

He saw a place where he might get up out of the gorge
and on to one of the hills. The option was still open to
him; already he had cut hours off Isparana's lead.

The sun seemed to resent that, and sought to bake him
like rock-bread, in the space enclosed by the glowering
cliffs.

The moaning rose in volume and increased its frequency. The tone was higher now, and seemingly human or, worse, preter-human; a doomed creature crying out its plaints of misery. Or . . . threats? And somehow gaining strength, too, as if nurtured by his presence here in its rockbound domain; as if feeding on every step of his incursion.

A lich? A *sand*-lich? Surely no corpse made such sounds!

He glanced back. His pack-horse pranced and sidled, tossed its head and rolled fearful eyes. They had come far, the Cimmerian saw. The gulch's shallow bend and gentle little curvings had blotted its entry from sight.

Half-way, the Cimmerian thought. *We've come half-way*. No use turning back, now.

The moaning came from behind him. The moaning rose before him, trembled around a shadowed curve in the passage ahead. It emanated from the towering walls of stone on either side and rose up from the sand beneath the hooves of his nervous horse. The sand twinkled and flashed like millions of tiny gems in the sunlight. The sand moaned. The moaning became a steady keening.

Badb and Nemain, but this was maddening!

His mount plodded past white bones, and Conan compressed his lips in a grim line. They were human bones. So were those – and aye, that was another pallid skeleton, sand-polished and sun-bleached. There lay a sword, not far from the segmented white twigs that had been a man's fingers. That was a dagger over there, and no stain marred its shining blade. He saw the skeleton of but one horse, while counting eleven human ones. The while, the moaning rose until it was a steady ululant assault on his ears, a disturbing tenor.

Twelve skeletons. Thirteen. Two Turanian helmets. More weapons.

His horse tried to shy from a fourteenth sprawl of bones, and Conan clamped both legs while he drew in the reins with his big fist. The moaning was no longer intermittent; it but rose and fell, while sounding steadily. As if it had grown stronger with his advance into the narrow, inescapable domain it haunted – or as if he were breaching its inner lair, challenging it too closely.

'Stop!' he snarled, glaring ferally about. 'Stop your

noise! Show yourself or be silent!'

His voice echoed at him from the rough stone walls flanking him – along with the moan-sound, now risen to a wail.

Conan blinked then, and jerked his head as if to clear it. He blinked again, disbelieving his eyes. Ahead and on either side of him, the gorge's sandy floor seemed to have come alive. It seemed to be shifting, flowing, the sands skittering brightly as if by little puffs of air. There was no breeze. In his pressing thighs, Conan felt the trembling of his horse.

And the sand moved.

The sand rose up then, swirling in its millions of grains, tiny spots winking and flashing. There was no wind; not even a zephyr stirred the air. The mournful howling came from no wind, and no wind raised the whirling dancing sand.

His mount whimpered, jerking its head, tried to turn and flee. Conan held it with a very tight rein – and the beast reared. Surrounded by rising spinning sand in refulgent motes, the animal pranced on its hind legs. It dropped again to all fours, bucked, and reared again. Conan clung, compressing his mouth and slitting his eyes against air clogged with ever-moving crystals.

When the horse rose up on its hind hooves for the fourth time, it also twisted.

Conan knew seconds of disequilibrium, saw the sky seem to dance and tilt. Then sand was above and sky below. Sand stung his hands. The reins tore free, cutting his fingers. Conan hit the ground hard.

Blinded by animated sand and by shock of impact, he heard loud whinnies – and galloping hooves. That sound retreated. His horses were fleeing, back the way they'd come. He had lost both horses, along with their packs.

He rose cursing and squinting against a blinding stinging sandstorm driven by no wind. The curses ceased quickly; he spat grit and clamped teeth and lips. He was a prisoner in a wailing, spinning cloud of never-still sand that rose up and up, billowing.

Sand-demons, desert-men called such when they saw them out on the deserts, spinning because of vagrant gusts of wind. It was only a figure of speech. Not, Conan thought, this time!

And then, immediately before him, the grains began to cluster, to billow up into a pillar. It spun, swirled, moaned, and that keening wail now hurt his ears. While his nape and armpits prickled and he sweated more than he had during a hotter period of that day, the sand coalesced, thickened. Every grain seemed trying to join every other, in that whirling column.

The column began to take on an anthropomorphic shape, even as it darkened.

It did. The sand had formed itself as a man, a dead-faced lich with a sinister dark gape of a mouth, dangling long arms – and no eyes. Though Conan's eyes were slitted almost shut and he could hardly see, he whipped out the curved eastern sword he had of a dead man of Samara.

The sand-lich did not pounce. It swirled, a chaotically spinning greyness in which that gaping mouth remained turned ever towards him, open and black within. The Cimmerian cut at it without effect. The sand seemed undisturbed by the sword's vicious slash through. There was nothing here to cut, nothing to hurt or kill; it was only a tall pile of sand!

It came over him then. It enveloped him.

Conan could not fight it, could not gain free, for it moved with him as though he were part of it. Sand stung his face, blotted his hearing and vision, pressed at his lips, and he knew he durst not breathe else he fill his nose and throat and lungs with airless grains of death. And the sand shut out all air, and Conan began to strangle, to smother.

He knew he could not hold his breath forever. He must expel it – or try to. And then would come the time when he must succumb to the automatic demands of his body. He would breathe in – and die.

He could not escape, could not twist or hurl himself free. The sand was a stinging, cloaking shroud that enveloped him, and it would be his death-shroud. His ears were full of a moaning wailing, but now the roaring from within began to blot and overwhelm it . . .

Words came then, and the Cimmerian knew that they

were not spoken, but that he heard them within his head, in his mind.

You have no soul!

I am dying . . . air . . .

You have no soul! No soul! Are you the thrice-accursed Hisarr Zul?

No! Dying . . . air . . . His-s-sarr . . . No! No, no!

Where is your soul?

Dying . . . can't breathe . . . Hisarr Zul has it . . . Desperately, aware that he had lost his battle, Conan expelled his breath between lips only slitted apart.

You are not Hisarr?

NO!

He has your soul! You have evil of Hisarr Zul?

Yes! Yes! Dying . . . must have air . . . Hisarr stole my soul – you steal my life!

The swirling pillar-shape, almost man-shape of sand spun away, retreating, freeing him. It withdrew some two feet. Conan fell weakly to his knees, and his gasps were vocal. His eyes bulged and his tongue was out – but now he could breathe. He could not talk for many seconds. He merely breathed, and the air was sweeter than new spring wine.

You live! Explain! The sand-lich stormed in his brain, and it was both command and yearning wheedling.

I am of . . . nowhere hereabouts. I am of Cimmeria, far and far.

You are not the accursed monster Hisarr Zul?

'No!' Conan bellowed aloud. 'It's he has my soul, my very soul!'

And though it was surely insanity to talk to *sand*, no matter that it resembled now a tall grey corpse all amove as with restlessly feeding maggots, the barbarian did so speak, and he went crafty. He was that anomaly, a man whose pride and code demanded truthfulness and would not brook an unkept vow – and one to whom lying on his behalf came easily. This . . . thing sought Hisarr Zul . . . and it hated him . . .

'I am sent by a well-born employer *for* the mage Hisarr Zul, for even now he rides hell-bent for Zamboula, having stolen our souls and an amulet of powerful sorcery. Only

I could have stopped him . . .'

The apparition moaned, seemed to diminish. It kept its distance and in a voice that issued scratchily, hollowly from that gaping black mouth in its sand-formed 'body', it . . . explained.

'Accursed Hisarr! He rides hell-bent, does he? Would that he were bound there in fact, him and his black heart and his blacker, treacherous soul! Listen, man of Cimmeria. Hear me, whom you see as monster! I am the shade of Hisarr's brother, I who was Tosya Zul! It was he who slew me and thereby doomed me to this partial existence, restricted to this place of my death! Give ear, man of Cimmeria, to a tale of treachery and the story of how I was *murdered*!'

If such a creature as this could be said to be sane or no, Conan felt that the sand-lich was mad, and with cause. The Cimmerian knew that he would listen, for he was in its power. Perhaps it would tell him how it might be laid, or how Hisarr Zul might swiftly be slain. He composed himself to listen to a story he realised the sand-lich was compelled to tell.

'None other has heard this story, Cimmerian. Attend. Together, my brother and I studied the ancient knowledge,' that scratchy, hollow voice said, 'and the arcane learning of long-dead mages. We learned those secrets known not in the abodes of men; the demonic lore of those formless horrors that dwell lurking in the farthest hills of the earth, in the very blackness between the worlds, in the ever-shifting sunbaked deserts, and in dark caverns where men go not. Incarnate and exotic magical intelligence became ours, and in our weening pride we sought power. What else is there? Already we had made ourselves wealthy. So we plotted for power, and we were found out – because my brother, as I later learned, could not keep shut his mouth! The khan of Zamboula learned of our plot against him, for his power to make Zamboula our base, and men came for us. Oh, they were right enough! Nefarious were our intents, and we were indeed brewing abominations in our close-shut house in Zamboula. They came to take us. We'd have been broken on the wheel, my brother and I; our nails would have been pulled out with pincers, and our eyes and tongues. I was out of the house when they came marching along the street with their weapons and their protecting little wizard – a minor bit of pulp who could weave only spells of protection and of seduction. I could have fled then! Instead, I risked my life to run along the streets as fast as I could, and in at the door and thus to our privy chambers to warn my brother Hisarr. Ah, would that I had fled without him, with nothing but the clothes I wore!

'We worked furiously to fill travelling sacks with the most precious of our gems and pearls, for so had we invested, rather than in land or the mere amassing of coins. We were trying to pack our paraphernalia and the books of our lore, the accretions of fifteen years of study and applied genius, *centuries of knowledge*, when the khan's men commenced hammering at the door. They bore torches. We could but flee, with the clothing we wore and our wealth. Yet we cursed and cast vile maledictions on the khan and his men, be sure; for the treasures we left behind were priceless, knowledge and objects and preparations beyond the wealth of men – and all we had was such. Trinkets, for buying. Normal men! We were hardly such, my brother and I! Indeed, we had been close on to learning how to remove the very souls from the bodies of men. He has that knowledge now, has he?'

'Aye,' Conan confirmed, through set teeth.

'Then he is close on to incredible power. With such knowledge, such an ability, all else becomes petty and inconsequential save the accumulation of power through . . . aye, now I say the word, after ten years of death: the accumulation of power through blackmail. Imagine what a man would pay to regain his very soul! Imagine what he would do, were it in the hands of another!'

I need not imagine, the Cimmerian thought bitterly. *I know. Get on with it, you who were no less living monster than Hisarr Zul!*

'Power over men of the city Watch, first, and then their commanders; over the counsellors and doxies of rulers – and ultimately over rulers themselves! For surely there was a way, my brother, my brilliant brother Hisarr said with those bulgy eyes gleaming like Black Stars, to gain the souls of men from some very personal possession of theirs. So we meant to do. We could have power over all Zamboula, and then over all Turan, over . . .

'But like dogs we fled into the night. Fugitives. We were fortunate to come upon a caravan, late the next day. They knew us not, and we joined them by giving the caravan-master no more than six of ten Iranistani lapis lazuli we had – he thought it was all our wealth! We could have bought his entire caravan, the fat fool! Hisarr and I travelled north with them, lamenting our loss, vowing to begin anew, vowing vengeance on Zamboula's khan . . . for, I see now, merely defending and protecting himself against us! I showed my brother those few preparations and writings I had brought out with me – a page from the very Book of Skelos itself! And he lamented, saying that he'd brought forth nothing in our haste to fly. And northward we rode, with my brother and me at the caravan's rear like common hangers-on.

'On the night we came to the hills called Dragon, I discovered that Hisarr had indeed brought certain writings – and had lied to me! He had kept them from me deliber-ately; I his brother, who had been his mentor and then partner for so many years – I who had *permitted* that viper to join me as partner. For Hisarr is my *younger* brother, and it was I who was the genius, the founder and instigator of our . . . ventures. Without me he'd have been nothing, nothing! Nor had I, in my weening interest in my studies and our future activities, any thought of the truth of our relationship . . . He hated me! He resented me my years, my seniority and superior knowledge! The thrice-accursed *viper!* And so that night I discovered and accused him, and we argued and all of it came out; his resentment and, aye, his hatred of me! We parted on that shocking note, both in anger, and on retiring I took certain precautions, ate of certain leaves and said certain words, for I was nervous and suspicious and sought to prevent my being murdered.

'I both failed and succeeded, as you see. That very night – or rather morning, for it was just at dawn – my clever brother did death on me, and afterward burned out my dead eyes with white-hot coins. I was left there – here! The caravan wended on. I was dead . . . but I never so much

68

as lost consciousness! Ah, my spell and my herbs had succeeded, for I was both dead and alive. Ah, the agony! A million times in these intervening years – how many years have passed, man of Cimmeria?'

'Ten.'

'Ten! And a million times during those *ten* years of long long days have I wished that I had taken no such precautions, that I had died as other men do, body and mind and soul. No. My body died. It is dead. It began to decompose, and I *knew*, I knew my body was rotting! I knew it when jackals came out of these hills and dug up my decomposing flesh, and feasted on it – on *me*! They ate me, barbarian, *me*! Some of my bones they took away with them, to gnaw in their dark abodes.

'But I remained alive. My soul is bound to this place. My mind, my *ka* is bound here, to bemoan my fate and think of peace, and revenge. And when men came, I attacked, for one of them might be my thrice-accursed brother, Hisarr the viper, the fiend! My will was strong, barbarian. It has gained strength with the passing years. I have gained control over the sand here. I have made it a part of me, subject to my will, so that with it I can form this semblance of a body you see; a body formed of sand! And so I have existed, dead but alive, and yet discorporeal. Nor can I leave this area of this accursed gorge where I was slain and buried, for here is my blood and here lie *most* of my bones. Again and again I have slain, seeking Hisarr – you do understand, northman, that I am surely no longer sane. How could I be?'

'I understand.'

Conan thought on the tale he'd had of the being from another world Yara the priest had kept in his fell tower in Arenjun. This sorcerous plotter was hardly so worthy a prisoner, hardly so pathetic and deserving of aid. Yet still . . .

'Upon the death of my brother, northman, barbarian, Cimmerian – is that it?'

Conan nodded, but the sand-lich had no eyes. 'Yes. Cimmerian. I am –'

'Upon his death,' the mad ghost broke in, raving, 'I too shall find rest. I welcome it now. No longer do I lust for life! This existence is horror! I have served my time in Hell, Cimmerian, and all the while I have been here on the mortal plane! And now . . . now, discovering that you have no soul – for I, a discorporate soul, know – I find the means for my deliverance. Hear me! Hear me, Cimmerian, for you too have cause to hate my brother and wish his death.'

Conan's face was like the stone statue of a grimly stern god, then, and his voice emerged as menacing. He spoke without disturbing the set muscles of his face: 'Yes.'

'Then hear me! You must capture him, make him helpless! He can be slain, Cimmerian, though not as other men may be done to death. The waters of the Zarkheba River will slay him, for that river of far south-western Kush flows with venom. Or any of his own . . . methods may be turned back on him, which is why he wears no weapons – is this true?'

'It is true.' *But where will I come by waters of some impossibly distant river, and how may such as I know how to turn back his own sorcerous weapons on him?*

'And he has learned to effect the stealing of souls.'

'Aye. His keep in Arenjun is guarded by men whose souls he took and imprisoned in mirrors . . . which he then shattered. But –'

'Ah. You can give them rest by stuffing the skull of Hisarr with earth, and his ears and nostrils, and then severing that head and seeing that it is burned – utterly consumed by flame.'

'His skull. But he lives . . .' And Conan thought: *You are mad indeed, lich of Tosya Zul!*

'He may be slain also by iron forged in Stygia over a fire of bones, for from that dark and demonic land came most of our spells. And he may be slain, too, by strangulation with the hair of a virgin slain with bronze, and made woman after the hair is removed.'

Conan said nothing. He felt his stomach lurch. What an abomination this creature without pity so calmly pronounced! Even for his soul, the Cimmerian knew that he could not murder a young girl and – do what else this mad monster specified. No, if necessary he'd spend years travelling to and through Stygia, to gain a sword of iron. Unless he found some way of turning Hisarr Zul's own evil back on the mage. That alone was promising; that alone seemed possible; yet it gave Conan little hope.

'And my own soul?'

'It is not important to me! I must have rest! Hisarr must die!'

'I vow on my mother by the gods my people swore by that I shall do all I can to slay him, Tosya Zul, and give you peace. But I want peace while I live. I want my body and my soul united!'

The sand-lich reared, shuddered, grew. 'I can *kill* you, little man!'

'I have no doubt of it, great wizard, as I stand here with no means of slaying you. But I am your best means of gaining peace. Aid me in overtaking him, and I will keep my vow. When you have told me how to regain my soul.'

'From him! He can return it to you in moments! Or by wrapping the mirror that imprisons it in the same tresses I have stated will kill him, and burying it thus wrapped in earth on which your blood falls. And by the simple means of causing a crowned person to break the mirror. For there is power in all those who rule, power that few of them know.'

'Then I must regain it from Hisarr himself, for I see no likelihood of holding converse with rulers of nations, and asking favours of them!'

'It is of no concern to me, man of . . . who are you?'

'I am Conan, a Cimmerian.'

'Why have you not told me? Never mind. Go now, and slay Hisarr Zul, accursed of all gods!'

'You have frightened off both my horses and with them all my water and food. Hisarr is already over these hills – for none uses this pass, now – and out on the desert to the south. I can never overtake him afoot.'

'There is an oasis but a day or two south of here, is there not? I remember dimly . . . ah, ye gods, what anguish is mine!'

'Yes!' Conan said hurriedly.

'Then it is he who shall overtake you, Coner of Simmon! For ten long years have I languished here dead but not dead, seizing on all who came in hopes that each is Hisarr at last! Now – now, Conum of Simmern, you can avenge yourself and *give me rest*! Take a good grip on your sword. Take several breaths and a good deep one *and hold it*! And close your eyes!'

The sand-lich of the haunted gorge was a raving madman, a pitiful *thing* – and yet Conan knew he was both a murderous monster – and a mage. He sheathed his sword and clamped his hand on its grip. He breathed hard, in and out, expanding his lungs, and sucked in a great breath. Holding it, he closed his eyes.

All around him then rose a sandstorm, and it rose, until it was a howling blinding fearsome horror that bore him up as though he were weightless, so that he clung to sword and breath and sanity and knew that he was being borne through the air at a hurtling speed. And he was. He was riding a sandstorm created by the master of the sand, and who was dead.

His belly floated within him and he fought back bile that would make him gasp for breath when there was only clogging, stinging, enfolding sand all about him, encompassing him and bearing him, like some grainy sorcerous cloak that formed wings for his transport.

The wind died then, or whatever force the sorcerous lich used to propel his sand, and gritty grains ceased to sting the Cimmerian's abraded hands and face, and he was dumped to the ground. And he smelled water.

As though from the dimmest reaches of the cold dark separating the world of life from that of death, Conan felt the words in his brain: *So you reach the oasis ahead of him, and lie in wait! And so I am exhausted, and*

The mind-voice of Tosya Zul faded from his brain, and the sandstorm was gone, and Conan lay in grass with the scent of fresh water in his nostrils.

CHAPTER 7

Isparana of Zamboula

For a long while Conan lay gasping and wondering. At last he lifted his head, and saw shade, and grass. Slender palms stood sentinel over a sizeable oasis that seemed to grow out of a large rock outcropping on an otherwise featureless terrain. Conan lay near the reed-edged water hole, which was a fair-sized pond.

Did I dream?

No; he had ridden into the Gorge of the Sand-lich; his horses were gone; he was well south, and in a large oasis. That one the Samaratan had said lay less than two days' ride from the Dragon Hills? He did not know. He could not be sure. He hoped so, and so he believed. Tosya Zul had presumably referred to the same oasis as had Arsil of Samara.

The Cimmerian grinned. Then surely, he thought, after all his troubles he was indeed ahead of the fleeing Isparana.

He drank, and gazed out on the sun-baked desert, and he thought on Hisarr Zul and on his brother. How sweet it would be to accommodate the latter! To exact his own vengeance, and Tosya's, and at the same time heroically lay the lich of the haunted gulch that so slowed travel! But . . . how? Conan turned over in his mind those means Tosya had detailed for ending Hisarr's life, and for the regaining of the Cimmerian's soul. He liked none of them. None sounded possible. How, then? Hisarr was a dangerous mage. He had but to break the mirror. And into that damned little tube of his, he need puff a single breath to accomplish Conan's doom.

Conan sat beneath a palm, his back against its slim, sturdy trunk, and stared at nothing. He waited, and he thought.

An old man came to the oasis that afternoon, with his

daughter and son and three camels. The son watched the Cimmerian with the dark, suspicious gaze of one ready to fight if necessary though too young to know that he durst not essay against such a man. The daughter looked upon him with fear, and something else that would not allow her to meet his gaze but, when it was directed elsewhere, would not let her look away from him. The father spoke quietly to the quiet, very big young man with blue eyes and a shock of raven hair, who had keenly watched his method of handling the camels.

Yes, the Dragon Hills and the Gorge of the Sand-lich were just two days north of here. No, they had seen no one. Aye, they were bound for Zamboula; would he care to ride with them?

No, but Conan accepted the food that to him was a huge gift, from these poor folk with so far to go. And while the old man saw to his camels Conan pressed on the skittish boy the sheathed dagger he had of a dead thief of Samara.

'I would not insult you by offering aught for the food you gave in friendship,' Conan told the father, 'but in friendship I have given your son a small gift of good metal.'

'It is well,' the old man said, 'and may Mitra hurry the steps of him you await, friend. Oh – beware. Some caravans leave ever at the same times, and last night's moon indicated to me that a caravan from Khawarizm should have been here yesterday. We have not seen it. Perhaps it will arrive this night, or on the morrow.'

When Conan continued to gaze at him, the old man said, 'Khawarizm is the southernmost port of Turan, on the Vilayet Sea. Slaves are traded for in Khawarizm, and carried north-eastward to such places as Khauran and Zamora.'

'How does this concern me?'

'Sometimes slavers are not altogether careful as to where they acquire their goods, or how, my young friend from Cimmeria. Where is your protection?'

Conan touched the pommel of his sword.

'Nevertheless,' the old man said, 'beware.'

And he and the boy and girl mounted two of their camels, and the other followed as they rode away southward.

Both younger pilgrims looked back. Conan made no sign.

He sat, and for a time he thought about how kind and good it was possible for people to be, and how few behaved so. Then he relaxed, and with the deadly insouciant patience of a stalking panther – or a northern barbarian – he gazed northward. Conan waited for Isparana, and plotted against Hisarr Zul.

While the sun wallowed low amid the deep gold of its setting, Conan watched the slow approach of a single rider and two animals, a mile and more away. While the sun went orange and then red that shot a spray of yellow gold up into the darkening sky, he saw that the rider was sagging, lurching, nigh asleep in the high-cantled saddle of a plodding camel. Another camel followed. The rider wore a dun-coloured jallaba over white robes, and was slim and narrow of shoulder.

Smiling, Conan belly-crawled through excellent grass, only muttering a curse when he put his hand down in camel dung. He reached his goal: the cluster of large russet-shot grey boulders just at the edge of the oasis; from them swelled the spring that created it. The sound of camel-bells grew steadily in volume.

From there he watched while, just at dusk, Isparana reached the oasis . . . and fell off her dromedary.

She had pushed herself far too hard, Conan thought. Good! Perhaps she'd glanced back to see him when he saw her, from the far side of Dragon hills. Good! She was certain he was behind her, then, and she was weary unto collapse. Her mount plodded on, carefully avoiding her with its big padded feet. It took a sip or two of water, seemed to consider, and began to crop grass. Its companion followed its lead. Conan watched.

For a long while Isparana lay, a bundle of white and neutral tan-grey.

Then she rose on to her elbows and wormed to the pool as if rising were far too much effort for her drained organism. Slipping back her sand-hood so that glossy black hair fell about her face, she let her head plop into the water.

Conan watched. He noted that she wore a long sword.

He watched while she at last rose wearily, and doffed the jallaba as if every movement was a great effort. Moving listlessly as one who had forgone sleep to gain her supposed lead, she hobbled her camels. Conan watched. Strands of hair like blackest night were water-plastered to her cheek and forehead, not unattractively.

Muffled in the loose white burnoos and yet distinctly feminine, she dragged her feet as she paced to the southern edge of the oasis. He saw her yawn. Once she stumbled and fell headlong, and with an ugly grin Conan heard her curse, by Erlik and by Yog. At the edge of the greenery, she stood and stared southward. It was obvious to Conan that she was striving to pierce the thickening dark with her gaze. The rising moon lit her face with soft white, and Conan saw that her features were soft-planed; a pretty face.

Conan watched. Never had he seen anyone so weary, so in need of sleep. He would wait. Surely good fortune was again with him.

Kneeling, the camels belched and chewed. Now and again one of the ugly creatures would stretch a leathery neck to tear off a few tendrils of grass to sweeten its cud.

Isparana was unable to see aught but the darkness, nor did the night bring any sound to her ears or the keener ones of the Cimmerian. She returned, like a shuffling ghost in her fluttering white garments, to the water-hole. Conan stared, just able to discern her in the moonlight softened and diluted by tall palm-trees. Then he saw what she was doing, and his stomach and throat tightened.

Unable to look away – he tried – he watched Isparana strip, a woman very alone in the nighted oasis. The languor of exhaustion added sensuousness to her movements and sight of her moonlit form made the Cimmerian covet more than the Eye of Erlik. The soft boots of red felt, yellow trousers and flowing white robes had concealed a most attractive female body, and Conan clenched his teeth.

Temptation rose in the youthful Cimmerian like a mountain freshet and he was unable not to consider wresting from this woman more than the amulet he must have.

Aye – the amulet. As she turned and slipped into the pool, he saw what she wore around her neck, on a rude

76

leather thong that had been slung under her voluminous clothing. A bauble dangled, winking, between the moving hills of her bare bosom, and two yellow stones gleamed from the pendant's abbreviated arms . . .

The camels, kneeling after the manner of their kind, chewed more and more listlessly, and slept. Soon one was snoring.

Isparana splashed about in the pool, no less listlessly. Conan swallowed again and again. His concealed proximity to so lovely a nude woman was torment for one of his years. He waited without patience, and sought glimpses that but added to his torture.

Nevertheless he entertained the thought that perhaps she was so weary she'd drown and save him a lot of trouble . . .

At last, a pale vision of loveliness in the moon's silver glow, she emerged from the water. Conan saw that even thus bathed and refreshed, she still dragged wearily. She shook out her long hair, black as the sky itself. Her standing with her weight on one foot unconsciously flouted her haunch in a way that made him close his eyes against the sight. She took her hair in her hands and wrung it. Water fell noisily at her feet and glistened on the grass like moonstones.

Conan ground his teeth and shifted restlessly. He had to work consciously to be mindful of making noise. That she was eight or ten years older than he was of no consequence. He was male, and young, and she was very very female.

With otiose movements she squeezed the moon-flashing midnight of her tresses in the hem of her burnoos. The robe she tedded on the ground. Slipping into her jallaba then, she let it open and lay wearily down. Conan continued to hold his rockbound position, and continued to watch.

Now there was nothing to watch. She must have fallen asleep instantly, not refreshed but relaxed by her bathing.

Both camels snored.

Conan kept his vigil. He was aroused, tempted. He was aware of the beat of his pulse before his ears, a strong hot surge. He waited. The moon lofted higher, a silvery three-quarter like a cradle suspended in the sky. Somewhere, Picts worshipped beneath it, as had women for long and long,

77

for they knew their kinship with the sky-hung Lady of the Night and were monthly reminded of it.

Conan waited, closing his eyes to rest them from their staring into the dark. The camels slept noisily. Conan was sure the woman slept. He waited.

Then a thief of Arenjun rose silently and crept upon the camels, who took but little note while, with great care for silence, he daggered away the bells of their harness. Squatting, he opened a large pack of provisions and transferred some of its contents. And a thief of Arenjun crept then upon Isparana of Zamboula; a thief who had plucked up costly ear-rings from a little table beside the bed on which their owner slept; who had robbed another woman while she lay with her lover less than ten paces distant; who had plucked a cloak off a sleeping man without so much as disturbing his snoring.

Only a skittish animal would have heard the whisper of the grass through which the thief of Arenjun made his way, without ever taking his eyes off the sleeping woman he approached.

He looked down at her. She lay on her back, the jallaba open to the ribcage and moulded to her womanly form. Conan's tongue touched his lips as, noiselessly, he slipped his dagger from its hide-covered sheath of oiled wood. Very slowly, mindful of any sound and without taking his gaze off her sweetly reposed face, he let himself slip down to his knees beside the sleeping woman.

The long dagger caught the moonlight in a metallic glint as the big hand that held it approached her throat. There pulsed her jugular, slowly, with her heart at rest.

And there lay a slim length of brown leather. Knotted behind her neck, it vanished into the bosom of the V-necked, pullover robe whose hood cradled her hair.

Conan used both hands.

She stirred while he sliced through the thong about her neck, and he went rock-still for long, long moments. She sighed; she did not waken. The camels' snoring did not interfere with her sleep, and neither did the feather-light touch of an experienced thief. After a time he took away the thong and, ever so slowly and with frequent pauses, the pendant it held.

78

Without moving from her side he cut away the knot, which he stowed in his mouth and tasted its salt. On the thong he strung the pendant he had already removed from about his own neck. It was identical . . . save that this substitution was without true value to her lord, the Turanian Empire's satrap in Zamboula.

Isparana stirred when he slipped the thong about her neck, and knotted it. He but tucked the pendant into the top of her garment; he would not torture himself and risk waking her by trying to tuck it deeper, into the warmth of her bosom.

His face tensed and he stared down at her while his eyes burned like blue lava. For a moment he was tempted to draw the leathern cord as tightly as he could and hold it until she thrashed and lapsed into a new sleep from which she'd never awaken.

He did not. He succumbed neither to the urge to enjoy nor to slay her. Barbarian he might be, and was called, often with scorn; he was nevertheless neither a rapist nor a murderer. Murder was sensible, under the circumstances; the Cimmerian, who was more animal than most men, was this time more human than sensible.

With a flex of his knees he pushed himself fluidly to his feet. Isparana slept the deep sleep of complete exhaustion, while a superb thief worked on. He turned and left as silently as he had ghosted to her side, and now Conan wore around his neck not Hisarr's copy but the real Eye of Erlik.

It felt no different.

For some reason known only to cameldom, Isparana's animals awoke without raising a clamour of ugly voices. Both even deigned to rise in response to his silent urging in which he copied the old man who'd tarried here earlier this day. The bells from their harness lay in the grass, well to one side. He had separated the contents of the main provisions-pack; he would not take all her food.

Conan sought to lead the humpbacked animals, the strange ships of the desert. They stood fast. He circled and sought to drive them before him, even slapping the flank of one with the flat of his new, curved sword. Its flying foot only just missed him.

Conan made his kick count, and the dromedary grunted and staggered on that leg. It turned to stare from beneath the long lashes given it by the gods to protect its eyes from the flaming desert sun. Conan returned the stare, not sullenly or icily but with the great malice he sought to convey to the beast so pridefully unlike a horse.

'I am going to lead you out of here,' he murmured to the camel Isparana had used as sumpter-beast, 'or drag your strangled carcass. Choose, old supercilious-head.'

The other dromedary, him Isparana had ridden, turned to stare. The Cimmerian gave it an evil look and showed the beast his teeth. The camel regarded him ruminatively. Conan moved back to its head and reached for its halter. The beast sought to bite and big, yellowed teeth grazed his wrist. Conan slapped its nose, hard. The animal made a throaty noise.

'Come.'

The Cimmerian took hold of its halter, rather than the rein. Beside its *jeml* head, the man paced forward. The camel plodded beside him! The other followed!

Don't know camels, eh? Conan mused in high triumph. *They understand mastery like any other, man or beast. They just have to have it proven to them differently, and they've more pride than horses – or less sense. Very well then, camels; I've more pride, and you feel it, don't you!*

The verdant grass of the oasis ended as he and the animals walked on, with Conan's face to the north. *Farewell, Isparana,* he thought. *I probably hope the slaver caravan comes – but for your sake I hope they have all the human goods they want!*

Conan had evidence that he possessed some sort of sixth sense, which had saved his life more than once. Whether he did or no was not at point; whether Isparana did was also unimportant; for whatever reason, at that moment the woman awoke. She sat straight up as if she'd slept for hours.

'Thief! STOP, *thief!*'

And she came racing around the water-hole, naked sword in hand.

Conan tried to spring on to her riding-camel, failed, tried to get it to kneel. Failing, he knew he was out of time. He turned grimly to face Isparana. He heaved a great sigh.

Around the pool she charged. One hand waved her sword so that it flashed in the moonlight; the other held her jallaba's skirt well up. Bare legs and feet flashed and she was muttering and cursing all the while.

'Wait!' Conan called. 'Stop!'

'*Stop!*' she cried, and her voice rose into a screech. 'While you steal my camels and leave me here to DIE?'

He was forced to let go the camel's halter and draw his sword. She came on, running with the new energy of adrenaline, both angry and as if mad. On the run, she swung a sweeping slashing stroke. He easily used his sword to deflect it, at the same time swiftly sidestepping. The charging woman's momentum carried her on and she slammed into the riding-camel. As she rebounded to fall asprawl on her backside, the beast decided it had enough of yells and now this untoward impact. It emited a grunting, bubbling roar and bucked, kicking in a most un-camelish display. One splayed soft foot caught the other camel in the foreleg. Both beasts complained. Then the second dromedary reacted to the shouts of Isparana's high-voiced screams and this sudden explosion of its companion into vicious action.

The pack-camel fled.

'No!' Conan bawled. 'Stop!'

The riding-camel then proved it was not wedded to the role of leader; it followed the sumpter beast. Never mind that camels were the most stupid and unarousably placid of animals; they were aroused. They made off into the night.

Yelling, Conan leaped after them. The rearward camel was frightened anew and speeded its gait. Conan lunged and missed; he fell sprawling in the harder-packed sand at the oasis's edge. The dromedaries lurched away into the darkness; ungainly or no, they showed speed.

As he started to push himself to his feet Conan heard Isparana's enraged cry – coming at him. He rolled as swiftly as he could impart the sideward motion. Her sword, already descending in a cleaving stroke, dug into the sand where he'd lain. Conan, on his back, hoisted himself on his elbows.

81

'Damn you, woman!' he snarled, and his sideward-rushing feet knocked both her legs from beneath her.

Then the Cimmerian scrambled up and raced northward into the night, after the camels.

He returned from the darkness on foot, not striding and looking thoroughly disgusted. He led no camels. Isparana stood waiting, glowering from a half-crouch. Her sword was up and quiveringly poised for a spitting lunge.

'Now you've done it,' he said. 'You frightened off the camels.'

'*I* frightened –'

'Aye. I think they're still running.'

'*I* . . . you filthy dog of a THIEF, you've trapped us BOTH here! I'll KILL you!' And she lunged in a rustle of enveloping jallaba.

Conan had to dive aside. He rolled. When he came up, his sword was out. 'Stop it, woman! We are trapped here, as you said. Better there were two of us than one.'

'But you – you . . . my *camels*! The *food*! The water!'

'Plenty of water a few steps away,' the Cimmerian reminded her equally. 'And I unpacked and left some food – what sort of man do you think I am!'

'What sort – dog! Mangy *dog*!'

'This is a big oasis and travellers are many, this time of year. We'll not starve before someone comes.'

'You – my cam – rotten filthy *dog*! Viper! How *can* you stand there and talk so – aarrghh!' And she charged him.

Conan appeared to brace to meet her inexpert assault head-on. At the last moment he faded aside, simultaneously whipping his sword out and down to intersect hers. The blades met with a ringing clash and metal scraped along metal with a shrieking sound. She was on the run, and plunged on unable to stop; her sword was carried out of her hand.

The Cimmerian was picking it up when she wheeled to face him.

'Now *stop*,' he told her. 'I have no desire to kill you. I will hurt you though, if you don't stay away and leave off these mad attacks.'

She stood and stared, and she wept, but not in softness

and despair; she sobbed in rage and frustration. Conan knew the feeling.

'You are very weary. You've not had enough sleep. I suggest you return to your burnoos and resume your rest. I'll remain across the pool, under that largest palm.'

She stood glaring, quivering in impotence. The energy of anger had to be channelled somewhere; she stamped and beat a fist into her palm. Then realisation: 'You were here. You *saw*!'

'Saw?' Conan sheathed his sword and transferred hers to his right hand. 'Saw what?'

'Saw . . . saw me . . . you saw me . . . bathe.'

'Oh, that.'

Conan shrugged, yawned, and turned to walk back into the grass and trees. He said no more, and did not glance at her, though he knew she still stared. He entered the oasis and sat at the base of the tree he had stipulated. He kept her sword in his hand. The air was growing cool.

She came, taking a curving path to stay well away from a man who both stole and insulted. Returning to where her burnoos formed a white patch on the grass, she stood a long while. At last she turned to face him across the placid water.

'Who are you?'

'Conan, a Cimmerian. And you?'

'Who sent you?'

'Sent? No one sent me. I was headed for Zamboula, from Khauran. I didn't know about the thing in the pass among those hills. Both my horses fled and I barely escaped with my life.'

'Worse luck for me! Expert at losing valuable animals on the desert, aren't you? You expect me to believe that you survived the Sand-lich, and are not mad?'

'I survived the thing in the gorge, yes. But surely no sane man would have been content with only your camels, once he'd seen you.'

'Save your compliments for the whores you doubtless know best! How came you here ahead of me, then?'

'Good fortune. As I emerged from the gorge, three people on camels were coming off the last of the Dragon Hills. They brought me here. Very kind people.'

'I saw them ahead of me, when I topped the first of those hills . . . bu they *left* you here?'

Conan gestured. 'I was not going their way.'

'But – to allow yourself to be abandoned on the desert, willingly . . .'

'It's a pleasant place. I knew someone would come.'

That struck her silent – for a few seconds. 'Monster! Dog! Son of a stinking cur! Grunting swine! You "knew someone would come"!'

'Aye. The Sand-lich told me how to lay him to rest . . . by killing a man named Hisser Zool, up in . . . Arenyi?'

'Arenjun,' she said automatically, in thought.

'Arenjun, yes. You know this Hisser Zool?'

'No.'

'Heard of him?'

'No. Of course not. I've never been to Arenjun. *Everyone's* heard of it. You belong there, believe me!'

So we are both liars, Isparana, Conan mused; *nor will I mention to you the caravan coming from Khawarizm . . . nor call you by name. Sleep, Isparana. Conan is weary . . . and durst not rest until you do!*

She sat, seeming to fold up. Though he could not see her features, he knew she was staring at him. Her exhaustion and her body's need for rejuvenating sleep overcame all her thoughts of him and food and the morrow; she lay back.

After a time she slept, and after a longer time, sitting propped against the tree, so did Conan.

She too was a thief, and quiet; she awoke him with the point of her sword at his eyes.

CHAPTER 8

Slavers!

'I'll not beg, woman,' Conan said, looking up along the shining blade of Isparana's sword. 'I'd give you something to consider, though.'

'I'm listening,' Isparana said.

'That is a caravan I see beyond you, coming up from the south. A few minutes more and we'll hear their bells. In less than an hour they will be here. Are you sure you can convince them you didn't simply murder me?'

She was wise enough to back two paces before looking southward. A glance was sufficient to assure her he had not invented the approaching caravan.

A nasty smile rearranged her features when she faced the Cimmerian again. 'If those are Zamboulans, dog, they will know and believe me when they hear my story – and you will die *slowly*, as you deserve.'

'Bloodthirsty wench! And if it's a party of slavers from Khawarizm? What then?'

She blinked. 'Why – they'll not harm a free woman of Zamboula, also of the Empire of Turan!'

'Hm. A woman without goods, animals, protector . . . hm. We could be a pair of runaway slaves. No, they'd not harm you – they'd just add you to their coffle.'

Now Conan's peripheral vision showed him that a party of horsemen had left the caravan and was coming in at the gallop; men to scout the oasis, he assumed.

'Erlik! That – that's unthinkable. But even so – what matters it whether I kill you or no?'

'What will it gain for you, so long as there's the chance I might die slowly, in Zamboula?'

'Revenge! But for you I'd greet them as one of property, with two camels and one laden.' Isparana's face tightened, and her eyes went hard again.

Conan sat gazing up at her. He did not think she would

kill him thus out of hand. Meanwhile, her ankles were just out of reach of his feet, his sword and dagger were sheathed, and five horsemen were rapidly approaching. He told her of them, suggesting that she hide aught she had of value. She spun, as the caravan guards, slowing to a ragged canter, reached the oasis.

'Ho!'

'Ho yourself,' Conan said, and rose while Isparana looked uncertainly from him to the newcomers. Her sword wavered in her hand.

'You two have this oasis all to yourself?' The mounted man looked around. 'Where are your animals?'

Conan stepped forward and slipped an arm around Isparana. He had to clench her shoulder, as she sought to flinch away. 'Stolen, by Erlik!' Conan said. 'My . . . woman and I came down here from Shadizar, up in Zamora. We were to meet her cousin, Arsil of Samara; he's a soldier of the Empire. Well, we waited for days – and when nine mangy desert rats stopped here, we were too kind. They made off with our animals. Two horses and two camels, by Erlik!'

'Thieving swine! And – her cousin . . . still not here, eh?'

Conan tried to dissuade slavers from enslaving thoughts: 'They arrived a few hours later. They hardly paused, but rode after the thieves.'

'Ah.' The man turned to say something to those with him, then paced his horse into the verdure. 'We saw no one.'

'No,' Conan said, 'they all rode north. You will doubtless meet Arsil and his men coming back soon. Carrying bodiless heads, I hope.'

'They left you that?' The horseman indicated the small pack Conan had meant to leave for Isparana.

'Aye. You from Zamboula, Captain?'

'No; Khawarizm.' The man dismounted. His beard, Conan saw, failed to cover several scars. A longtime mercenary then. 'You're not offended by the sight of . . . human trade-goods, are you?'

'Your business,' Conan said, 'is yours, and ours is ours.'

'Of course. We will tarry a few hours – then you may join us.'

'We'd best just wait here,' Conan said easily, 'for Arsil and his Imperial soldiers. Don't you think, Kiliya?'

'Definitely,' Isparana said, swift-mindedly following his lead. 'Arsul will be back soon. Perhaps the captain and I can discuss the possibility of our buying a horse.' She turned a smile on Conan. 'I can await you in Zamboula, my love.'

'I'd not think of your travelling all that way south alone, my love,' Conan said, smiling just as sweetly.

Also smiling, the mercenary stepped forward so that he was on the side of Isparana opposite Conan. 'Perhaps it's your accent, northman,' he said, 'but I note you and, uh, Kiliya do not agree as to her cousin's name. I am also no such fool as to believe that five soldiers of far Samara would ride so far north to meet a mere *cousin* of one of their number.'

'Unless she's the cousin of the ruler of Samara!' Conan said in an even tone, and he too managed to maintain his smile. 'You can understand that we did not wish to tell you so, Captain. Though your trade is guarding camels and slaves, you must know about such things as state secrets.'

For a moment the mercenary captain looked most unsure. Then, 'Aye . . . and now I'd hear you tell me the name of the ruler down in Samara.'

Conan, who had no idea, held his open expression. 'Tell him, my lady.'

Isparana stared imperiously at the guardsman. 'I am not in the habit of being interrogated.'

'Hisarr Khan rules Samara,' Conan said, hoping that the captain did not know, either.

'Wrong,' the man from Khawarizm said.

'Damn,' Conan said, and stepped away from Isparana with hand on hilt.

'Ha! I know not the name of Samara's ruler – but neither do you!' the captain said. He gestured to his mounted men. 'These look like two escaped slaves to me! Here is where we earn our employer's promised bounty. Take them!'

Conan drew sword with one hand and yanked Isparana

away from the man with the other. 'Better use your sword, my lady! And pray for Arsil's return!'

Isparana had never sheathed her sword; the mercenary captain was reaching for his; a rider came at Conan. As he leaned down to hack with the big club he wielded rather than sword, Conan lunged beneath his horse in a headlong dive. He was up on the other side before the mercenary had recovered from his heavy swing. His twisting in the saddle was too late; Conan cupped a hand under the man's foot and tipped him off his horse. At the same time Isparana, noting the captain's attention was on Conan, stabbed him in the left armpit.

With cries of shock and rage, the others spurred forward, and hands clutched for swords rather than slave-taming clubs.

'Get the one on the ground!' Conan yelled, and though the horse from Khawarizm turned three-quarters around, the Cimmerian hung on and dragged himself up into the saddle.

At his words two of the three attackers reined towards Isparana. Conan booted his new mount hard, so that it plunged between her and the charging Khawarizmi. The sword of one was already raised on high for a downward stroke to split the woman; without pausing Conan slashed his belly open from hip to hip. The man cried out in pain at the same time as Isparana sworded the one Conan had tumbled off his horse.

'Get that horse!' Conan yelled, yanking his grunting mount around to drive at the other two from the caravan.

Unfortunately they swerved so that he passed between them. He took a cut high on his left arm while he slashed the other horseman across the face. While he fell back with a hand to his scarlet features, Conan again yanked his horse around. The man who'd cut him was doing the same. And Isparana, somehow, was mounted, with her jallaba open to the navel and hiked to the hips.

'Take him from behind, "my lady"!' Conan called, looking past the last foe.

The mercenary's eyes went huge. Without glancing back he jerked his horse's head rightward at the same time as he clapped heels to its flanks. The beast bolted. With his four companions sore wounded or worse, the terrified Khawarizmi fled back to the slaver caravan.

'Five hardly worth their pay,' Conan snarled. 'Just let me snatch up this bit of provisions, "my love", and we'd best head north, at the gallop!'

Then he looked her way, saw her sword rushing at his face and her contorted features behind, and ducked desperately. The sword missed; Isparana was already kicking her mount into a gallop on a south-westerly course, to avoid the other caravan guards. Conan, meanwhile, had no occasion to know that she would never make it. He not only fell, but bashed his head on the large old palm. For Conan, the sun went out.

Five men, in matched cloaks and spiked helmets sat their horses and watched with disapprovingly set faces while a caravan plodded by on its way north. The five soldiers led two extra horses; the caravan led four, and some twoscore shuffling slaves on a single chain attached to the left ankle of each.

'They seem to have lost some guards,' one of the soldiers said. 'I see only six, plus two wounded men and four riderless horses.'

'Good observation, Kambur. Perhaps we'd best ask them if –'

'Arsil! Arsil of Samara!'

'Tarim's eyes! Who calls – one of the *slaves*?'

'Arsil! Conan the Cimmerian needs help!'

As Arsil's eyes isolated the man who'd shouted from the very end of the line of shackled slaves, a mercenary guard rode at the big man, raising a whip. Arsil's arm leaped out, finger extended at the guard.

'Strike him and *die*, mercenary! Caravan master: call a halt! Kambur, Sarid – to the end of the slave-coffle, and bring his horses. Be ready to fight, if these swine insist on denying our blue-eyed friend's claim to freedom! After me!' And Arsil's heels kicked, and his horse bolted for the caravan's head. Two of his men followed. Leading the two horses they'd easily captured just north of the Dragon Hills, the other two rode for Conan. He brought up the very rear of the caravan save for two mounted guards.

A few minutes later one Iskul, caravan master, was expostulating. 'He slew two of my guards and sorely wounded two others! He's lucky we didn't kill him!'

'Lucky?' Arsil's hand loosened his sword in its sheath; Iskul's eyes followed the movement. 'Would you rather be dead or enslaved? Speak up swiftly, citizen of the Empire I serve; I can accommodate you in *one* of the choices.'

The man from Khawarizm swallowed, took some time to think, and made another attempt. 'Captain, Captain! We are *merchants* here, acting for other merchants to enrich the same Turanian Empire you serve – too. You have no authority to stop us and demand one of our slaves! As well demand the other trade goods.'

'Did you steal it, too?'

'Captain –'

'You had ten guards. One man, you say, slew two and wounded two others. We are five, on a mission for the Empire,' Arsil said, stretching fact a bit. 'In my possession is my khan's document empowering me to accost thieves and return their loot – and you know *my* khan is the King-Emperor's wife's cousin. By Tarim, I believe my writ could be made to apply to you. I will have the Cimmerian, sir. Will you give the order or must we embarrass the Empire of Turan by drawing steel?'

Again Iskul was silent, thinking. And again: 'Look here, Captain, we need not talk so. He's a big strapping fellow, and his price will be excellent! Perhaps you and I could strike a bargain. I am no poor man –'

'Just,' Arsil said, 'about to be a dead one. I do not bribe, fellow.'

'Ah! Demons take you both! He's surely a rebellious type anyhow. *Fars!* Loose that last one. The dog has a friend.'

'And the woman the bastards captured with me!' Conan yelled, before he took time to consider what a fine slave Isparana would make, who had enabled him to be taken – and then failed to outrun the other mercenaries anyhow.

After a brief confrontation, Iskul bawled a second order. Fars, flanked by two of Arsil's men, dared do no more than open Conan's shackle, then Isparana's. Grinning, the Cimmerian looked up at the soldiers.

'Kambur of Iranistan! My deep thanks. And you even brought my horses. This,' he said, laying a hand on Isparana's shoulder, which was bared to the sun in punishment, 'is the woman I sought for my master. Those two camels – there, see – are hers. She's going south as you are; here, Isparana, is a fine escort for you – brave men, and my personal friends.'

She glared darkly at him. The Eye of Erlik flashed on her bosom; the false Eye. Conan whirled to Fars, whom he passed with a snarl so animalistic that the Khawarizmi mercenary fell back, wide-eyed. He made no demurrer when Conan took two weapon-belts from his saddle; each bore a sheathed sword and dagger. Conan first strapped on Isparana's, then his own. He looked up with a bright smile as Arsil came cantering to him.

'Arsil my friend, I am indebted to you forever.'

'Just claim nothing and no one else here, Conan,' Arsil said, 'else we have rebellion within the Empire! You'd make a rotten slave anyhow, blue-eyes.'

'Would I not indeed! Now Isparana here – methinks she'd be a perfect slave. Yet I am weak and overly gentle, and could not let her remain coffled. Why, one of those two camels is actually her own!'

Arsil turned his head a bit to one side. 'And the other?'

Conan spread his hands. 'I told you I followed her for my employer, up in Shadizar. She had several little items of his – but all are in the pack on the sumpter-camel's back – my *employer's* camel.'

That brought life to Isparana for the first time in the day and a half they had been slaves; she had been as if dazed, and the sudden appearance of friends of the Cimmerian thief and the opening of her iron anklet had been just as perplexing. Now she rounded on the grinning Conan.

'Animal! Son of an animal! Dog of a thief – that is MY camel! Both are and you know it. Captain – look at me. I am on a mission for the khan of Zamboula himself. How can a soldier of Turan allow this – this –'

'Best cease your habitual lying, my love,' Conan said, 'lest I claim too that bauble you wear around your neck.'

Isparana's voice broke off; Isparana's eyes widened; Isparana's hand clamped over the amulet made by Hisarr Zul to confound thieves – a bit too late. Isparana's lips, too, clamped.

Conan smiled up at the mounted Arsil. 'Did you find aught at the oasis up yonder?'

'Nothing. The caravan you mentioned must have done something with the bodies you left. Naturally, they also appropriated the camels. A fine *gift*, to them.'

Conan wagged his head. 'I do feel responsible, Arsil, and I am in your debt. Here.' He unstrapped the sword he'd taken from Uskuda the Samaratan thief. 'Take this; it is proof to your khan that you met and slew Uskuda and his partner.' He turned to his own sumpter-horse, and swiftly unstrapped a smallish pack. 'You know what this contains, Arsil, and you know whence it came, though you'd have let me keep it. Take it too. This way you return proof of Uskuda's death as well as a goodly portion of his loot.'

'Conan, you were born too low! Come with us; a man of your abilities and noble nature will soon be *my* superior in the Guard of Samara!'

'*Noble*,' Isparana muttered – and both Arsil and Conan stared until she looked away.

'I will never forget you or that offer of employment,' Conan said, and he paused to show his pantherish strength and suppleness by pouncing on to his horse. 'But I *must* get myself up north, now. My employer does have a certain . . . hold on me. "My lady" – you do think swiftly and you are good with a sword – too bad we cannot remain a team!'

'Speaking of swords, do – uh, Conan –'

He clapped a hand to his, which had been hers. 'Ah, you'll not need one, dear girl – these big Turanian soldiers will take care of you! Do fare well down in Zamboula. Oh – Arsil, my friend: get her to show you how well she swims!'

And Conan urged his horse into a trot, with the other, a little more lightly laden, hurrying along behind at the end of his lead. Behind him swift-plodded Isparana's dromedary. All along the line of the caravan Conan rode, grinning, and paused only for a long, long moment in which he stared down at Iskul of Khawarizm.

'Some day, fat one . . . some day I am going to come down to Khawarizm, and open up your belly to let the air out, and burn down your whole rotten slaving city!'

Then Conan galloped northward, and he made but one small divergence on his direct route to Arenjun. At a certain oasis, he paced a hundred steps eastward into the desert and there dug up a nice little package he had buried.

CHAPTER 9

Black Lotus and Yellow Death

'So, Conan of Cimmeria! You are back in much less than a month,' Hisarr Zul said, his brows arching above exophthalmic eyes. 'You have succeeded in your mission, then?' The mage stood rocking on his toes, his hands clasped behind his back as Conan had first seen him.

'Aye,' the Cimmerian said, and he glanced about the Green Room to which Hisarr's eerie guards had conducted him. Once again he was weaponless; those were down by the manse's rear door. Aye, there it was, he saw with a qualm and a renewal of that inner sensation of emptiness. There in the cupped hands of the statue of a black demon rested the little mirror containing his soul.

Conan gestured. 'I'll have that mirror emptied, sorcerer.'

'Will you! Nothing simpler – for me. But first the proof of your success in retrieving the amulet.'

'I do hate to part with it,' Conan said. 'I've worn it for a week now.'

'Hmm. And the copy I gave you?'

'It has been in the hands of her who stole the real Eye from you. She is doubtless still on her way to Zamboula – with the five-man escort I arranged.'

'How resourceful you are, Conan of Cimmeria!'

'Not resourceful enough. I have no waters from that river down in Kush, or Stygian iron, and I am not the sort to slay a maiden for her hair!'

The blood drained visibly from Hisarr's face. 'How did you – what sort of nonsense is this you speak?'

'You have already slipped, sorcerer. It's true, then. Those are the means of your death. And all the souls you have stolen may be liberated by stuffing your dead skull with earth and burning it to ash, eh?'

Hisarr Zul was shaken, and literally staggered: he backed a pace on watery knees while he stared into deadly blue eyes. 'You . . . but one person knows those things!'

'And I am he. The other has been dead ten years. Ask no more, Hisarr Zul. Return to me my soul,' he said, fighting so as not to falter over the word, 'and I shall tell you where to find the amulet.'

Regaining control though still pale, Hisarr shook his head. 'That will not do, Conan. I must see the Eye before I free you.'

'And how will you know that it is the real Eye?'

'I will know. So would the Khan of Zamboula – but he will never have the opportunity.'

The Cimmerian thought of Isparana, on her journey over a thousand miles south to Zamboula. 'No?' He moved to place himself between his soul and its . . . keeper.

'No.'

Smiling, Hisarr moved to his long, high table. There, muttering the while, he took up a carven chest of russet-coloured wood. From it he took, showing each to Conan, a ruby and two black-barred yellow stones, and a quantity of gold dust; the components of the Eye of Erlik. He dropped them into a bowl that appeared to have been wrought from a single piece of amber larger than the Cimmerian's fist. He filled it with oil from a large stoppered jug, and struck spark to tinder. He lit the oil, which flared up bluely, with tongues of yellow.

'When the oil is consumed and the flame out, the bauble I made will be but a blob of yellow metal in which three gems are embedded. True gems, mind; I made the copy to place here and confound thieves. As you should very well know, my northish lad, experienced thieves know gem-stones from glass!'

Conan nodded. He reached within his tunic. 'This will not become slag.'

The sorcerer's dark eyes brightened and seemed to bulge a whit more. 'No, no, it will not. You have accomplished your task indeed, my good servant! Do you fetch me yon mirror, and we will soon have you whole again. A soulless man is a sad thing.'

Conan said nothing; his agreement need not be expressed. He went to the statue and from its clawed, cupped hands of black jade plucked the mirror. With great care he conveyed it to the sorcerer, who stood across the table from

95

him. There Hisarr presided over his alembics and crucibles, his powders and liquids, statuary and strange tools and that potent oil of a man who had within him the means of gaining control of the world, via the systematic stealing of souls. His eyes were fixed on the amulet Conan wore on a simple thong around his neck. It would be Hisarr Zul's means of controlling his first ruler, and Zamboula. A mere start.

Conan placed the mirror on the table before the wizard, with great gentleness. He gazed across the board at the mage, from sullenly threatening blue eyes. Smiling, Hisarr Zul hefted a rolled strip of parchment. It was bound with a cord at either end so that it formed the customary tube.

'You are in some trouble with Arenjun's authorities, I now know. I have acquaintances among them; the magistrate, for instance. In this parchment lies the solution to all your problems, Conan of Cimmeria.'

He held it high, balanced on his palm with his thumb atop, so that as Conan leaned forward to take it he was looking into the end of the tube. Conan took a deep breath . . .

So did the mage. Swiftly Hisarr Zul's head bent and he set his puckering lips to his end of the tube. He blew.

Conan knew instantly what the tube contained: death from far Khitai. Nor did he bother to cry 'Dog!' at Hisarr's trick. Having assured himself that his unwilling agent had returned the Eye of Erlik, the treacherous wizard would swiftly slay one who was manifestly dangerous to begin with and who now knew far too much. He blew hard into the tube –

And Conan blew with all his might at the other end, just as the deadly powder started to emerge. Then he turned and ran as fleetly as ever he'd run, not tarrying or looking back to watch the cloud of the black lotus's yellow death envelop Hisarr Zul's face. Conan exited the room by the same door Isparana had used, and barred it just as she'd done.

Conan sucked in a great breath – and grinned. He had blown all the deadly cloud back on the sorcerer – using Hisarr's own means against him as his dead brother had specified – and the Cimmerian felt no ill effects. He had blown so desperately in time.

He saw that he had entered a room of dark portent and shuddersome occupancy; on various tables lay the corpses of those guards he and Ajhindar had slain in this keep of sorcery and death – and none had decomposed! The room also contained their clothing and weapons, and a horrid chemical odour.

A new endeavour of that monster, Conan thought, but otherwise ignored the grim corpses. He seized on a sword, whished it through the air, tried another. First cutting off a goodly piece of thick drapery, he left the room by the corridor door. He grinned evilly at the single guard outside the Green Room. Mechanically, the soulless creature drew his sword, and again steel rang in the manse of Hisarr Zul. In less than a minute the guard bled from two wounds; the second was fatal.

'If all has gone well, your soul will soon be liberated to go – wherever the souls of the dead go,' Conan said, and he pressed the doubled scrap of velvet firmly over his mouth and nose. Then he kicked open the door to the Green Room.

Hisarr Zul, having collapsed instantly into unconsciousness, had had no opportunity to get at his antidote. More than twice two minutes had passed since Conan had left him enveloped in the cloud of greenish-yellow death. The powder still dusted the wizard's face and robe, like golden pollen.

He lay on his back, and though his eyes were closed for he'd been unconscious, he was dead.

So much for a sorcerer's nasty tricks, the Cimmerian thought, *and so much for world conquest. And what a hero I am; I have just laid to rest the demon-lich of the haunted gorge!*

An hour later, having used the sorcerer's own potent oil to burn his earth-stuffed skull to white ash, Conan left the keep of Hisarr Zul. He bore a huge pack, and two swords, and several daggers. Too, he wore an excellent cloak. In the pack was much valuable loot. And, wrapped many times in fine velvet, was a small and most valuable mirror under a thick glass dome.

Conan had the Eye of Erlik, and the wherewithal to gain the attention of a ruler of men, and his soul. Behind him, flames danced higher in the manse of Hisarr Zul.

97

Conan the Mercenary

PROLOGUE

The old man's skull gleamed in the lamplight that picked out brownish spots scattered over the tight-drawn skin. Pale yellow light emanated from four oil lamps set in a complicated sculpture suspended from the ceiling; daily a servant lowered the fixture on its chain to fill the lamps, which he later lit from a taper.

The hairless dome thus unflatteringly lit belonged to my lord Sabaninus, Baron of Korveka. His chain and medallion of rank hung heavy on the breast of a robe of wine-dyed woollen. The robe was high of neck and long of sleeve, though neither weather nor this chamber of his office was cold.

Slowly the baron lifted a wrinkled and liver-spotted hand to the jaw-long strands of hair that hung at his ear, framing his skull in a lank fringe the colour of cream. Even the last mocking remnant of his former mane was yellowing with age, as were his nails. Korveka's lord blinked, leaning a bit forward across his desk to look at his visitor.

Was it sheer imagination that there seemed an aura of malign genius about this man from so very, very far away, however dimly the baron saw him?

Sabaninus blinked again. The Baron of Korveka thought that no one discerned his failing sight and daily headaches; the truth was that none who more than glanced at him could fail to note how he blinked, and squinted, and strained ever forward in his effort to distinguish the details his eyes refused to report.

The lord baron was certain of one detail concerning his visitor. The man's skin was yellow as a dying flower or as gold seen at sunset.

The lord of Korveka had never before encountered a yellow-skinned person. This one he was delighted to see – almost to see – because the younger man had made the baron an offer; a most strange and tempting offer indeed.

In silence, Sabaninus considered it. The two men gazed at each other. Neither moved. Above, the lamps burned

silently. None would interrupt; so had Baron Sabaninus
ordered. Sabaninus pondered the offer, and his past – and
his future.

The lord of the far north-western uplands of Koth was
a widower. Nor had either of his wives borne him a son
to inherit the demain of meadowland that produced such
fine crops at the foothills of rearing mountains. Not even
a daughter had his wives produced, a girl he might have
wed to some other noble's son, to preside over Korveka
and produce sons to carry on the line; even that were
better than the situation in which he found himself. The
baron was no happy man.

Sabaninus knew that at court in Khorshemish he'd long
been referred to as 'Baron Farm-lout' and 'Lord Bumpkin'
and, of late, That Wrinkly Old Farm-lord of the Blue Lake
Country. Other nobles of the ancient Hyborian kingdom
plotted incessantly. None had approached Sabaninus for
years. Neither his support nor his advice was any longer
sought. His produce was valuable; he was harmless. He
was neither an intimate of king and court, nor out of
favour. None sought him as ally and none sought his
counsel. People of other lands knew Koth for its superbly
made armour; none came from Korveka. The barony's
fertile land, fed by clear lakes and rivers emanating in the
mountains, was effectively cut off from the rest of the
country by that natural wall of granite. Here the land was
too hospitable to animals and foodcrops to be wasted in
the production of aught else. Even as far as Hyrkania
across the Vilayet Sea; even as far as Zamboula to the south,
men of weapons wore Kothian armour. Who beyond Koth's
capital knew of Korvekan lettuce or cabbage or olives? What
people truly appreciated those who fed them, in their cities
and palaces? When Sabaninus of Korveka was thought of
or mentioned, it was as that quaint old provincial noble
from over in the mountains; the hermetish old fellow who
sent such fine produce to the palace and markets of Khorshemish. Oh yes, Korvekan wool *is* superior – have you
heard the latest about that handsome guard captain and
the queen's cousin's wife . . . ?

Royal decree had long forbidden his trading with his

neighbour, the little kingdom of Khauran, a wedge nestled up to Korveka's easternmost border. Fierce sky-reaching mountains separated Korveka from Corinthia and Zamora to the north. Korveka, which might well have been a kingdom of its own, was all but forgotten.

'Khauran,' Sabaninus muttered.

'Aye. Khauran of the Unhappy Queens,' his visitor said in his glutinous voice.

Ah, Sabaninus thought, if only he could have made alliance with the current queen or her predecessor – however fat, after *her* widowing. What a hero he'd be in Koth; in Khorshemish! Koth's narrow-eyed, plot-wary kings had long given jealous and calculating thought to the diminutive eastern neighbour. With a Kothian on its throne – a Korvekan! – alliance might well develop into . . . more; into a sort of annexation of Khauran; a satrapy whose future ruler would be of Kothian blood.

My lord Sabinamus, son of Sabaninus, Lord of Korveka and King of Koth!

A smile flirted with Sabaninus's sagging mouth. Such a prospect, along with his becoming instantly honoured hero, meant more to him than did wearing Khauran's crown.

It was his own people he had ever wanted to impress, during all the twoscore years since he, at forty-two, had inherited his father's medallion and title. The medallion of sapphire-set gold had grown steadily heavier, and its chain; the meaning of the title had not appreciated. To be invited into the glittering palace in Khorshemish! To pass between lines of admiring and envious nobles; to be announced and honoured, welcomed and praised by a grateful king! Never again to be indicated as a bumpkinish upland farm-lord! Oh, aye! He'd gladly make the long ride down to the west to such a purpose, such a reception!

His visitor smiled. 'And perhaps my lord baron is wise at that; as king over Khauran you would be but consort, and ever aware and wary of Koth, and justifiably nervous of invasion.'

'You know my very thoughts, man of Khitai?'

'I have many abilities, Baron, but the reading of minds is not one of them. I am merely no fool; a wise man would know how you would think, having heard my proposal and taken time to reflect.'

'*Youth.*'

'Ah.' A smooth, gold-sheened hand rose, first finger uplifted as if in admonition. 'Not youth, Sabaninus of Korveka. The *appearance* of youth; the feel of it. That we can obtain for you. Inside, you remain the same man, and you surely cannot be offended by my pointing out that Death still has his burning eye on you.'

The baron sighed, staring intently, and the sigh wheezed out through a mouth in which less than half the teeth remained. One ached even now.

'My hair . . .'

'Full, and brown.'

'My . . . my mouth . . .'

'Firm of lip. Were your teeth white? They will be whiter.'

Sabaninus lifted his hands and regarded them, turning them. 'My –'

'Smooth and strong. The hands of a man of . . . I can remove two of each three years of your age, Baron. Yours will be the hands and hair and teeth – and the sight – of a man of thirty. Are these enough, Baron of Korveka?'

The old nobleman swallowed hard. 'Baron of the Mountains of Gloom; Baron of the Farms; My Lord Sheepherder.' Perhaps his eyes were rheumy as he uttered the harsh words so softly spoken; perhaps tears sparkled there. He closed those eyes in a long, long blink.

'To me . . . to be the age of thirty is . . . is as adolescence to others, Khi Zang.'

The yellow-skinned man sat in silence. They two sat alone in the baron's room of office, and would not be interrupted. Light flickered on bald head and on the visitor's old-gold skin.

'You are . . . certain, Khi Zang, that this can be accomplished?'

'I am. It is not without cost.'

The baron showed attentiveness while maintaining silence. The Khitan made a brief, dismissive gesture.

'It will cost a life; one life for *Koth*! There is no danger to you: none. Once the transformation is accomplished, you will of course be wise to move swiftly, for though your appearance will be that of such a younger man, you will still be . . . you.'

'It is not enough, of course.'

'Of course it is not. Youth is the goal of all; its *semblance* is but a mocking reminder of what was. Yet you do not need me to remind you that neither is death enough, nor lack of proper recognition for one such as you.'

'Aye. After fourscore and two years. But to seem to be thirty . . .'

'Aye, Baron. It is not enough. But what man has even so much as the *appearance* of being younger?'

The baron stared at the man whom he saw as through a thick morning gaze, or through an ell of water, however clear. 'Khitan . . . Khi Zang . . . you? How old are you?'

Strong white teeth flashed in a yellow-bronze face as the Khitan laughed. 'I wondered when you would be minded of that! How old do you think I am?'

'I –'

'Do not dissemble with me, Sabaninus,' Khi Zang said, the first in many years to call the other by his name. 'I know you see but poorly, and strain even for that!'

Sabaninus was a while assimilating that, and wondering if others knew. Probably. He had lied even to himself. And now . . . was this young visitor from a land so far away as to be considered legend by many . . . was he lying? Was it a trick? Was Sabaninus of Korveka once again but the butt of a joke, of contempt?

Most desperately, he did not want to believe that he was; he wanted to believe Khi Zang of Khitai. 'You appear . . . little more than . . . thirty.'

The Khitan said equably, 'My son is older than that, Baron. Indeed, Zang is nearly fifty. And aye, I have come thousands of miles to visit you. My years are not gone from me; they are no longer visible. Nor do I feel them – save in the mind.'

'You remember all?'

'I do.'

'And you have journeyed all this way to offer me y – the appearance of youth?'

'I have.'

'Why?'

Khi Zang sat forward. 'At some time in future, Sabaninus of Korveka, I or my son will have business in Khauran. We will ask nothing that you – or your son? – cannot give, in willingness. A temple. That is in future, Sabaninus; how much future have you? Presently, I will have a saddlebag of you – one saddlebag, Baron – filled with that which you have hidden here in quantity. Gold.'

'Gold! You know even of –'

'I do. The fortune of the House of Saban, and of what value is gold to a man who dies old and alone and heirless?'

'You are in my home, and you are cruel, Khitan!'

Khi Zang saw that there was strength and fire in the baron yet, and he bowed his head. 'Cruel. Aye, honesty is cruelty, to the old. What need is there for men so old as we to avoid facts lest they be "cruel", Baron of Korveka? Come, Sabaninus. Had I said, "What would you pay for youth?" you'd have blurted, "All I have!" For the appearance of youth, then, and the opportunity it brings . . . what? The twentieth part of all you possess? A deed of gratitude to be paid by the queen and prince you leave upon dying; a debt to be paid by architecture? Your soul and your fortune, remain yours. Sabaninus of Korveka.'

Do they? Sabaninus thought, and his brain was amoil. He said, 'O Lady Ishtar! How can I refuse you?'

This he asked helplessly, feeling that he should. The Khitan was right. His life was all that a man possessed of real value; that and his honour and his dreams. Gold and some future claim; these were not comparable. Nor even was wisdom and further reflection. Tonight, tomorrow, next month might bring the fulfilling of his years on this plane. Sabaninus considered, and reflected, and cast consideration and reflection from him with a saddlebag full of gold.

What was gold? But – what was this about . . . a life? Immediately he became wary again; surely the man would not demand the son he hoped to get on Queen Ialamis?

He had said, 'How can I refuse you?' and Khi Zang said nothing.

'I will do it. What must be done? Tell me in detail. Life? What life is demanded?'

'Open to us the final keep of this keep; your underground

chamber of final refuge. Fetch, bring, lure to us there – for the how of it does not matter – a maiden. You will be present, and you must be careful to do as I direct.'

'I . . . I am not to slay . . .'

'No! You are to be still, and silent, and to observe. You are afflicted with a concept of what is Good, and what is Bad. Tonight you must put such superstitions from you: for yourself, for *Koth*! These things that I have stated and they only are required of you, Baron of Korveka. Of me: my skills. Of her: her unimportant life.'

'You keep reminding me . . .'

'Yes. I will not lie or dissemble to you, Sabaninus. I have not found that which is free in this world; have you, in fourscore and two years? Your gain – perhaps Koth's gain – is to be bought at the cost of another life. So it must be, and so you must understand.'

The baron raised tremulous, liver-spotted, spindly hands before his sunken old face. *I am not a bad man. I have never been a bad man. It is for Korveka, and for Koth!* Through his hands his voice was low, muffled:

'I will do it.'

Nateela of Ophir was eighteen and she had been slave for eighteen years.

Happiness had begun for her the day a man in rustic attire had bought her in Khorshemish. Knowing then only that he smelled of sheep and was some far lord's steward, she had been more than apprehensive on the long trek east and north. Beyond those menacing, difficult mountains she had gazed upon a land of lovely lakes and rolling greenlands dotted with sheep and kine. As the party of her new owners descended, she saw that laboriously constructed fences of grey rock blocked the grazing animals from the land under cultivation. There grew crops and the people seemed happy enough. Then she knew new fear, when her escort headed for the great baronial manse, bearing city-bought supplies, clinking saddlebags, and . . . the new human property: Nateela.

There had been no need of fear. She had been eleven then, and for seven years Nateela had known happiness and peace, good food and adequate rest, and never a beating.

Now she did not care ever to leave the domain of the baron of Korveka. She secretly loved the man, as an uncle or father. Her woman's love was an altogether different matter, and was reserved for Vanirius, son of the steward. Not that that handsome young free man took note.

This night Nateela did not know why the baron had been so long below, in that mouldy keep of keeps, with his strange guest. Nor did she question, or much care. She had been told – by the baron himself – to fetch them not wine but cider, about the time the moon was over the shearing enclosure.

She was not anxious to descend into the darkness of the underground chamber designed so long ago as final haven for the baronial family in the event of siege. She went. Her lord was below; she trusted her lord and served him willingly. He was no bad man and now surely had but few years left him. It was strange that he'd wanted wine, down there in the dark and the damp, to allay such pains as that in his left leg and his right elbow and left shoulder. They plagued him much, she knew. She wished she were a sorcerer, to rid him of his pain.

He was so old. It was stupid to talk, as some philosophers were said to do, of 'average life expectancy'; for the number of years thus arrived at averaged in the many many who died in the first year or two of their lives – and the many women who succumbed to childbed fever. Even so the lord baron of Korveka had lived beyond the span gained by very few men, and fewer women. Nateela was aware of this, and the only apprehension she now knew was what might befall her after his inevitable death. Inexplicably he had chosen no successor, adopted no one; the King in Khorshemish would surely take the lands and send another lord to preside over them. Or perhaps one would accept the lands and their revenues, but remain on the other side of the mountains rather than live so far from the capital. Then nothing would change, for the steward was no mean man, and his son Vanirius . . .

Nateela did not think on it. She but served the lord Sabaninus well and loyally, and with love.

The air as she descended was thick and musty, smelling of earth – though she smelled, strangely, the burning herbs of incense. That was nice, though a bit thickly cloying. The old, old steps were dark. From below, candles or lamps flickered in invitation, and she heard the two men talking. Crouching a bit to avoid cobwebs, she descended slowly and quietly, with care though without stealth.

She heard the baron's voice, and then she could distinguish the words: 'My steward has been told that you and I depart very late tonight, alone, for Khorshemish. So have I told my household overseer. Both have retired, probably thinking to try to aid me on the morrow. Meanwhile, two men await the appearance of you and my *nephew*, Sergianus. They are – or had better be! – at the stable, with horses and provisions prepared for us four.'

'You appear to have arranged well.' Nateela heard the deep, accented voice of the strange, yellow man. 'And the girl?'

'Ishtar forgive me,' the baron said in a low voice more tremulous than usual. 'She should be bringing us refreshment now. Your preparations are complete?'

'They are, Sabaninus.'

Nateela wondered at their words, but forgot them in her astonishment at hearing her lord called by name. Never before had she heard that done, in his presence. She descended, and bethought her that it were wise to make a sound. A good servant, she coughed.

'Just do remain by me within this circle,' the Khitan went on.

'Perhaps –'

'Save it, Baron of Korveka; that cough is a good servant's announcement of approach.'

Oh good, Nateela thought; the poor old baron probably hadn't heard.

The Khitan's voice rose in volume: 'And none too soon; this musty air below ground does dry a man's mouth and throat!'

The two men fell silent, then. Nateela was glad that the strange yellow man had heard her. The lord baron doubtless heard little more, these days, than he saw. Poor man, poor old man with neither wife nor son nor daughter; *how my heart goes out to him! And a good man, too!*

She stepped down on to the floor of the keep within the

keep. A gasp escaped her, for the earth was cold and hard beneath her feet.

'Good sweet cider, my lords.'

'What a lovely gift from such a lovely child, my dear,' the Khitan said, and he smiled.

He was not unhandsome, she supposed. His colour, the glossy blackness of his coarse-looking hair, the strangeness of his almond shapes of eyes; these aspects of his appearance were new to her, and different and undreamt, so that Nateela could not be comfortable in his presence. She managed a tiny smile and was aware of his black eyes on her while she carried her salver to the baron.

The lord of Korveka wore a full-sleeved white blouse and a particularly loose scarlet riding-jupon over leggings just as loose.

Both men watched her appreciatively. Though some slaves were left bare above the waist for the good of their spirits and the delectation of their masters, this was not true in the household of Sabaninus of Korveka. True, Nateela wore little. Just as true, that fact made her more interesting to look upon than had she been bare-chested. The yellow-trimmed halter of Kothian green swayed and jiggled with her steps, and the sway of her hips was sensuously visible above the low-slung drawstring of her long skirt of the same hue. Save for a copper bracelet and an amulet suspended on a simple cord about her neck, Nateela wore naught else.

'How beautifully made you are, my dear child,' the Khitan said, as if he were much older.

She flashed him a smile, her lashes lowered, while he took the large mug of cider from her tray.

He stepped back from her, one pace towards the baron. He spoke strange words in stranger inflections. Nothing he murmured was in any language she knew or knew of, but strangely fluid and not unlike a song.

'Thank you, Nateela,' the baron said in a quavery voice. He looked as if he were in mourning. 'You are loved, Nateela.'

'Thank *you*, my lord,' the Ophirean said while she felt her heart would burst with happiness. What a lovely thing for him to say! What a dear lord she had!

Hearing a sound behind her, she took no note of how the Khitan swiftly knelt to draw a short arc; it completed the circle in which he and Baron Sabaninus stood. Nateela looked around.

They were no longer alone in that underground chamber so fitfully lit, and she was too fear-stricken even to shriek. Nor was the newcomer anything that approached the human form.

An awful croak boomed from the thing. Its bulk was massive, a huge dark form in which details were not clear; it was a slice of night. All Nateela saw clearly were terrible glaring eyes and immense, gleaming fangs. It . . . *hopped*, once, towards her. Only then did the Ophirean cry out and back away –

A hand set itself between her shoulder blades, and she was thrust violently forward.

'NO!' That from behind her; she recognised the baron's voice and though her brain was no longer working well, she knew gratitude that it could not have been he who pushed her.

'Hold, you fool!' the other man snapped. 'Move from this circle and you too will d –'

That was all Nateela heard. The thing blotted out all vision with the blackness of an utterly moonless, starless night, and then all sound too, and, after an instant of agony, all feeling as well; for it tore her in half before it ate her.

The Khitan had clamped a hand on one arm of the baron while he renewed the voicing of incantations. Abruptly the horrid thing vanished forever from the domain of Baron Sabaninus. Of Nateela there remained only the few splashes of blood the demon or Dark God had not had time to lap up, ere Khi Zang sent it back into whatever gulf of dreadful darkness it habited.

And then Baron Sabaninus, too, vanished.

The man who stood where he had been wore the baron's clothing, but on this erect, far younger man neither leggings nor jupon hung loose. Holding his arms crooked at the elbows, he stared at the hands he turned and turned before his face. Then his eyes lifted, to stare over his fingers at the Khitan.

'Ishtar's curls – *I see you clearly!*'

'And I see you clearly, Sergianus!'

'Every feature . . . oh ye gods! Oh Lady Ishtar of my fathers . . . I am I . . . and I am not!'

'I see what a mirror would show you,' the man from Khitai said. 'A man of thirty, tall and straight. Chest and calves bulge with firm young muscle that tunic can barely contain. A shock of rich brown hair from which the morrow's sun will strike glints of red. A face far from homely and far from old, and keen young eyes. None will know you!'

'Ish . . . tar . . .'

'The goddess of that ivory image in your room of office? Only she might recognise you now! Remember that horses await. They await . . . whom?'

'Me! No – I mean yes. Aye! The horses await Sergianus, my nephew – the nephew of Baron Sabaninus of Korveka. Sergianus . . . *I* am Sergianus!'

'So are you then, my young lord Sergianus.' Khi Zang's sweeping gesture encompassed more than the dim-lit subterranean chamber. 'Nothing interests or keeps us here, Sergianus. Let us away – a queen awaits!'

'Aye!'

And Nateela was forgot in that instant. 'Aye!' Sergianus repeated in a strong voice that was at once mature and far from old. 'A queen awaits!'

Laughing, trembling not with palsy but in excitement, Sergianus strode to the steps and mounted them. The smiling yellow wizard from Khitai followed. He closed the door behind them.

The snowy ball of the moon moved but little before they were mounted. Accompanied by two young men whose ambition and greed would make them trustworthy long enough, they rode eastward across the nighted barony. Behind them they led, strangely, but two sumpter-beasts. All four men wore daggers, though only Khi Zang and Sergianus bore swords.

Eventually one of them would part to travel, somehow, the thousands of miles to his home, there to wait years for the accomplishment of his goal in Khauran: the future transplantation of a ghastly god from the dark mists of Khitai's ancientmost history. Of the other three, but one would complete the journey to the capital of Khauran of the Unhappy Queens. By that time, three would have died for his dream.

CHAPTER 1

Death in Shadizar

The tall youth walked the nighted streets lithe as a jungle cat on the hunt. The fingers of his big hands remained slightly curled, ready to draw sword or dagger or both. His eyes moved constantly in an effort to spy out the darkest shadows, pools of squid's ink on this poorly-lit street on the perimeter of the city's Watch-patrolled areas. For all his height and powerfully-constructed bulk, he moved almost silently. Eyes watched him from well back within a hallway dark as a well at midnight; the footpad appraised his probable lack of wealth, sized him up, and let the big youth pass.

The young man crossed that perimeter then, reaching the corner of Bazaar Way and, without hesitation, turning left into the Street of Erlik Enthroned. It was both narrower and darker.

The moment he'd rounded the corner, he grunted at impact of a rushing body. A lissome young woman had run full into him. Sleek and slippery, she jiggled wildly in a few strips of scarlet-dyed homespun and shameless gauze sewn with copper coins too small to tempt any but the very lowest of thieves. Her light panting and wild eyes told him she'd been running though not for long, all silent on bare, filthy-soled feet. His arms did not go around her; with a hand on each of her upper arms, he pushed her gently back a pace to look into her face.

'Here girl, where –'

Despite his big hands on her arms, the chestnut-skinned easterner writhed away, ducked, and hurried on past him. The youth did not even turn. With a little snort and a whimsical jerk of his head, he walked on. His hand left his dagger and his eyes squinted as he scanned upper-storey windows.

'Boy. Ho there, big one!'

He half turned to look back. A slim hunting panther to his black-maned lion, the girl stood in the centre of the intersection, where it was safest. Her hands rode bare hips and she faced him.

'Don't go that way unless you don't mind blundering into someone else's trouble!'

A young male addressed a young female: 'You think I'm wearing this sword to pare my toenails?'

She snorted and tossed her head so that purplish-black hair flew. 'Huh! No, and you're big enough. It's just that smart folk avoid others' troubles, and you're headed for some. Three or four blades, at least. Where came you by that barbarous accent?'

'Not on the other side of the Vilayet like you, girl.' He glanced around, a broad-shouldered near-giant whose massive chest strained the cloth of a tunic not made for him. He was bronzed by the sun and the tunic was the colour of desert sand. 'Why warn me?'

He was wary, and justifiably. He knew Arenjun well, and Shadizar's reputation was little better. Such a helpful and tempting young woman could easily be distracting his attention whilst a silent confederate stole upon him with cudgel or club or worse. He saw no one. The Street of Erlik Enthroned was quiet and apparently untenanted. The cult's adherents either did not meet this night in that big building they had converted into a temple, or they were quiet about the conducting of their rites.

She shrugged. It was a jerky gesture, boyish save for the movement it imparted to her bosom, which was more bared than clothed; less clothed than adorned. Homespun and gauze indeed; she was poor as a temple cockroach!

'I ran into you, and you didn't grab me or try to pin me up against a wall. Why not?'

'Not because I did not find you attractive,' he said, perhaps hopefully, for the city was new to him and she was comely. 'Show me the way to a place to get better acquainted, then.'

Her reply was a scornful chuckle. 'You haven't that which attracts me, fellow!'

'I'm a year or so older than you, and strong enough to protect such a girl as you!' Even as his chest swelled a bit, he checked again down the Street of Erlik Enthroned. It remained empty, in the darkness.

'Huh! So are scores of others, hill-boy, and all with big hot hands that want to roam like stray dogs! It's good coin that *I* require.'

'Go your way then, and find a fat grease-headed merchant with coins to spend on a girl so poor she can't afford silk. I require good coin too.'

She started to say something else – perhaps to remind him that he was bent in a way opposite the city's moneyed area – but changed her mind. With another of those interesting shrugs and a toss of her long thick hair, she turned and padded away along Bazaar Way, towards the sprawling inner city plain that made up the Bazaar. He noted that she contrived to add an exaggerated sway and grind to her girlish hips.

'Women,' he muttered, in the manner of a man of experience, and he disregarded her advice. He resumed his prowl away from the better-lighted, patrolled area. He knew this city was wicked. Perhaps he was, too. He was confident.

The capital of Zamora was not idly called the City of Wickedness, Conan mused.

In the Bazaar that was the city's culmination of the great caravan route called Road of Kings, every commodity was available from produce to baubles both of stone and metal and flesh and blood. Above that sprawling market flanked by stalls and shops with brightly striped awnings, every manner of vice was readily available and even hawked like goods – for a price. Most of the vices were exotic and unbridled; the prices were high. No matter how curious he waxed, no matter how tempted by his eyes and the murmurs of extolling hawkers – and tales told in his inn – Conan eschewed the expensive esoterica of Shadizar the Wicked.

True, the strapping, almost hulking youth was a man of property, with two horses in a guarded stable behind the inn. Yet he cherished those possessions; they were hard-gained. Nor was his business in Shadizar to spend. Conan had other business. It involved his soul . . . and profit, rather than expenditures.

Having set up as a thief in Arenjun once he'd worked his way down here from the hills of Cimmeria, he had just spent the better part of two months to little profit. Indeed, he had suffered the loss of not only that fraction of his life, but of a prized part of himself as well. Though blessed with an easygoing barbarian insouciance and the open-eyed optimism of his few years, he was hardly the happiest person in Shadizar of Zamora, or without cares.

He had come here with ambivalent hopes and goals. While he cherished a desire to gain audience with the sorcerer-ridden king, he sought too to vanish. He'd soon learned that the lord King of Zamora was not seen by some foreign youth without the laying out of a good deal of money to various intermediaries in fine robes. Too, he'd not needed to investigate or query to know that he could not long afford to stay in the Upper City. He'd found lodgings on the other side of the bazaar, in that area of the walled capital known as the Desert. He stopped at the inn under the sign of the Foaming Jack, as often called the Leering Jackal.

This night, as on the night before, he prowled.

His pacing was not aimless; Conan moved ever uptown, out of the Desert. Why then had he turned down Erlik Enthroned? He was not certain. Here were companions, and anonymity unto invisibility, but no real attractions for an ambitious thief. And so he must be, to gain the wherewithal to bribe the robed slime that oozed between king and those who hoped to gain his ear.

The winding, narrow streets of the Lower City were dim even by day. The dingy human-constricted caves shadowing them were tenanted by refugees from the authorities and angry rulers of a dozen lands and other cities and city-states. Here were thieves whose activities had made other abodes far too unhealthy for their continued tenancy and newly-bearded mercenaries and deserters (or newly-shaven, had they worn beards afore) fighting off the shakes ere they sought new employment; here brooded shadowy, un-worthy temples of a score of cults whose adherents would be unwelcome in most of the rest of the world. The cults of Shadizar were often artificial, manufactured to feature and support various vices in lascivious rites. In the Desert, night-companions ranged in age from the just-nubile to time-ravaged, pitifully old whores. They swayed among cultists and pleasure-seekers and the merely curious drawn by Shadizar's reputation; and deviants, refugees, and outlaws of every ilk and persuasion, predilection, and unrepentant reputation. Cut-purses and armed bullies prowled the streets and infested hallways dark as their souls. So too did cult-shills, temptresses and others: women of all ages more than ready to sell themselves by the hour, or for the time necessary to travel elsewhere with a protector strong of thews, or purse, or guards and reputation. For many who remained in the City of Wickedness were not all that happy; they just could not or dared not seek to betake themselves somewhere else.

Last night the big Cimmerian youth had said nay to nine women (one of whom was sixty if she was a day, while another was surely not yet nubile), four boys and two men. One of the latter pair had been so obstreperously insistent that he'd had to be refused with vehemence and finally with strength. 'You should be flattered!' he had told Conan, who wasn't.

During the course of the same evening Conan had heard described the most abominable rites of the Temple of Set-Ishtar Reformed and United, and the unequivocally voluptuous ones of the Temple of Derketa Cloaca. Too, he had seen a swaggering big Nemedian mercenary neatly and swiftly knifed by a boy of no more than thirteen, and him face to face with his victim. Later Conan witnessed the upending and sound spanking, in a public inn, of a young woman attired first in wisps of violently red silk and then in nothing save her brace of bangles. Afterwards she was tossed – aye, literally tossed – easily to two sombre, black Stygians who swiftly hauled the blonde to their dingy quarters.

Conan had eschewed involvement. This was solemn resolve. He was here on important business: theft, and the regaining of his soul. He would not involve himself in the problems of others. And he would have care as to whom he sought to rob!

He had been too much involved in too much of late. A few too many persons down in Arenjun desired his company if not companionship. Events and his own straightforwardness had resulted in his reducing Arenjun's sorcerous population by two, and in destroying both their abodes. Ensconced in the Mall where thieves held revel by night – which in Arenjun was only a lawless section, while it seemed to comprise half of Shadizar the Wicked – he had got word of those who sought him.

There were men of the City Watch, of whose number he had slain one, wounded another, and destroyed both dignity and commission of an officer, all on one night some two months ago. The former prefect and his friends quietly sought the huge hillman with his smouldering blue eyes and short temper. So did uniformed men of the Watch, and one un-uniformed agent. Next came intelligence that a trousered, khilat-wearing man of far Iranistan was also asking guarded and knowledgeable questions as to a certain Cimmerian youth's habits and whereabouts.

At that point Conan decided that Arenjun had grown lamentably small.

With his new possessions, he had departed the city by night. He rode north to Shadizar. He could have brought a willing female friend; Conan did not share her willingness.

Oddly, he had taken a longish route, avoiding the Road of Kings that directly connected the two Zamoran cities.

Though Shadizar was the capital and its gate sentries suspicious, few questions were asked of anyone by anyone, once a newcomer was within the walls. Too many here had too much to conceal; 'Best not to ask, lest one be asked,' was a common phrase in Shadizar. In Arenjun one never knew who was plotting and who might be deadly danger. In Shadizar, one assumed: all plotted, all were lovers of vice and probably bent on wickedness. Conan preferred Shadizar. It was not difficult for him to be on his guard at all times.

Walking now that city's nighted streets, he smiled grimly. Purely as practice, he let his right hand dart across his muscular midsection to snatch out his sword. It sheared the air before him within a second, and he returned the blade to its oiled home with another smile. All in the space of a few heartbeats.

'Nothing worth stealing here,' he muttered, in a sound that approached a growl, from the throat. 'Best head back uptown.'

He had come out of the affair of the Eye of Erlik –

which was not finished – and of the mage Hisarr Zul – who was – with some small wealth. He'd left the wizard's burning keep with several weapons and a bolt of good cloth, hastily snatched. Too, he had acquired two horses and a like number of camels, along with a few stolen goods from far Samara. The horses remained. A youngish girl of astonishing skills and an older, far more crafty woman of Arenjun had assisted the youthful mage-slayer in relieving himself of the surly camels and the silver they brought, along with a few other items. He was left with memories and a new philosophy concerning women, and a vow he honestly believed he would keep, as had many a youth and man before him.

The guards at Shadizar's gates and the proprietor of the Foaming Jack had accounted for the rest of the Samaratan booty (which Conan had gained as a result of defending himself against their possessor, who had stolen them). And now he had been in the City of Wickedness for two days.

For two nights, departing his inn just after sundown, he had wandered the Zamoran capital.

He had not been challenged. Though obviously a youth with his erect posture, smoothly muscled arms and face free of lines, he was nevertheless manifestly formidable. The sheath of worn shagreen leather at his left hip was not new. It showed wear. The hilt standing from it was not ornamented, hinting at a serviceable sword. Neither was there ornamentation on the bone handle of his dagger. A glance into his eyes, a swift appraisal of his posture, his gait, his roving gaze, his huge, ready hands and their thick wrists below extraordinary biceps; these told potential accosters they were better advised to seek prey elsewhere. Something about this young man bespoke that the dagger had been used on meat other than cooked. Surely the sword would be sharp, and wielded with expertise and power, and had in past been wiped of scarlet smears.

Conan was reconnoitring, seeking. He was about his business.

Part of that business was stealing, and he felt himself above mere footpads and cut-purses. He was swift, and could climb and be stealthy. An integral part of his chosen profession involved sniffing, observing, reconnoitring in the manner of a good general or military spy. He would be both, eventually; just now he was not quite eighteen, and still learning.

He was an agile and facile thief who had learned a certain wariness and cleverness – not without cost. Certainly he wished he'd never sought to rob the Elephant Tower of Yara the priest or the keep of Hisarr Zul the wizard!

He reached the end of the Street of Erlik Enthroned, and now he saw that which the nameless girl had fled, and warned him against.

Why the cross-street was called Khauran he did not know; who owned the decorated and curtained litter resting against the far north-west wall he could not say. Nor did he care. He knew not whether the litter was occupied – or if it were, whether that person was alive or dead, wounded or swooned. Conan did know that the foreigner who had himself carried about this part of the city at night was stupid: two men had borne the litter while one guarded. In the Desert of the Lower City, three were not enough, and doubly so when two of them were not trained men of weapons.

One bearer was down, twitching in his blood when Conan came upon the scene. The other fled up Khauran Way in the manner of one who'd not even pause for breath until he was somewhere in the eastern hills of Brythunia, Zamora's northward neighbour.

None of the four attackers pursued him. Three beset the mailed, helmeted guard, who'd got his back against a wall and was sweeping his sword in horizontal figure-eights low enough to keep from being skewered. He could not maintain that rapid exertion forever, and his assailants knew it. Now the fourth was leaving the body of the downed bearer, to join them. He carried a trencherman's dagger and another; the second had a blade as long as his forearm. It dripped. Two of the others had swords, no matter that such were so expensive; the fourth, to the beleaguered guard's right, was also armed with two daggers.

'Never mind,' one of the attackers told the fourth. 'We have him – just drag the rabbit out of its burrow and start stripping it of jewels. If it resists – see if it bleeds! Uh!'

The speaker had said too much, partially turning his head

towards his companion of the bloody dagger. No poor fighter, the guard swiftly altered his sweeping defence just enough, advanced one foot just enough, to send the first inch of his blade slicing through the man's throat. He staggered back, unable to speak, and dropped his weapon to clutch his neck. It was leaking badly. Making hideous gargling noises, the man continued to stagger away. Conan watched him sag.

I salute you, warrior, the Cimmerian thought, and decided it was time he took a stranger's advice and followed her back up towards the Upper City.

It was then that the man with the bloody dagger laid hand on the curtains concealing the litter's interior. A beringed and braceleted wrist flashed from within. The thief cried out in shock and pain as his hand was slashed by the short blade of a dagger whose jewels flashed even in the dimness of the street and the flickering light of a pole-set lamp.

A woman, Conan realised – and one of wealth! That bracelet was of gold. Even so it was gem-set, and the rings were surely not glass. She even stabbed at an attacker with a jewelled knife! To aid such a person might be more profitable than stealing – and surely little more dangerous, judging from the ragged appearance of the three assailants.

A complication arose even as the Cimmerian arrived at that intelligence. Bleeding from one hand, the thief clamped it against his tunic while he obviously prepared to send his long blade stabbing through the curtain into the litter.

What Conan bawled out did not matter; perhaps it was 'KAWAAAH!' or somesuch. Only the sound was important, and he was on the move even as he shouted. Naturally, the man beside the litter interrupted his activity to look around.

He saw six or so feet of broad-shouldered, thickly muscled man rushing at him, black hair blowing about his head. His long sword was carried at the waist with wrist turned slightly outward. Even so the fellow was foolish enough to stand and meet that rush, and it was necessary that Conan strike twice rather than once. The first blow clanged his swordblade against the other's dagger with such force that the man grunted in pain and the weapon went flying to clang off a stone wall, striking sparks, and clunk to the street. There it skittered and fetched up against the wall's base with another clang.

Conan's second stroke was in truth merely the backswing of the first: it sliced the man open from right hip to left. The thief hadn't even dropped to his knee ere Conan was swinging away, knowing him done, and turning his icy-eyed gaze on the other two thieves.

Neither had as yet got past the guard's defence – which, Conan was impressed to note, was not yet faltering. Nor had either been so much as wounded.

'Which one shall I run through from behind?'

The horrible question was snarled in Conan's most vicious gutturals. Had there been twenty with their backs to him, all must have turned. One of the attackers was wise enough to skip several paces aside while he turned; the other forgot all and twisted his head about to snatch an over-the-shoulder look.

Once again the litter's guard saw opportunity, and swiftly took it. In truth it was beautifully done; he took this man just as he had the other, with the very tip of his blade across the throat. It was enough; bone and vital artery were opened, and another man gushed blood on to the street called Khauran.

Grinning like a snarling wolf, Conan pounced to within three feet of the other, showing the guard his unprotected left side. He stared into the eyes of a sword-wielding thief in a dirty brown tunic – who had set out this night with three companions and was now ineffably alone.

'See to your employer,' Conan said, without taking his gaze off his chosen foe.

'Ha!' The thief, a Kothian sure, struck at Conan, who sidestepped and watched the sword rush past. He watched the backstroke, too. It was awkward; the fellow had so little knowledge of combat that he began the necessary twisting of his wrist far too late. A fair enough thief, perhaps, Conan mused; but the fellow was a complete failure as a swords-man.

'You'd better run off,' the astonished Kothian was told.

'Here, that's my business,' the guard said. 'I'm paid to –'

'Tonight,' Conan snarled, staring at the thief but answering the guard, 'you were paid to die by an employer too mean or too stupid to hire adequate protection for this part of town by day, much less at night! You were a *dead man*, Shemite; think on that! See to your heartless employer now, lest she cut herself on one of her precious damned jewels – hunh!'

The final grunt was occasioned by the remaining thief's attempt to take off Conan's head with a magnificent sweep of his sword. That all-out beheading stroke made the Kothian's blade a speeding horizontal stripe of silver.

Both Conan's knees bent to drop him straight down into a squat below the mighty cut. He heard the wind-noise of the rushing blade, too close above his head. And then Conan showed the Kothian thief why such a mighty cut was unwise, too great a risk: straightening, the Cimmerian faced him and, before the now desperately begun backstroke was fair under way, struck the man straight through the middle.

The backstroke was never completed. The Kothian's arm twitched and wavered; his eyes went huge while he sucked in an audible sobbing gasp. Backing mechanically off the cold sliver of steel that had opened his stomach and belly and those organs it found within, he thumped against a mud-brick wall. It alone supported him. Glowering, his chest heaving, Conan waited.

The man's arm dropped. Slowly the swordhilt eased from the grip of fingers going helpless. Just as slowly, the Kothian thief of Shadizar slid down the wall. His head hung bowed while lifeless eyes stared at what came out of him, in shining bloody coils.

Conan paced over to his first foeman.

'Hurt?' the Cimmerian asked. 'It will never heal, but you needn't die slowly, in stench and pain.' He slew that man then, and wiped his sword with care on the hem of the corpse's tunic.

'Name of Ishtar,' the guard said in a low voice. 'You're a bloody one!'

Conan stared at a tall man, young and not unhandsome, in yellow-plumed helmet and a fine coat of Kothian mail, though he was no Kothian.

'It's called mercy,' Conan said quietly, and sucked in a great breath to still his voice's slight quiver of excitement;

adrenalin still flooded his system. 'Is there no mercy in Shem? Would you leave a man to die slowly of so awful a wound, with his guts starting to stink with green rot and him screaming in agony and smelling his own death?'

It was then that a ring-bedizened hand swept aside the litter's curtain from within, and the hand's owner thrust forth her head to spew her vomit on the street. Conan stepped back two paces, mindful of the splash.

CHAPTER 2

Employment for a Thief

Shaking his head, Conan glanced around. No one was astir on the streets of Khauran or Erlik Enthroned. Those within the buildings lining both avenues had heard the sounds of combat, and not only remained inside but had probably extinguished whatever glims they had lit. Naturally anyone who'd been approaching was now heading precipitately in the other direction.

Again he looked down at the woman who hung out of the grounded litter. Now she dry heaved over the noisome pool that had been her dinner. Her appearance was most unusual indeed, even to Conan. He knew he'd never been in her homeland, or seen another from there either.

Her black hair was so high-piled that he realised its glossy sheaves must be wrapped about a cone of some sort, perched atop her skull. Pearls were woven into the sheaves, and the star-like gleam of gems against hair black as the night sky meant they formed the heads of long pins. A carcanet of gold wire, cloth-of-gold, and what appeared to be a million pearls surrounded her neck and covered her upper chest. Its bi-lobate lower curves were carelessly trapped in a bandeau of white silk that revealed the flesh tints within. Her great heavy girdle was also jewelled, and supported a long and voluminous skirt of pale yellow, shockingly side-slit. The leg that emerged from the little chamber formed by framework, roof and curtains atop the litter poles was handsome, and narrowed into a small foot shod in a gilded sandal. Its lifted heel clacked when she set it down. Gold wire pierced each of her earlobes to dribble two strands of four large pearls. The lobes were elongated from years of bearing such gemmy weights, and the face that looked wanly up at Conan was that of a woman of perhaps twoscore years. It was a handsome face, rather than pretty, with fine cheekbones and startling eyes under long black lashes stiff with lacquer.

Both her arms were half-covered with jewels.

'One bearer fled,' Conan blandly informed her, 'and I'd say the other is dead. No wonder; you came down here wearing what looks like crown jewels, and guarded by only one man.'

She gazed up at him from beneath those long stiff lashes. They glistened.

'Why . . . you're very young, aren't you?'

Conan stared whimsically at her. 'That is what you have to say to me.' He gave his head a jerk and looked at her bodyguard.

'Who are you?' that man asked.

'And that is what you have to say. You both live because I ignored a warning to avoid this area, and you can say only that I am young and unknown to you.'

A movement caught his peripheral attention; he looked aside and down to see a hand extended up to him, a hand bearing four rings, though thumb and forefinger were bare. The nails were scarlet. Conan deliberately took his time sheathing his sword. Just when the extended hand started to waver, he took it and drew its owner up from her litter. Her Shemite guard was nigh as tall as Conan; even in her noisy heels, the woman was short. Perhaps all her people were, and thus the elaborate high coiffures.

'I am the Lady Khashtris, of Khauran. This is my personal guard, Shubal. And we are indeed very grateful to you. Tug my rings, and they will come off.'

'I am Conan, a Cimmerian. And I'll not strip your rings, Lady Khashtris.'

She released his hand and used her other to strip the right of three of its four rings. She held them out in her fist; after a moment's hesitation, Conan accepted them as the price of her life.

'They are only baubles,' she said. 'You have saved my life, Conan, Cimmerian. Both our lives.'

He opened his big fist to inspect its flashing, faceted contents. 'You mean these are not gold and silver set with a topaz, and a moonstone, and a ruby?'

'Oh yes, Conan, they are that. And now they are only tokens of gratitude. We came up from Khauran to purchase cosmetics and other goods from eastern lands. Though one of my guards lay ill, I was foolish enough to want to traverse this particular street – Khauran Way – ere we depart for home on the morrow. Another guard fled when this attack began. You did not see him, I suppose. I am not so heartless and greedy, you see. And Shubal is easily one of the two bravest men in Shadizar; he stood against four, which obviously meant his death. It would be my good fortune now if you were to be seeking employment, Conan, Cimmerian, at say twenty coins of the best silver for the next month, for then I should have both the bravest men in Shadizar to protect me from the lawless ruffians of this wicked city, of a land foreign to me and hardly so gentle as Khauran.'

A bit long of wind and hyperbole, Conan thought – even while being charmed by Khashtris's pretty speech. In addition, she seemed sincere. It was only that she tended to speak at such length, he supposed. Khauran might be a land a man might swiftly tire of. Within a month, perhaps . . . That she had cited his calling her heartless was nothing he saw as cause for embarrassment or concern. If she showed anger, he'd consider apology. She did not, and he did not.

'You are talking about employing us both,' he said, noting the dark look given him by Shubal of Shem.

'Of course.'

'And Shubal, who has seen me rewarded, of course has a reward coming also, as the bravest man in Shadizar.'

The Lady Khashtris of Khauran nodded. 'Of course. You are forward in all things, aren't you, Conan of . . . is it Cimmeria? Is that a city?'

'A country,' Conan told her with studied aplomb, 'north of Aquilonia . . . *and* the Border Kingdom. It is no more than twice Zamora's size,' he added, exaggerating. 'Is Khauran a city?'

The Shemite turned his face away lest his employer see his smile. In truth Cimmeria, Zamora and Khauran could have been stuffed into sprawling Shem, with room to spare for Khoraja and perhaps more territory as well.

'A country,' milady Khashtris said equably, 'about half the size of Zamora – and I am sorry not to know your land, Conan. But why not see for yourself, and enlighten me as well? We leave for Khauran on the morrow. Will you join us, then?'

'I suppose I could get my affairs in order by . . . noon,' Conan said, just as coolly. 'I have a pair of horses . . . but my chaincoat is being repaired.'

Khashtris of Khauran looked at him from beneath arched black brows and lacquered lashes. 'We too have horses . . . and no bearers.'

'You do not ride, Lady?'

'I do not.' She looked at the litter, and back at her saviour, who noted she had not lowered her eyes to sweep the corpses around them. 'As for tonight . . .'

'Guardsmen to a noble lady,' Conan advised, 'do not of course carry litters. If you will walk, though, I shall carry your chair.' Stepping past his employer and ignoring her look of surprise, he lifted her empty conveyance with ease, and soon had it adjusted on one shoulder. 'Shubal: well met! No bad blood exists between Shem and Cimmeria, or Cimmeria and Khauran.'

'Nor between us, Conan,' the tall Shemite said, for his dark looks had vanished with Conan's affirming their co-employment and pushing Khashtris to promise a reward.

'Milady,' Conan said, bending forward just a little and tilting rightward away from his load, 'well met. Do we go now to your inn?'

'Shubal,' she said, and then, 'No, wait; do you follow with me betwixt you. I shall guide Conan. Will you join us, Conan?'

'I have my own accommodations,' he said, realising that he was surely in for considerable walking. While the Foaming Jack was but a few streets away, the noblewoman must be staying in the Upper City, in far finer surroundings.

They set off up the Street of Erlik Enthroned. Mailed, helmeted Shemite bodyguard; huge, bronzed, black-maned Cimmerian thief carrying a side-turned sedan chair; and between them the short, heavily bejewelled woman with heels that clack-clacked loudly at every step and elaborate coiffure that stood nearly a foot above her head.

When they reached better lighted areas they found others abroad. Most stared. None, however, challenged or interfered with the strange trio. And Conan was right; the inn at the sign of the Thirsty Lion was indeed far uptown, and he had a long walk back. He spent the rest of the evening squandering the topaz ring on a woman of Shadizar with more paint and cheap jewellery than clothing or culture. Still, she was beyond girlhood, and Conan learned much from her. As she was charmed by his youth and massiveness – as well as the ring of real gold set with a real gem – the exchange was more than equal. Ring or no, bruises or no, both considered it a night well spent.

Next day Conan, who had no mailcoat at all, parted with Khashtris's ruby-set ring. Armour was not cheap. In addition to the mail-arrased, peaked Turanian helmet, huge white cloak and a crotch-protector of woven chain over leather over cloth, he was able to purchase only a sleeveless mail-vest of no great length. Happy with the ring, the merchant made a to-do of adding a padded coat to be worn under the thirty pounds of linked chain.

Conan advised the pleased merchant that he also required two bearers for the litter of a smallish noblewoman; he did not name her nationality or their destination. The man swiftly procured two Ophirean brothers down on their luck. Conan spent a few minutes carefully questioning them and several more assuring each that lack of loyalty would result in their employer's having the unpleasant chore of wiping a lot of blood off his blades.

The mailcoat was new and the helmet had doubtless once adorned the head of a bluish-bearded man now dead. Conan liked them well enough. There was something manly in their weight and sheen.

He cut quite the figure and knew it, riding so tall in his mail through Shadizar. He bestrode one horse while leading another, apparently accompanied by two retainers from the meadowlands of a nation whose knights oft wore gilded armour. These wore sleeveless shirts of saffron and of blue, breechclouts, long daggers, strapped sandals, and a good deal of hair.

Conan's chin tilted and his eyes automatically narrowed to appraise upper-storey windows. *Stupid*, he reminded himself. He was no longer a thief. He had a patron whose moonstone ring he wore on his left little finger; he was employed as guard to a noble lady. And what might he have done with himself otherwise? Broken into the so-called temple of Erlik Enthroned, where white kittens were turned red in sacrifice to the yellow-eyed god of death?

The edge of Conan's mouth twitched, though he did not quite smile.

Erlik.

His right hand rose to toy with the leathern cord about his neck. The amulet it supported, under tunic and haqueton and mail-vest, was nothing: a diamond-shape of moulded clay or glazed pottery set with a bit of glass; a barbarian's amulet that any would assume furthered some northern superstition. Anyone could see that it was a nothing, worthless.

Conan's mouth set grimly. Aye, a nothing . . . for which several had died including a mighty wizard, and which was sought after by the rulers of several countries. The Cimmerian had cleverly disguised the valuable Zamboulan amulet called the Eye of Erlik. So it would remain, embedded in hardened clay, until he decided what to do with it, this thing he had of a sorcerer of Zamboula who was more lately of Arenjun . . . and still more lately deceased, with Conan's aid.

The Eye of Erlik, he mused. Well, just now it was of no importance to him or his needs. He had a far more serious need. It involved his very soul. His hand moved behind him, to touch the carefully-wrapped packet behind his saddle; apparently a leather-wrapped cushion in the Iranistani style. No cushion, surely, had ever been of such importance to any individual.

Thus reflected the Cimmerian while riding through Shadizar to the Thirsty Lion, accompanied by the two he had hired on behalf of his new employer. With both one guard and one bearer having run off last night, Lady Khashtris was of no great competence at choosing men, he thought — without taking into consideration her employment of him.

At the inn, he found Khashtris disappointingly swathed in travelling robes of white and yellow. She and Shubal were ready to depart — with two new bearers they had contracted with. Both men were of Shadizar, though a parent of one had certainly come here by way of Stygia.

'Good,' Conan said. 'We will need four bearers, to spell each other. Let us hope they can fight too, if need be.'

And that was that. He was outsized, and forceful, and not ill-favoured; the Lady Khashtris was wealthy and inclined to accept his word, even considering his youth. He had after all saved her life, and was beautiful in helmet and that arm-baring jerkin of linked chain.

Conan asked, 'And the guard who fled last night?'

'Not a sign of the white-livered dog,' Shabul said.

'Hmp! I'd not expected him to be here, to try to hire on again,' Conan said and he and the Shemite exchanged a look and a tiny smile: two men of weapons who had downed four, they would inspect the hue of the coward's liver if ever they laid eyes on him.

Milady's other guard remained ill. He must remain here and travel home alone when he could. Khashtris had to be back, for her cousin awaited some of the goods she'd purchased. Conan nodded, noting her four well-laden sumpter beasts. He appraised Shubal's horse, a handsome bay that would surely have been welcomed as mount by a knight of Aquilonia. The Cimmerian magnanimously announced that the off-duty bearers could take turns riding his sumpter-horse.

'Would be so much easier if women rode horses,' he said, while he and Shubal assisted Khashtris into her chair with its curtains of yellow, broidered with a red-fruited tree in green.

'A noble of Khauran does not bestride a horse,' she said, with a natural austerity that was not sententious or insulting. She drew in a bare leg.

'Not even the men, Lady?'

'Only to battle,' she assured him.

Conan nodded. 'Lady . . . might one ask if the Noble Khashtris knows the King of Khauran?'

She sighed and her face took on an expression of pensive sadness. 'Khauran of the Unhappy Queens has no king,' she said. 'The queen is daughter of my mother's sister.'

Elation leapt up in Conan like a cool spring. Cousin to a queen! And the horrid theft perpetrated on him by Hisarr Zul could be righted only by one who wore a crown. Aye, so had said the mage; a crowned *person*, he had said, not king, or even man! Conan stared into her eyes and spoke most earnestly.

'Lady Khashtris, there is that which only your cousin can do for me. For her it is nothing; for me, everything. Aid me in that and I will return your ring and serve you half a year without wage.' And he held out her moonstone-set ring of graven silver.

She could not miss the intensity of his gaze or tone.

'Why, Conan . . . there is no need of such rash promises. I live today because of your bravery and sword-skill of last night. I will see that you meet my royal cousin, and I will intercede for you. You will tell me what it is that only she can do; queen of a land you heard of only yesterday?'

'Noble Lady, I will!'

And he caught up her hand to press the ring on her. Stepping back then, Conan saluted the surprised woman with the loyalty sign he had offered no one since that day over two years ago when, just before the attack on the invaders in Venarium, he had been proclaimed warrior.

He had far more reason than a few pieces of gold to protect the life of this woman; she represented the return of his soul!

And so the lady Khashtris, queen's cousin of Khauran, employed as bodyguard the son of a barbarian smith, and with a gesture he pledged her a depth of loyalty she'd not have accepted, had she known the sign. As it was, smiling, she turned in her seat and drew the curtain. She was lifted on the shoulders of all four bearers. Before rode the Shemite, Shubal; behind the litter paced five sumpter-beasts, four laden, and behind all rode the giant in the arm-baring blued steel and the peaked Turanian helmet with its steel curtains that left bare only the forefront of his head and throat. The cavalcade paced through Shadizar and was soon passed through the south gate, on to the Road of Kings.

A bit later that afternoon, others followed.

CHAPTER 3

Swords in the Dark

Once they were on that broad caravan track called Road of Kings, Conan and Shubal rode just behind the litter. An off-duty bearer rode Conan's second horse and held the lead-rein of the first pack animal; the others docilely followed.

Shubal was of the *asshuri*, a Shemite warrior clan, Conan learned while the two men conversed. Soon they would swing west off the broad road, and into Khauran.

'Why "of the Unhappy Queens"?' Conan asked.

'The curse. Long and long ago a queen of Khauran mated with a demon. I believe the result is assurance of royal fecundity and Khauran's continued independence, or some such; I am not sure. The blessing carried with it a curse: once in each century a queen gives birth to a demon-child, a witch. She is easily recognised by the crescent mark on her bosom.'

'Every time, eh? What a belief!'

'Don't scoff, Conan. It's true. Each one is named Salome, after the first witch – and each is slain. Seven years ago, Queen Ialamis bore twin girls. One had the mark. She was given the dread name, and exposed to die on the desert. Princess Taramis, the witch's twin, does not know. She will be told during her Rite of Womanhood, in five or so years when she reaches age thirteen. Khauran's Queen Ialamis the Sad is a lonely and unhappy woman, widowed soon after she caused her own daughter to be slain. It is the dual curse of the queens of Khauran, for they seldom keep consorts long.'

'Someone should console Ialamis that she has saved her daughter; the princess is at least spared any possibility of bearing a demon! And who do the queens of Khauran wed, then?'

Shubal said, 'Strong and brave men!'

And they rode on, with Conan reflecting dolorously on the unhappy woman whose aid he so needed. They met a large caravan, and towards sundown a squad of uniformed horsemen, Zamoran soldiers, passed them. Later still, Conan cursed when a couple of youngsters galloped past, exciting his and Khashtris's beasts and raising a cloud of yellowish dust. They departed the road then, to make camp.

One horse bore tents; they set them up so that Conan and Shubal shared one and the four bearers another, while Khashtris had the tall green one to herself. They were on their way again shortly after sunrise.

Eventually the small cavalcade was pacing into the rich farmlands of little Khauran. Khashtris avowed that the very air was sweeter now, and had her curtains open. She even emerged now and again to walk for a space. Conan kept careful track of which bearer's turn it was to ride, and he and Shubal were not unhappy at having nothing else to do but watch the flash of their lady's fine legs.

On one of his employer's emergences from her litter, Conan dismounted to walk beside her.

'It is fine fertile country you are blessed with, Lady.'

'Aye, Conan – and just hear the birds! See how the farmfolk smile and wave when we pass. All are happy in Khauran . . .' And she stopped suddenly, frowning.

'Except the queen herself,' Conan said.

'Aye.'

'Shubal has told me of the Curse of Khauran's Queens. Would that I could break it, Lady, for you.'

'Think you so much of me, Conan?'

'You are certainly neither insensitive nor heartless, Lady Khashtris! I admit I'd defend you against odds, though, because of your promise to present me to the queen, with my petition.'

'Will you tell me of it now?'

'Aye, in brief. In Arenjun, I fell afoul of a certain mage, Hisarr Zul,' Conan said, seeing no reason to mention that he'd been engaged in trying to rob the mage at the time, and had fallen into a trap. 'He stole from me my very soul. I –'

'Your *soul*?' Khashtris was incredulous.

Conan glanced around, then at the plump cushion behind his saddle. 'Aye, just so. I think I've not smiled since, nor known a perfect night's sleep. My . . . soul is encased in a mirror. Thus the mage forced me into a mission for him. In the course of that I succeeded in laying a ghoulish ghost, a sand-lich on the desert between Arenjun and Zamboula. From that thing I learned the means of causing Hisarr Zul's death. When I returned he sought to slay me, but I turned his own poison-dust back on him. He is dead. My soul, my very essence, remains trapped in the mirror. He could have removed it, but I had to slay him or die myself. If the mirror is broken, I am soulless, yet alive. I have seen such creatures: such served the wizard, and I had rather be dead and eaten by vultures! Yet if the mirror is broken by a crowned ruler . . . my soul is returned to me. So said the sand-lich, who has been Hisarr's brother, and murdered by him.'

'Oh, *Conan*! Ishtar and Ashtoreth – how horrible!' Khashtris paused to turn to him, her elaborate coiffure spiring high as his forehead. 'Would that I wore a crown, that I might make you whole, my poor unfortunate! My cousin will end your torment, though, on our arrival. There is no doubt or question, Conan. It will be done.'

And now you know, my most attractive lady of twoscore years, why I would defend you against Old Set himself, Conan mused, and returned to his horse that he might be in better position were he needed as mercenary bodyguard, rather than companion.

He was not so needed, that day.

That night, Conan awoke to sounds that should not have existed. He knew what he had heard. Though Shubal lay a few feet away, breathing heavily in sleep, Conan elected to make no sound. He rose silently. Without taking time to don padded shirt or mail-vest, he buckled his weapons-belt over his breechclout with a silence few would have believed. Just as silent, he crept from the tent. Even thumping Shubal with his foot might bring the man awake with a cry or a groan, and someone outside was most interested in stealth. Conan adopted the same measure.

No more than ten good paces separated Khashtris's tent from his and Shubal's. Beyond it and angled a bit so as to form a triangle, the bearers' tent loomed against the night sky. He was just able to distinguish men there – and another less than five paces from him, his back to Conan. This one bent over still another, and a slender blade dripped on the fallen form. Conan knew he had heard a muffled yelp of pain or dying. The moonlight brought a glitter to upturned, glazed eyes, and Conan recognised one of the Ophirean bearers he had employed.

The Cimmerian crept forward like a stalking panther.

Seconds later there were two corpses on the ground. The man Conan had just slain was one of the bearers hired by Khashtris; he had murdered the Ophirean. Crouching, a snarl twisting his face, the Cimmerian peered about. The other three had not heard this killing. They were moving, very stealthily, upon Khashtris's tent.

Conan made instant decision, faded around his own tent, and came in behind Khashtris's, so that it was between him and the skulkers. Four, eh? Someone had followed them, then – someone in league with the two litter bearers the lady had employed. Now Conan squatted behind Lady Khashtris's tent. Moments later the fabric was neatly slit.

The queen's cousin awoke with a huge hand covering her lower face from cheek to cheek, from nose to chin. Her struggle was stilled by a brief whisper:

'It's Conan. Be still.'

With her heart pounding and her mouth covered and his brawny arm a heavy pressure on her breast, the high-coiffed lady waited in the darkness, and wondered whether she was being protected or menaced. The darkness and silence had become horror, so that her heartbeat sounded like the tympani of a marching army. She felt the swift beat of his heart too, beneath the massive chest bare against her bare back.

The flap of her tent was drawn aside from without, to admit a pallid pool of moonlight. A stooping man entered as if walking on eggs. Another. Another, bearing a sword. Conan thrust his noble employer roughly from him as he rose. In the silence and the darkness of the tent his snarled words were as a ferocious growl to freeze the limbs of any skulking murderers.

'What seek you, murdering dogs? Death?'

And he pounced one step to strike such a blow as he'd

never have risked against sighted foes. He could see dimly, and they had just entered the tent and surely could not; he risked. His sword clove meat and a man groaned horribly. Instantly Conan was twisting his blade free of its victim's flesh and muscle. He pounced aside then, and there came the sound of a falling body.

'Who – who struck? Baranthes?'

'*I* struck, slimy dog. You've come to do murder – do it!' The voice was as much animal growl as human, and the skin of Khashtris horripilated no less than that of the two men.

'Son of Set – it's that *Conan!*'

This time Conan said nothing; squatting, he extended his sword and swung. The arm was two feet long, to the wrist; the sword it wielded added nearly three feet more of reach. When the rushing edge struck, no groan arose; a man howled hideously in the dark as his calf was chopped more than half through. Even while he toppled, the silent Conan moved again, this time with unerring instinct towards Khastris. Leaning towards the tent's flap, he chopped down towards the floor as if seeking to split a fallen log. His blade did not reach the ground, but was arrested by a semi-yielding bulk. The ugly bubbling sound from a human throat told him he had found either lung or neck of the man he had already crippled: a treacherous litter-bearer from Zamora by way of Stygia.

Conan did not care which; he twisted free his steel and lunged rightward.

The *whish* he heard to his left was the third man's sword; did the fellow know he was now without companions?

'Best flee, slime,' Conan told him, growling low. 'You are all alone. I've slain three this night, and both Shubal and Khashtris live!'

Rather than accept sensible advice, the man struck wildly. Conan was already amove. With a loud chopping sound, the would-be murderer drove his sword into the tent's single pole with such force than he groaned at impact. The pole crumpled.

As the tent came down over them and Khashtris squeaked in terror, Conan pounced. He did not stab another unseen foe in the dark; he found an arm, which he broke, and then a neck. He broke it, too.

The Cimmerian stood alone, with the sagging tent draped over him so that he formed a human pole in a darkness that was absolute. The third stalker of Khashtris lay at his feet. Again the lady of Khauran made a squeaky, whimpering sound.

'There were three,' Conan said, and forced his way towards her voice, and squatted. The tent fell over them. Grasped by a shivering Khashtris, Conan held her close, and remained. Hardly old, the woman was nevertheless more than twice his age. But no woman, Conan learned, was old, in darkness.

Just at dawn a horrified Shubal hauled the tent away, and stared. Conan showed him an animal's ugly grin.

'Good morning, Shubal. You do sleep soundly.' The Cimmerian waved casually with a hand whose little finger wore a band of silver set with a moonstone. 'Drop the tent again, will you? Just for a few moments.'

Unable to speak though his mouth was open, Shubal did. Conan reared up to form a human tentpole, while the Lady Khashtris hastily clothed herself.

CHAPTER 4

Soul of the Cimmerian

Conan, Shubal and Lady Khashtris occupied a camp in which they were the only humans alive – though they now possessed two additional horses, bridled and saddled. All four bearers lay dead, the Ophireans murdered and the two hired by Khashtris slain by Conan. One lay under the woman's collapsed tent; the other two men there were unknown to Conan.

They were known to Khashtris and Shubal. The corpses were of her other two bodyguards, he who had been 'ill' and he had fled the thieves' attack in Shadizar.

'These two plotted it,' Conan mused aloud. 'Both of you and your bearers were to die. Perhaps these dogs made agreement with those thieves of Shadizar, or hired them. You travel with too much wealth and not enough protection, Khashtris.' He had called her by name without giving it a thought; Shubal noted, but made no comment. The noblewoman did not so much as compress her lips. 'That failed, and so they put two likely bearers in your way. You hired them –'

'Foolishly!' Khashtris said, in bitter self-accusation.

'Aye, foolishly,' Conan said, as though she were not his noble and wealthy employer. 'The two traitors followed us. Those tik-nuts the Stygian half-breed gave Shubal were a drug, or drugged. I didn't like the things, but he didn't know I'd spat them out, for I had no desire to insult him. I spat about ten times more to rid my mouth of their foul brown taste! Both Shubal and I were to sleep through your murder and robbery. Who can be sure why they first slew the Ophirean bearers?'

'Ishtar damn me for a fool!' Shubal blurted. 'Beat me with your sword, Conan!'

'Better we both beat our employer for hiring only two trustworthy men – and four treacherous midden-heap rats!

Better still, let us beat no one or our breasts either, but be on our way. Men have died afore, and I have killed afore. I reckon I will again. I may even make a mistake or two, some day. My noble lady: this time we leave that silly chair-on-poles. You will ride like a human and not a priest of Set, or you will walk while Shubal and I ride. Crom's name, we now have eight horses! Shall I tie you to one, or help you to mount?'

She gazed at him, large-eyed and blinking. 'I – I've never – my legs –'

'The legs of Noble Khashtris are better than those of any girl of fifteen or of twenty! Come, be human; be a wench, for once! You might enjoy it.'

Khashtris stared at him, and chewed her lip, and then suddenly she was smiling.

Thus rode the three into the walled city of Khauran, capital of Khauran, and along its broad main thoroughfare. All bestrode good mounts, and Khashtris sat tall with much display of fine bare leg. People stared; the noble lady held high her chin and her brows, and looked straight before her.

Between marble-walled structures the trio rode, leading five other horses. One was laden with the weapons of dead men. Conan was no stripper of corpses, but neither was he one to leave good weapons lying about to rust or fall into the hands of farm children.

They rode to a house of greenish marble and black pillars near the palace, and here was the Lady Khashtris made welcome by her household. A restive Conan suffered himself to be bathed while his armour and tunic were dusted. Nothing here was large enough to fit the Cimmerian, who clad himself again in the same tunic, over which he drew his padded jack and new shirt of mesh-mail. His lady employer still was not ready. He occupied the time of waiting in the downing of a huge cup of wine and the hurling of japery at Shubal, who wore a silver-bordered tunic of snowy white and a brocaded short-cloak for which Conan saw no purpose.

Once Khashtris had bathed and been coiffed anew and clothed she appeared – and at once pointed out how filthy

Conan's voluminous white cloak was. Rather than wear a cape such as Shubal's – who was smirking – Conan doffed the travel-soiled garment and refused to don the one she proffered.

Lady Khashtris and her bodyguards went to the palace, where a messenger had already carried word of her coming.

Many eyes watched the strapping near-giant with the hot blue eyes and the mop of square-trimmed black hair as he accompanied his gemmed employer and fellow bodyguard to the lofty structure housing Khauran's royalty. Despite the popularity of beards in Khauran, Conan had scraped his face smooth. The new mail-vest had been polished, and shone. Though its owner had slain four since purchasing it, the armour had yet to turn a blade or be blood-splashed.

Through the lofty marble halls of the palace they paced, accompanied by the clack-clack of Khashtris's shoes. Her yellow skirts rustled. Past doors arabesqued in gold they walked; past bronze-cuirassed guards who seemed to see nothing; past servants whose eyes rounded while they stared at the trio; by all these they passed in silence. They came to two tall doors plated with silver. On them some watery-eyed fellow had doubtless spent a year of his life inditing various scenes from the past of the Ashkaurian dynasty.

Khashtris was expected. She hardly gave the annunciator time to call out her name before she swept within. Conan followed her into a large chamber of pennon-hung walls of pink marble veined with red and grey, tiled floor strewn with carpets brought from the east, and an impressive number of burning lamps in ornate cressets of brass enhanced with gold and onyx.

Here were no guardsmen. Here were gathered six adults and a child of six or so years, who was gowned like a miniature queen. Her Conan saw but briefly, as she departed the audience chamber in the company of her nurse. He gave her but a glance: the child-sister of a dead witch, her hair black as that of her Cousin Khashtris's, though not piled and teased up into the Khaurani cone.

Cousin or no, Khashtris genuflected to the woman seated on the dais carpeted in scarlet. Just behind their employer, Conan and Shubal bowed.

The woman on the throne of Khauran bore signal resemblance to her cousin. Her black hair was coiffed identically to Khashtris's, if more ornately dressed; so was the hair of every noblewoman of this land. The queen's crown surrounded her high-spiring hair and its gems, yellow and smoky topaz, twinkled as if winking at Conan. Only her face and palms and fingers were unclothed; the youngish woman was draped in a pile of brocaded velvet and shining satin of rich hues. As to her form Conan could be sure only that she was of a broad-hipped plumpness.

High of forehead, the queen of Khauran affected tiny lines of eyebrows that were hardly the preference of the barbaric hillmen of cold Cimmeria. He liked her wine-coloured lips well enough, and her fine nose with its thin wings, even as he saw that her face was that of no happy woman.

Her attire was magnificent. Broidery of cloth-of-gold flowed inward from her shoulders in arabesque loops to the high collar of her bodice of mauve velvet, and up on to the high, stiffened collar. Bare round arms flashed from sleeves slashed from shoulder to wrist; each was cleverly caught just above the elbow by a few stitches and encircling bands of beaten gold. Thence each sleeve flowed down into a tight cuff that descended in points on to the backs of her hands. Ending in loops, the points were secured to the bases of her middle fingers, so that she seemed to be wearing matching rings of red-violet.

Below swept many yards of shimmering satin the colour of ice seen through turquoise. Over it the mauve bodice continued downward in a broad central panel. This fell to the skirt's hem, where it was purfled in silver in the Finquese style of Bakhaurus. A bandeau of scintillant cloth-of-silver circled the bodice over the bosom, sewn there and clasped with an ornate pin of shell and pearls and silver wire. From this outer bandeau draped a sort of third skirt, long behind; in front it formed a deep, inverted V whose arms flowed down the queen's legs and thighs like folded wings of mesh-mail.

From the royal lobes cascaded prodigiously ornate eardrops like bursts of incandescent light. Elsewise her jewellery was but a single ring formed of a serpent of gold and another of silver, intertwined.

Conan swallowed. She was only a few years older than he, and the mercenary who was bodyguard to her older cousin did entertain an interesting if silly dream or two...

Gathered with the queen were the City Governor, Acrallidus, whose beard was grey though his hair was not, and his son of about fourteen years; Krallides; and robed in dun and red, the queen's adviser Arkhaurus, a man of about forty-five. A huge carnelian seal hung on his chest from a chain of twisted silver wire. The handsome young man so near to my lady queen's right hand was Sergianus, duke's son of Tor, in Nemedia. A great sapphire-set disc of gold was suspended by a gold chain to flash on his chest.

The young noble from afar was enamoured of the queen and attached to her, Conan saw almost at a glance; he noted too how Queen Ialamis looked at that same Sergianus. The queen had a suitor then, come down from a land well to the north-west. A smith's son forgot his dreams.

All gave listen while Khashtris told of the adventure in Shadizar, of the later plot, of the loyalty of Shubal and the heroism and prowess of the Cimmerian. Eyes appraised the big youth anew. Now Conan saw respect and interest in those gazes. He was silent. In this, his first visit with such a collection of high-placed personages, he sought to look older, the brave and noble bodyguard.

He hoped that wise-eyed Acrallidus could not recognise a thief when one stood before him, however mailed and lauded!

Khashtris finished her glowing narrative, and all were silent while Queen Ialamis the Sad gazed upon the tall newcomer.

'Conan of Cimmeria: you have twice saved the life of our beloved cousin, and we are more grateful than may be expressed in words. Name a boon, warrior: what would you ask of the Queen of Khauran?'

Perhaps Conan appeared disrespectful to some; it was merely that he spoke instantly: 'My soul!'

The queen blinked, stared. Some of those around her looked questioningly at each other, but still none other spoke.

'He speaks literally, Lady Queen,' Khashtris told her

142

cousin. 'A certain Zamboulan sorcerer in Arenjun had the means of stealing souls from their living owners and lodging them in mirrors. Now the sorcerer is dead, but Conan and his soul remain separated. Should the mirror be broken, he will be . . . a horrid purposeless creature which he has described to me.'

'Incredible,' Acrallidus murmured, while the queen all but whispered, 'Horrible!' And Sergianus lifted one eyebrow as if in doubt: 'Sorcery? Separate soul from body? It is incredible, indeed!'

'So is the curse on the rulers of Khauran,' the ruler of Khauran said in a passing quiet voice. 'Conan: what is it you need us to do?'

The Cimmerian showed them the leathern package he had strapped to his belt; it resembled a well-stuffed pillow, covered in leather and crisscrossed with thongs, knotted and knotted again. He squatted to place it on the pink-tiled floor, a few feet before the three steps to the queen's dais.

'The mirror is contained here, Lady Queen. It must be placed in your hands.'

'Need I unwrap it?'

'No, Lady Queen,' Conan said.

While all watched, he untied, broke, and slipped the thongs. Next he unwrapped four folds of what was now revealed to be a large, broad strip of well-tanned and unusually supple leather. Within, thong-bound, were two plates of metal. Soon he separated them to withdraw a package wrapped in the dark green velvet that had draped a chamber of Hisarr Zul. There was much of the stuff, and while Conan unfolded its windings with care, the eyes of everyone present stared in expectation.

At last Conan had unwrapped that which he had protected so well against accidental breakage; the smallish mirror of Hisarr Zul.

'You had it wrapped well enough, Cimmerian!'

Conan looked at the speaker, the man called Sergianus of Nemedia in his sleeved, long, wine-red overtunic belted over a slightly longer tunic of green.

'Nothing in the world has been of more importance to

me, Lord Sergianus, save only my life.'

'Yet you risked that to rescue our cousin,' Queen Ialamis said.

'Aye. And she has brought me to you, Lady Queen. Only the wearer of a royal crown can end the spell and return my soul to me. If the mirror is broken, I and my soul are parted forever. If it is broken by a crowned ruler, we are united.'

The queen was leaning forward, her gaze moving from the squatting man to his mirror and back again to his face. 'Then we must break it for you, Conan.'

'Wait.' This from Arkhaurus, the royal adviser, and Conan's eyes narrowed. 'Wait, my queen. Suppose that all this is part of a sorcerous plot? – that some awful sorcery will be loosed on our lady queen *by* the breaking of the mirror? Dare we place faith in – '

'Lady cousin and Queen! I owe this man my life, twice over! I refuse to believe that he can be doubted, or that any plot is afoot against you. *He* is the unfortunate . . . and Arkhaurus wrongs both him and me.'

'Queen of Khauran – ' Acrallidus began, and the queen lifted a hand. The City Governor broke off, and none spoke, for they'd been silently commanded to silence. The queen studied Conan in obvious contemplation. At last, with a brief nod, she straightened.

'Bring me the mirror, Conan of Cimmeria.'

Taking up the small bit of wood-framed glass in both hands, Conan carried it to the foot of the dais. Standing on the floor at the base of the three-stepped marble platform, he did not have to look up to meet the eyes of the seated queen. He held out the mirror with both hands; with both hers she took it. Royal fingers touched his. Conan noticed that they felt no different from any other fingers, unless softer. Conan's mind accommodated that intelligence by shifting a bit, and never again would he stand – much less kneel! – in awe of royalty.

Queen Ialamis looked down into the glass of a dead sorcerer, and a wordless exclamation escaped her red-tinted lips. Then: 'Why – there is a *man* in this glass, a tiny youth with – it is you, Conan!'

'Some think it more I than what stands here of me,' he

said, without himself fully understanding the twisted meaning of those words.

'Sorcery!' Arkhaurus said, in a low hiss.

'I want to see!' That from young Krallides son of Acrallidus, and he pressed forward.

The queen did not afford him that privilege. Holding the mirror with care, she stood. Conan moved aside as she descended the steps of the dais in a rustle of satin. Three paces she took along the carpet bisecting the floor of rose tiles and she stopped. Lifting the mirror with both hands, she looked at Conan.

'Lady Queen,' Sergianus said urgently, 'flying glass –'

Conan glanced angrily at the man just as Ialamis hurled the mirror against a wall of stone.

The Cimmerian heard the crash, and jerked as if struck; for he felt a great surge within him; a sudden *wholeness*, as though his body had encompassed emptiness now filled. And then he was staring at Sergianus, and Conan's eyes were large and his face showing astonishment. The hairs stood up along his arms and on his nape. None other noted; all stared at the mirror.

Perhaps the others underwent similar reaction to Conan's; they saw the mirror shatter against the audience-chamber wall, and yet they saw no flying shards of glass. All *floated*, eerily, just before the wall whereon the mirror had shattered – three feet above the floor.

The gleaming slivers and bits of glass seemed to dance like refulgent dust-motes of many sizes, or spilled gemstones. And then gasps sounded, for each tiniest bit of glass burst into flame. All flared brightly so that every watching eye squinted – and then flame and glass vanished.

On the floor near the wall lay the wooden frame of Hisarr Zul's mirror of sorcery. Not one trace of flame could be seen; not one particle of glass. No faintest hint of the scent of fire remained in the chamber.

Now all looked at the Cimmerian. They saw how he stared at Sergianus, who, also noting, frowned. Then Conan blinked. He seemed to stagger. He gave his shaggy head a jerk. After shooting Sergianus a disbelieving look, the Cimmerian turned to the queen. When he lifted his head, Shubal and Khashtris saw Conan smile, naturally and far from bestially, for the first time since the dark-maned giant had entered their lives.

'Lady Queen, it is done. I am in debt to Khauran and its royal house. *I felt my soul return to me!*'

'I but repaid a debt, Conan,' the queen said, forgetting the royal pronoun. 'You are welcome in Khauran, saviour of m – our cousin.'

CHAPTER 5

In the Tavern of Hilides

Conan and Shubal had been walking about Khauran for a couple of hours when the Shemite guided his younger companion on to a street of taverns and inns. They approached a door under a broad-striped awning of orange and bright green. The awning was particularly horrid and hurt Conan's eyes; the shop was not and did not. Small, cool and clean, it barely housed two longish trestle tables and benches, and four other tables: three-legged, for two people who wanted more intimate converse. The two bodyguards, their charge safe within the palace, sat at one of the latter tables.

'Shubal! You've not been here in awhile!'

'That's because I've been up in Shadizar with my lady,' Shubal told the burly, ruddy-faced man with the large pot belly and eyes like new-tanned cowhide. His brown hair and beard looked as if someone had recently hurled a handful of sand into each.

'Ah! Oho! Shadizar, eh? Eh? And you came *back*,' the fellow said. 'Why, from all the tales I've heard of that place, your return is a miracle! Just yesterday Verenus made his delivery, and said Pertes's son went off to Shadizar – a month ago! What was it Verenus said; how do we keep good Khaurani boys on the family farm after they've seen Shadizar City of the Wicked, eh? Eh?'

'The miracle that brought me back is this little fellow with me,' Shubal said, tapping Conan's shoulder. 'Since Verenus was just here, Hilides, fetch us a mug each of that watery ale of his.'

'Done. It was tapped this morning. What do you mean, he's a miracle? It's a miracle a lad that age grew so big, mayhap, and suffers himself to be seen in company with such as you! Is that it? Eh?'

'Shadizar wasn't hard for me to leave,' the Shemite replied. 'Noble Khashtris and I were nearly killed there.'

Hilides set glazed earthenware mugs before the two without so much as a thump. The fellow had the arms of a woodman or warrior, Conan thought, and the belly of a king.

'Oh! Got a story to tell, do ye? How'd it come about, Shubal? Whorehouse brawl? Irate husband? Hoho! Eh?'

'This braying mule-brain is our host, Conan: Hilides. Hilides: Conan, a Cimmerian. Noble Khashtris's new bodyguard – with me, of course.'

'Cimmeria.' The big taverner looked at Shubal's big companion. 'Conan. Co-nan. Welcome to Khauran, Conan. Sorry about your taste in friends. A passing nice corselet you have there. You're not from Shadizar, eh?'

Conan shook his head. 'The mail is,' he said, and drained his mug. 'Small cups you use, Hilides.' Then he made a face.

Hilides laughed. 'Does go down easy, don't it! Took it too fast; stings the tongue that way! And wait'll it comes back; you'll jump a mile when you fart. Verenus Clingcoin's brew. Shubal swears he waters it.'

'No, I don't Hilides; I swear *you* water it.'

'Ha! Hoho!' Hilides slapped his gut, which Conan saw was solid and firm as a thigh. 'Only thing I water is my garden! *I* think Verenus brews it from alfalfa, Conan. Oddly though, it's popular.'

'That's because it's cheap,' Shubal said, 'and Verenus's daughter is coming on to be a beauty! Uh, be careful about drinking much, Conan. Noble Khashtris is . . . sensitive about that.'

'I've barely dampened my throat,' Conan said. 'Fill it, Hilides, or a man-sized mug, if you have one. This will go on Shubal's bill until our lady parts with some coin, unless you'll make a chit for me, too.'

'For a well-employed friend of Shubal, Shem's gift to womankind, I will. You look good for it; you could buy Verenus's brewing for a half-year with that mail. As a welcome to Khauran, though, I'll buy the second one.'

'The second?'

'Aye – you knocked back that first mug so fast you didn't even taste it, and I'll not support such waste!'

Conan chuckled while Shubal laughed. 'But only,' Hilides called back, 'if I hear about Shadizar and your adventure there, Shubal!'

'Huh! Try to stop me from talking about it,' Shubal said, looking around. He nodded at one man, threw up his hand in greeting to another. At this hour of the afternoon, only three others gave Hilides business. 'Oh – Hilly! A little Shemite sausage?'

Conan blinked. 'This little place stocks sausage from down in Shem?'

'Not really,' Shubal said smiling. 'Hilides adds some pepper and sage and a bit of honey to the Khaurani summer sausage his wife makes, and calls it Shemite. He doesn't charge any more for it, and I think I'm the only one who knows any different. I don't say anything. It's a popular treat here. It is good, Conan. Put hair on your chest.'

Conan said nothing. He had no hair there as yet, and wished he did. It was not a favoured subject with him. He was sitting back, leg asprawl; now he leaned forward and thumped a pair of meaty forearms on the small round table.

'Shubal: What do you know about that Sergianus?'

'Hardly anything. No one else does, I think. It bothers me a bit now; today is only the second time ever I saw him, and this is the first time I've set eyes on that medallion he wears.'

'It bothers you?'

'I think I recognize it. Or I've seen its twin.'

'And –'

'Well, where I've seen it certainly wasn't in Nemedia, Conan; never been up there. Or one just like it – as I remember.'

'You think maybe he's a thief? Or buys stolen goods, maybe?'

'I haven't thought about it at all, in truth. As for buying stolen goods – most of us do, at one time or another. No, I don't think anything. I just don't remember where I've seen it – I mean, one like it.'

'Did you notice anything . . . unusual about Sergianus, Shubal?'

'Certainly. He has an odd voice – and a suicidal bent.'

'What? Why do you say that?'

'Conan, he is paying court to our queen. I do believe, judging from the looks they exchange and his concern for her, that they two may love each other.'

'One *larger* mug of Verenus's beer,' Hilides said, 'on me. And a bit of the fiery sausage of Shem.' He stood at Conan's elbow.

'Thanks, Hilides,' Conan said, hardly glancing at the man. 'Shubal . . . why is that suicidal?'

Hilides, half-turning away, paused. 'Suicidal?'

'Conan,' Shubal said, 'the unhappy Queens of our Khauran have more to contend with than the Curse of the Witches. They also have a hard time keeping consorts. Our Queen Ialamis was wed at fourteen, delivered of twins at fifteen – '

' – and one of them the Witch,' Hilides said, lingering.

' – and widowed when she was only seventeen. A fever carried off her husband, and almost killed her. She lay abed for months.'

'Months,' Hilides said, standing over the little three-legged table and imperturbably injecting himself into the conversation. '*Months*, and was wan and slow to move for a full year. Some think she's never recovered; it's been four years now. Lord Arkhaurus feels that the problem is as much in her mind as in her . . . body.' The taverner hesitated over the final word, and lowered his voice, as though it might be worse than untoward to use such a word in speaking of the queen. 'This young dukeson from Nemedia doesn't worry about that though, does he?'

'That's just what we were talking about,' Shubal said, around a mouthful of deceptively pale sausage, dotted with red. 'Conan and I are just come from the audience chamber, and Conan asked – '

'The audience chamber! And then *here*? My benevolent stars – Hilides is honoured today!'

'Oh stop, Hilly. Anyhow, Conan asked if I noted aught unusual about Noble Sergianus. I told him aye, the man's plainly suicidal.'

'Oh.' Hilides grinned and wagged his head. 'For hanging about our queen? Mayhap he is, eh? Are they thick? So I hear. In the meanwhile, though, I also hear that she's happier than she has been in years. Or so they say, eh? *I* don't spend my time loitering about the audience chamber, rubbing elbows with our sovran and her charming visitor from Nemedia.' He glanced around. 'Merkes – our Shubal's just come from an audience with Herself!'

From across the room a man said, 'Ishtar? Don't be silly. She doesn't speak to Shemites!'

'I meant the queen . . .'

Shubal half-turned to call to the man named Merkes. 'Or anyone as ugly as you, Merkes! For your information, though, Ishtar is a Khaurani import: Herself is a Shemite goddess.'

'I meant the queen,' Hilides said again, trying to regain control of a conversation that wasn't his to begin with.

'Bosh and cowfeathers!' Merkes said from within a vast black beard. 'She was born right here in Khauran, right where Her temple stands now, across from the palace.'

'You damned chauvinists,' another man said; the one Shubal had waved to. He sat in the far corner, rear. 'Ishtar's from my own Nemedia!'

Shubal shook his head, laughing. 'The ignorance of the clientele this place attracts! Everyone knows that Bel was born in Shumer, of Shem –'

'Who's talking about Bel?' Hilides asked.

'– precisely four thousand nine years ago, which is the day before the world began.'

'Bel was born in Shem before there was any Shem?' Hilides said.

'Ishtar,' Shubal went on, never having glanced at the tavern's owner, 'is claimed by the Pelishtians – *also* of *Shem* – who say the city of Asgalun was begun on the site of her appearance, full-formed, from a stone of the earth that was split by a single bolt of green lightning. Even her priests agree that this was two hundred years after Bel's birth, for Shem was lonely for a woman's touch. Stars above, can you imagine what a people would be like, with only a single god, and him male? Oho!'

'Did you know that Bel's the Turanian god of thieves?' Conan tried.

'That's what's wrong with Stygia,' Merkes said, dropping

the subject of Ishtar's place of origin. 'All those mid-nighters have is that noxious *Set*!'

'Ah,' Hilides grinned, speaking quickly and raising a big hand for attention, 'but you are forgetting Derketo! That thrice-sensuous creature is most definitely female, and Stygian! No, for people with only a male deity, you have to go to those desert tribesmen, the Habiru.'

'Up in Nemedia we call her Serketo the Stygian Serpent-Slut!'

Conan sat silent, trying not to guzzle the new-made beer while the others talked about nothing. Gods! Who cared! Where he came from, gods were plentiful and chief among them was Crom. Nor did that god, never called father, care what happed with an infant, once it was birthed. What self-respecting deity would concern himself – aye, or herself – with the affairs of humankind? It was for humans to concern themselves with the affairs and preferences of the gods, whom they blamed for half that which went bad and most of the good that befell. Derketo did sound promising! Meanwhile, the Cimmerian wanted to find out more about Sergianus, and his own eerie vision in the queen's chamber.

'. . . spider-god over in those old ruins called Yezud,' Merkes was saying.

'Shubal,' Conan said low and fast, 'what's the name of that fellow from Nemedia?'

'Sergianus.'

'No, dolt, the one over there who says Ishtar is Nemedian.'

'Ha!' Hilides essayed again; 'You can tell these two are friends – Conan just called Shubal a dolt!'

'Anyone that big,' Merkes said, 'can call me double-dolt, if he wants!'

'Oh,' Shubal said, 'he's Nebinio.'

'How long has he been away from Nemedia?'

'I don't know,' Shubal said.

'Say, these two are ignoring us, eh? Eh?'

'Neb!' Shubal called. 'How long since you were in Nemedia?'

'Too long, by Mitra! What's that have to do with any-thing?'

Conan twisted his neck to look back at the chestnut-haired fellow in the corner. Nebinio wore a tunic that had probably begun – years and years ago, when last he'd had his hair trimmed – at white, and a faded half-cloak or cape that was either filthy or unwisely dyed the colour of dust.

'Wondered what you thought of this countryman of yours at the palace,' Conan said. 'Son of the Duke of Tor.'

'Where're you from, big fellow?' Nebinio said, a bit surly.

'Cimmeria. My name is Conan.'

'Well, I make it a rule never to argue with a man wearing sword and mail,' Nebinio, who was perhaps five and a half feet tall, said, 'and I don't know this man whereof you speak – Sergianus, isn't it? But Tor's no duchy.'

Conan turned himself a bit more around. 'Sergianus is duke's son of Tor, in Nemedia.'

'Well,' Nebinio said, 'mayhap he's just making himself more important. Tor's a barony. Presided over by a baron. Baron Amalric is about . . . oh, fifty, perhaps. Has a son who will succeed him, also named Amalric.'

'No other sons?'

'Of course he has other sons! Who knows anything about second and third sons, though, noble or no? Hilides, unless you're going to spend the rest of your life there by their table, I'd like more wine here, and a slice of the black.'

Hilides departed the table of Conan and the Shemite. The other drinker, the quiet one near the door, plunked down a coin and left. Shubal said:

'Why are you so curious about a Nemedian, your first day in Khauran?'

Conan looked at him very seriously. 'Are you not curious about him? He may well be your next king.'

'No, no – queen's consort. But I see what you mean.'

'A baron's severalth son, elevating himself to ducal rank, and who you think is wearing a medallion you've seen somewhere other than in Nemedia. Mayhap he's one of those accursed Zingaran adventurers – or a Stygian sorcerer, old as the hills themselves, in disguise.'

'You believe in sorcery?' Shubal shrugged. 'I'm probably wrong about the amulet he wears. You about through, here? We'd best be getting back. We *should* be at the palace right now, waiting, and we'd better be about when Noble Khash-tris is ready to return home.'

'I need another jug of ale just to cool my mouth after a bit of that damned sausage of yours! My tongue is numb and my throat feels like one of the flame-eaters in the bazaar in Arenjun!'

Shubal laughed. 'I'll just finish it for you, then,' he said, scooping up the remainder of Conan's sausage. 'We can't all have strong stomachs.'

'Strong! Yours must be lined with brass!'

'Come, Conan; we can always try to beg a cup at the palace.'

'Hmp.'

They rose to depart, despite Hilides's expostulations; he'd not had the story of what he called Shubal's 'adventure' in Shadizar. Tomorrow, Shubal told him. The two companions left the little tavern.

Four blocks later they short-cut through a marketplace crowded with awning-shaded trestle-boards and bins and baskets, loud with hawkers of various fresh edibles. Conan inhaled air redolent with the aromas of a dozen vegetables and fruits, and as many condiments. Shubal shouldered Conan, making a sudden change in their direction. The man from Shem ambled to a fruit-spread table beneath a plain scarlet awning. In its shade sat a moon-faced old woman with much fat and few teeth. Standing beside her was a young woman, plumply attractive, uncommonly chesty in her loose blue outer shift and apron.

'Sfalana!' Shubal called brightly. 'Miss me?'

The young woman gave him a cool look from under thick, arched brows. 'Oh, have you been gone?'

'Evil wench! You know I have, and that you've missed me.'

'I've managed to keep myself occupied,' Sfalana said, giving Conan a dark-eyed appraisal. The old woman shook with her ridiculously high-voiced laugh. The sound reminded Conan of that of a jackal on the great Turanian desert.

'Counting melons, doubtless,' Shubal said, unfazed. 'How about a hug?'

'I'm busy, Shubal.'

'He just wants to squeeze your melons,' the old woman shrilled, and made her jackal laughing sound anew. 'Why not buy two of these instead, Shubal? They won't keep you warm, but they're all the way from Korveka, I swear.'

'Oh, of course,' Shubal scoffed. 'I can just see you importing melons from . . . Korveka . . . that's it!'

They looked at him, the old woman and the young, and at the tall youth standing silent beside him.

'Korveka!' Shubal repeated.

'I swear,' the old woman said, and laughed.

'Believe her and you'll believe Derketo is a virgin,' Sfalana said. 'Where have you been, anyhow?'

Shubal reached across the piled fruits and seized her hands. 'Shadizar, with Noble Khashtris. Just a shopping trip for her – things for her and the queen. But for me – it was nearly death. We were attacked, and –'

'Oh, Shubal!'

Oh, Conan thought. Now he understood why Sfalana had been so cool and distant with Shubal; she loved him and he'd gone off without telling her. Her eyes and tightened hands showed her concern.

'Aye. Four bandits slew one bearer, and the other fled. The other two guards were part of it, Sfalana! One played sick so that there were only two of us that night, and the other one ran off the instant the attack began. He was part of it too, we later learned. This – oh. Sfalana, this is Conan. He's from Cimmeria. He saved my life, and our lady's.'

Sfalana turned huge dark eyes on Conan. 'Ishtar smile on you, Conan of Cimmeria.' And instantly she returned all attention to Shubal. 'Were you hurt?'

'Not a scratch, I swear. Tell you about it tonight?'

She nodded. 'Come for dinner?' She glanced at Conan, as if she thought perhaps she should ask him too, but didn't really want to.

'Uh . . . no, I'd better show Conan a few things, first. He's joined Noble Khashtris's service, too, and hasn't even seen his bed; we're just back. And we'd better be on our way. Noble Khashtris expects us, at the palace.'

'The palace!' the old woman cried, and laughed.

'Of Korveka,' Conan told her, and winked. He was tired of being a less than comfortable bystander.

She laughed again, then: 'What know you of Korveka, big lad? You from Koth?'

'No, Cimmeria. North—'

'Ah! Cimmeria! I've heard of it. Cold! I've never met anyone from Cimmeria before. My name is Mishellisa, Conan of Cimmeria. Come along with Shubal tonight and I'll show you a good time!' And she jackal-laughed, to assure him that she only jested. Conan thought it best to continue his sentence without taking note of hers.

'—of here. I'd never heard of Korveka until you mentioned it. I just said it because you said these were Korvekan melons.'

'You hear that, Shubal, you doubting Shemite! Your big friend believes me!'

'You believe her, Conan,' Shubal said, 'and you'll believe Derketo of Stygia's a virgin!' While the old woman cackled, Shubal looked at Sfalana. 'Later.' He glanced at Mishellisa. 'Go to bed early, grandmother.'

Her high-voiced, ululating laughter followed the two young men as they moved away. Shubal glanced at the sky.

'We'd best stride out,' he said.

Conan did. 'What's Korveka?' he asked.

'A barony of Koth, right up against our western border,' Shubal said. 'By rights it ought to be part of Khauran. Khauran was once part of Koth, you know. Back in their Empire days.'

'Umm. You seemed excited to hear about it.'

'Your pardon, lady. Oh, aye! Seeing Sfalana and thinking about tonight I almost forgot again. Aye, Korveka! That's where I've seen that medallion — I mean, one just like Sergianus's—before. Around the neck of the Baron of Korveka, of Koth! I passed through his domain several years ago, on my way here.'

'Look out where you're going, lout!'

That to Conan from a bustling man in a violently chartreuse robe that was loose everywhere save over his paunch. Conan stared; the many-chinned fellow betook himself off with alacrity, muttering the while.

'What does my lord of Korveka look like, Shubal?'

Shubal barked a short laugh. 'Not like that handsome Sergianus! His son, perhaps. It has been five years—old

Sabanitus – no, Sabaninus, Sabaninus . . . he's probably dead by now. A very old man. A *very* old man, Conan. Sergianus barely looks old enough to be his son.'

Conan thought on that, and on his vision in the queen's audience chamber, while they strode through Khauran's capital to its royal palace.

CHAPTER 6

Sorcery!

Once Conan had been introduced to the four members of the house of Noble Khashtris, Shubal led him to the room they would share. It was larger than many the Cimmerian had slept in, and larger than the huts of many, many peasant families. The fat dumpling of a blonde maid iterated and reiterated her assurance that his pallet was clean and fresh.

Conan removed his vest of mail and the padded jack beneath. The fat dumpling of a maid's fatter sow of a mother, also blonde, measured him. The mistress had instructed her to make two tunics for the new member of the household. Evriga muttered while she measured. When her daughter wondered aloud if the big youth was big everyplace, Evriga ordered her out of the chamber. Daughter left; mother rounded on the Cimmerian.

'You are not to lay so much as one of these huge hands on that girl, do you hear?'

Conan had not considered it, and might have done so only were he and the girl marooned on a small and unpeopled island far out to sea, with certain knowledge of remaining there, alone, beyond six months. Nevertheless he replied without rancour, without smiling. (Beyond Evriga, Shubal was making ridiculous faces at his fellow bodyguard.)

'I hear and obey,' Conan said quietly.

'Hmp. Glibly spoke,' Evriga said.

'Would you like me to swear?'

Evriga reiterated her 'Hmp' and resumed her taking of measurements.

Standing very still, towering over Evriga, Conan swore not to touch her daughter: 'This I vow by Crom, grim Lord of the Mount, and by Badb, and Lir and Macha, and Manannan and Morrigan as well, and Nemain, Venomous Nemain.'

'I never heard of any of them,' Evriga said. 'Ishtar – what *arms*!'

'I swear too by Ishtar, who as all know is of Nemedia, and by Set and I swear too by Derketo –'

'Never *mind* that Stygian slut-god, barbarian!'

'And by Yog,' Conan solemnly intoned, 'King of Demons.'

'All right,' the woman said, 'all right.' And measurements completed, she left them.

Immediately Conan and Shubal fell to laughing. Shubal interrupted to assure Conan that it was Evriga who truly had designs on him, and erupted anew. Conan did not reply; Evriga might have made a fair mother, he thought, or an excellent mattress.

'Two tunics! I have never owned three tunics at once in my entire life, Shubal!'

'All that long!' the Shemite grinned. 'How old are you, Conan?'

'Twenty.'

'Um. In a way, I'd have thought you older. In another, you seem younger. I too am twenty, my fellow guardian of the body of Khashtris.'

Conan, who was eighteen, nodded and they went to take the evening meal. Spartus, Khashtris's head of household, presented the newcomer with a single silver coin.

'Three of these would purchase the sword you wear; eight would buy a good mare, Conan. This is against your wages, that you might not be penniless in Khauran.'

'What,' Conan asked of Shubal, 'is the price of a mug of ale at Hilides?'

'Two for a copper. That silver coin will exchange for twenty good coppers.'

'I am almost rich enough to be drunk,' Conan said, and made the silver Queenhead vanish.

Shubal rose laughing, said he had business, and departed. Conan, who knew the nature of that 'business', knew longing. He also felt that he was new, and on duty, whether in Khauran there was danger to Khashtris or no. Finishing his dinner, he went out to examine the gardens behind the house. He sought to pass the time of evening with the gardener. Amid the cool verdure, beneath gently rustling trees, that man had no care for a stranger's need of companionship. He affected rude manners and talked but little.

It was not pleasant to be new in a city, and to know that one's only friend was with a woman, and to have no companionship whatever. Conan returned to his and Shubal's room.

Shubal was very absent. There Conan abode, sitting and sprawling and restlessly pacing by turns. He gave much thought to the day's occurrences and to what he had learned – and regained – and to what he had seemed to *see* at the instant of his soul's adjoining his body. These reflections troubled his mind. He was doubly troubled: he was intensely aware of what Shubal was doing, this night, with Sfalana of the melons.

He was vehemently aware of Khashtris's presence in this large nightbound house. *Her* house. The house of *Noble* Khashtris, in which she was employer and cousin to the queen, not a frightened and grateful girl-woman under a collapsed tent.

Eventually his mind and body were so troubled and restless that he had to escape the room. It seemed to have shrunk and at the same time become too large for one person alone. Its four walls leered at him.

He left it. The house was dark and silent. Silent as a panther the Cimmerian paced along rug-strewn halls of coloured stone floored with marble. He let himself out by the rear door. Trees rustled and the grass and shrubbery filled his nostrils with a fragrance that was green and fresh and cool. Soon, pacing in shadow-haunted moonlight, he had memorised the shrubbery, trees and garden-plot. He'd have been delighted if an assassin or two had come slipping over one of the walls. None came. The branches of the trees seemed to whisper of love.

After circuiting the house, Conan ascended to the porch and sat for a time amid square-based columns painted the blue of the sky and decorated with plumey strutting birds in green and yellow and blues.

That, too, palled. He rose. His attempt to enter was blocked by a locked door. *Good*, he thought, for he was employed as bodyguard to a noble who trusted him, and he went around back.

That door, too, had been barred from within. Good . . . but . . .

Well, Conan mused, *no one knows I came outside, and the moon is high. The night ages. A very efficient steward, that damned Spartus!*

Conan spent the night in the garden.

Just after dawn he was on the porch, his stomach rumbling while he awaited the awakening of the household of noble Khashtris. Eventually the door was opened to the day. Conan explained, and Evriga laughed at him as he entered. That was enough; while he breakfasted, alone, he was advised by cook that his tunic stank. That was more than enough.

'So,' the seated Conan said quietly without looking up from his wooden bowl, 'does your breath. Now hush and give me more of that only fair gruel else I consider telling our employer how you imbibe wine intended for cooking, even of a morning.'

He received another bowl, in silence, and was left in peace.

Shubal entered the little room as Conan was finishing. They exchanged smiles, and the Shemite winked, but neither man said anything. *I had rather be in someone's army than have this job,* Conan mused as he left the other man to his morning gruel.

Conan had nothing to do that morning, and did not enjoy not doing it. Just after noon – at last – he and Shubal un-necessarily escorted their employer to the meeting house of the Advisory Council. It was there, while Khashtris was within, that Arkhaurus came walking out among the lofty columns covered with swirling multicolour patterns. He approached the Cimmerian.

'You stared hard at my lord Sergianus on yester day, Conan,' the Adviser to the Throne said. 'All the while that our lady queen was performing the act to rescue you from black sorcery. Why stared you so? '

'I – might I answer question with question, Arkhaurus? How came that noble lord here?'

'Ah – you think you knew him afore, then?' Arkhaurus's eyes were so dark as to be night black, and they seemed to

161

pierce like sharpened bits of onyx. Today he wore a longish white tunic over dun-hued leggings, and the silver chain supporting the carnelian seal on his chest. When Conan said nothing, the rangy man spoke on.

'As you are bodyguard to the queen's cousin and something of a hero for having brought her safely home from that wicked Shadizar, I will tell you. The men at the western gate saw him first. They beheld a frightsome apparition: a man in fine clothing that was torn and stained, and him all bloodied and afoot. He identified himself. He was believed because of his manner and the medallion he wore. It is obviously no trifle, or new either. The sentries brought him to Acrallidus whilst we two were conferring. We soon saw to his bathing, and provided him with a robe. Over wine, he advised that he had been assaulted by robbers who had slain his two retainers and fled when they heard a dog barking. Thinking others were coming, the bandits fled with the mounts of the dukeson, Sergianus and his retainers, and his sumpter animals as well.'

'He was injured?'

Arkhaurus shook his head. 'He bore no wounds aside from a smallish cut on his sword-hand.'

'He fought, then. The blood on him came from his own sword, which must have wounded one of his attackers.'

'I see that you do know combat, and do think as well. Good for you, my boy. Begging his indulgence and patience, we sent men to look. He was lordly austere about our wish to corroborate his story, but nice enough. He is in truth a pleasant fellow. Our men returned to report that they had found the corpses, and blood, and the marks of many stamping hooves. Tracks led west, to Koth.'

'*To* Koth.'

'Aye. The fleeing bandits.'

Fleeing horses, anyhow, Conan mused, and nodded in silent invitation for the man of five-and-forty or so to continue.

'One sword, bloodied, lay at the scene; otherwise the bandits had taken weapons and horses.'

'Without killing Sergianus.'

Arkhaurus pursed his lips, giving Conan an admonitory

look. 'The lord Sergianus,' he said, with a bit of stress on the title, 'said that once his men were downed and he unhorsed, he lay as if dead. For surely one man afoot cannot fight three. They were coming towards him to be certain of his death when they heard the dog. One opined aloud that such a sound doubtless meant people, and they hadn't after all come bent on murder, but on booty. The three galloped off. '

'Did *the lord* Sergianus say that one was wounded?'

'Two, indeed, he said bore wounds. Once they had gone, the duke's son arose and made his way here, afoot. We accompanied him then to the queen. He told her his story in our presence; all was the same. Our good Queen Ialamis kindly offered him clothing and lodgings as the son of a foreign noble, far from home and so foully robbed in our land. That was just under two months ago; he has remained.'

'Paying court to Queen Ialamis.'

'He is very good for her; everyone sees that. Our queen has long been a most lonely and unhappy woman, Conan. At her next birthday she will be one-and-twenty. Yet she has endured the burden of the crown and her misfortunes these seven years, and borne but once, though they were twins – you know of this?'

'Aye.'

'And of the curse on the royal House of Ashkaurus?'

'Aye.'

'And that it was our poor Ialamis who bore the witch in this century, and made the bravely logical, and yet terrible and soul-tearing decision – all alone – concerning that doom-bearing child of her own womb.'

'I know it, aye. And that she was widowed within a couple of years.'

'Aye. Well then, you can perceive that it is no happy queen I have advised since then – and, indeed, been as father to. She looks older than her years, Conan, and looked older still, before the arrival of the Nemedian lord. She had much trouble sleeping, and suffered horribly from nightmares in which she heard her dead babe crying out to her from the desert. The child was Salome, a witch, and she represented horror and evil. Nevertheless, my lady Queen had carried the babe within her, and it was her own child she ordered slain.'

Conan nodded. Once he fathered a child, he could not imagine himself slaying it, no matter the reason or logic; not in infancy, at any rate.

'Yes,' he said. 'I understand, and thank Arkhaurus the Royal Adviser for taking so much of his time to tell me of Khauran. And then the son of the Nemedian duke came.' *Except that there is no duke over Tor in Nemedia.*

'The young Duke of Tor, aye. I have seen years fall from our queen as dead leaves from a strong tree, leaving it to bloom and thrive anew in spring. I have seen life return to her haunted eyes, Conan, and now she is cheerful, at times almost girlish again. My lord Sergianus, Conan, is the best thing to happen to Queen Ialamis – and thus to Khauran – in many years. As you are, to her noble cousin, for you saved her life. My queen and Dukeson Sergianus are smitten each with the other, methinks, though they are *not* lovers.'

'Not yet, anyhow.'

That came from Shubal, who had joined them without Arkhaurus's noticing. Conan had noted the Shemite's approach, but had seen no reason to interrupt the queen's adviser. Now Arkhaurus turned those awl-sharp eyes on Shubal.

'The prospect of a landless Nemedian, then,' Conan hastily said, 'as Khauran's lord does not disturb you.' He did not quite make it a question.

'No,' Arkhaurus said.

Shubal said, 'Better, for the matter of that, a landless adventurer than one who may be kin of the king of a country that has so long eyed this little nation.'

'Shubal,' Arkhaurus said, 'refers of course to Koth. Surely we cannot call Dukeson Sergianus an "adventurer", though.'

'Oh no, no,' Shubal said, 'I meant that even if he were, that would be preferable to a Kothian. Koth would gladly trade off her western provinces for dominion over these rich farmlands of Khauran!'

'Umm,' Arkhaurus said noncommittally. 'But Conan . . . you have not answered my original question: why stared you so at my lord Sergianus? Have you seen him afore-now?'

'No, I – what I saw was . . .' And an idea was in Conan's head like a new flashing gem, or as if the plan had been writ on an arrow shot into his head. 'Arkhaurus . . . do you read Turanian?'

The statesman looked puzzled, but nodded. 'Aye,' he said, and went on in the Turanian tongue, 'Aye, I speak it, read it, and can write it, Conan. Why?'

'Because,' Conan said, 'it is the only language I write – and that not excellently. Shubal . . . you have letters?'

Shubal did not look his most comfortable. 'I am, uh, fair in Shemite – '

'Which I cannot read,' Arkhaurus said.

'Nor I,' Conan said.

'Well, actually,' Shubal went on, 'I write pretty well in Shemite, but only fair in Kothic.'

Conan knew that Kothic was the tongue of Khauran, with a few modifications; the written language remained even closer to the original.

'Then I want to conduct an experiment. Shubal . . . without saying his name, will you write a description of that man we spoke of yesterday, who had the medallion?'

'Sergianus?'

'No, the other – and without his name, Shubal.'

'Oh. He's probably dead by now, Conan. It's been over four years. Nearly five.'

'Indulge me.'

Shubal would; they went into the whitewashed building. The aged scribe just beyond the portico was none too happy to turn two strips of freshly scraped vellum over to a pair of ruffian mercenaries. As they were Noble Khashtris's men and the request came from the Adviser to the Throne, he could hardly refuse. Soon Conan and Shubal, each with his back to the other, were painstakingly writing out descriptions. A mystified Arkhaurus waited with his patience on a short rein. His appearance was that of one just short of anger.

Pausing now and then to scan their memories for details or perhaps words, Shemite and Cimmerian dipped their quills frequently and scratched away. Each cursed more than once in a language different from that in which he wrote.

Conan finished first, and Shubal but moments after. Arkhaurus looked his enquiry at the Cimmerian, who bade Shubal read what he had written.

'Better I than Arkhaurus, with my spelling! "He is very old," ' Shubal read, haltingly as a boy even over his own just-inscribed words. ' "Most of his head is bald. His hair is white unto yellow and hangs down lank like a fringe. His skull has spots on it, sort of orangey-tan. So do his hands and he squints and I think he does not see well. His left eye droops. So does his mouth and it has deep lines around it. Teeth are yellowed and two are missing on the right . . ." '

'Above or below?' Conan interrupted.

'Below. "His moustache is white, and fuller on the left" – no, it's the right – "than on the left. He is terribly thin. His hair is yellowish with age and there is none on his hands at all and the veins are very large on the backs of them. They quiver." '

The Shemite looked up. He shrugged, finished.

Conan seemed to have paled. 'And that describes . . .'

'Sabaninus, lord Baron of Korveka, in Koth.'

'Look here, Conan, what is the purpose of this . . . boy's exercise?'

'Arkhaurus, there is sorcery here. A man said on yester day that Tor is a barony in Nemedia, not a duchy. Does Sergianus elevate his rank, or does he *not know*? And Shubal recognises his medallion – *my lord* Sergianus's; he saw it or its twin five years agone on the baron of Kothic Korveka.'

Arkhaurus heaved a sigh and gestured with both hands, palms up. 'What matter these niggling points?'

'This,' Conan said. 'Sergianus spoke just as the queen started to break the mirror of sorcery for me. At the instant my soul returned, I was looking at him. And . . . he *changed*. I saw another man there where he stood, in the same clothes and medallion. I have never been so far south-west even as Khauran City afore, and never seen Korveka's lord. But here is what I saw standing beside *your* queen on yester day, Queen's Adviser.'

And Conan read aloud from his own vellum:

' "A tall, lean, very *old* man with a bald crown dotted with age-spots and yellowish-white hair hanging down like a ragged curtain all around his head. His moustache, also aged white and now yellowing, has a gap on the right side; and his left eye, his moustache and his mouth all droop. Lines mark his face like gulleys, especially around the mouth, which is missing two lower teeth on the right. His hands quiver and great standing veins on their backs look like worms under the skin, which is hairless and shining. They are also marked with the same brownish-orange spots that dot his skull above the hairline. Finally, he has a small brown wart in the fold of his cheek beside his left nostril." '

'So has Baron Sabaninus!' Shubal practically shouted. 'That . . . what you wrote sounds just like him!' He scratched his chest. 'But how —'

'Sorcery,' Conan said.

'Impossible,' the Queen's Adviser said. 'Coincidence. That might describe many men of great age. What could the meaning be of such a situation? What can it matter?'

'It could matter to Khauran! Suppose that it means just this,' Conan said: 'that somehow a Kothic noble has been given the appearance of youth, and sent here — most likely by the king you say covets Khauran — to charm and wed your lonely queen.'

'To deliver Khauran to Koth!' Shubal burst out.

'Sorcery,' Conan said. 'And I, a victim of sorcery until yester day, was enabled to see through this spell at the instant of my deliverance from my own.'

The three men were staring at each other when Khashtris came rustling out among the particoloured columns, ready to return home.

As dusk shadowed the palace with rose and a deepening mauve within its chambers, Ialamis sat very close to Sergianus. He was discoursing on a proposal of Acrallidus. The young lord stared straight ahead; her eyes held their gaze as if fastened on his face, on his lips. Her lids dreamily shaded those dark eyes, but did not conceal their luminosity, their sparkle of love. Some slaves gazed so, at their masters.

Her knee moved ever so slightly to rest against his, and

he glanced at her. He spoke as if in accusation; certainly not as if to a queen:

'Ialamis! Are you hearing my words?'

'Yes,' she said softly. 'If you believe it is a bad idea, I will tell Acrallidus, and that will be an end to that.'

'You sound as if you're in a dream, a trance.'

'I am.'

'Can't you pay more attention to the concerns of your own realm?'

'Not while I am alone with you.'

'Can't you stop staring at me that way, woman?'

'No, Sergianus,' she said softly. 'Should I?'

He gave her thigh a careless pat, a fleeting touch. 'I must go.'

'Why?' she asked softly. She swayed closer and her lips remained parted.

He touched, only touched, her soft lips with his. His hands, clamping on her upper arms, held her back, as if at bay. 'Because I must,' Sergianus said, and rose and left the Queen of Khauran.

She stared dreamily after him, and she sighed.

The moment he was out of the room, Sergianus's face relaxed into a triumphant smile. *I have her!* he thought; *and with this pose of coolness, I'll soon hear her begging!* And he grinned, and went to his own palace chamber.

There awaited Arkhaurus, Adviser to the Queen of Khauran.

CHAPTER 7

Rosela . . . and Assassins

On the following evening Khashtris went to the palace to play at cards with the queen and others; she would remain overnight or be escorted home by royal guards. Conan and Shubal were at their ease for the night. They walked down to the tavern of Hilides.

Over the evening's first mug of ale, Conan was still stubbornly insisting that they'd been followed when the girl appeared in the tavern's doorway. She looked about fifteen. A childish mass of walnut-hued curls capped her head above a tiny-chinned heartshaped face with eyes like matched spheres of jasper. The flippy little yellow tunic that hardly covered her elfin body was torn so that one small shoulder was exposed. Conan saw that the wide-eyed girl was panting as if she had been running. Her gaze swiftly roved the interior of its patrons and abruptly she ran to Conan. Before he could so much as exclaim, she was on his knee with her arms around him.

'Please pretend I'm your girl and if a man follows me, look mean at him!'

Conan was more than willing to wrap an arm around her. It half covered her back all the way across, with room for his hand to hold her waist; indeed, his fingers lay on her narrow little belly.

A man did step into the doorway. He too panted as though he had been running; chasing. His eyes sought within the tavern; Conan glowered. The man clenched his teeth while he stared at the huge arm shielding the girl's back – and at the icy blue eyes that were like dagger blades, levelled at him over her shoulder. Grinding his teeth, the young fellow departed into the night.

Her name was Rosela and she was lovely, and a short time later Shubal departed for he had become as the third horse to a double-hitch; the Cimmerian obviously had in

Rosela all the company he needed. Last night Conan had been very alone. Tonight he felt no sympathy for Shubal. He did not even watch the Shemite's back as he left the tavern.

Seconds afterward, a cry arose outside. It had not faded before there followed the clangor of sharp blades. The diminutive Rosela slid off his knee as Conan rose with a curse.

His sword was in his hand before he reached the doorway.

A man lay dead or dying on the dim-lit street just outside; two others, masked, assaulted a fourth. He was Shubal, and he called Conan's name. That prompted one of his attackers to glance around.

The man turned in time to catch Conan's heavy side-armed stroke across the throat rather than the side of his neck. His severed jugular erupted and he staggered back five or six paces, looking astonished, before he fell.

Conan's and Shubal's swords struck the masked and cloaked second attacker at the same time, neck and belly.

Three men were down in their blood, and Conan had not so much as parried a stroke. He saw that blood came thickly from a nasty sword-bite in Shubal's left forearm. Thrusting the second wight through the middle, Shubal left his sword sheathed there, standing, while he clamped his hand above the cut on his other arm.

'Had to defend myself with something,' he said apologetically. 'It was get this arm hacked or lose half my face.'

'Just don't faint. Sit down.' Conan looked around to see a wide-eyed Rosela in the doorway. Other faces peered from behind her, all male. 'Push back through those goggle-eyed geese behind you,' Conan said in a feral snarl, 'and get a cup of wine out here. Out of her way, you behind her. Back!'

He turned back to find that Shubal was not sitting, but asquat beside the first fallen man. 'It's poor sour old Nebinio,' the Shemite said. 'They killed him just as I came out.'

The Nemedian, Conan thought, and looked up at a dancing light and the sound of men tramping and clanking. Four came, matching of arms and armour.

'Here! What goes on here? You two are both foreigners, aren't you?'

Seeing that they were men of the Khauran City Watch, Conan said, 'Why, yes,' and, feeling mean: 'Don't you like foreigners, then?' He squinted at the young man under the high-held lanthorn. *A strutter*, Conan thought. *So damned self-important in his uniform he's like a game-cock.*

'Not when I see what appear to be three corpses! Consider yourself under arrest.'

'Consider yourself in trouble if you make any other such noises, *sub*-prefect. I am Shubal and this is Conan, and we are bodyguards to the Noble Lady Khashtris who even *foreigners* know is cousin to *our* Queen Ialamis. Close your mouth and open your eyes and you will see that two of these men are masked. Is that a clue, *sub*-prefect, as to whom you might want to be detaining?'

Conan held his smile. He'd not seen Shubal handle himself so, before. He was impressed and pleased. The four men of the watch were standing silent; three stared at the subprefect, who appeared to be encountering considerable difficulty in getting his mouth closed.

At last he said, 'Shubal, you said?'

'I did. And Conan. I didn't quite hear your name.'

The man availed himself then of the opportunity to squat beside the man in the cloak; that way the name he muttered was not clear. Conan's glance met Shubal's. Shubal still clutched his wounded arm, the bloodflow from which had slackened. The two smiled.

'Masked, aye,' the squatting Watch squad's commander said. 'Dead, too. This your, uh, sword, uh, Shubal?'

'This one's dead, too, Prefect. Throat's slashed out.'

'Yes, it's my sword,' Shubal said.

The sub-prefect straightened. 'Thieves?'

'Assassins,' Shubal said through close-held teeth. 'They murdered this man. He isn't even armed.'

'You know any of them?'

'This is Nebinio, a Nemedian who's lived here for years and years, a worker in leather. Those two are still masked —here, Conan, what're you *doing*?'

'Be still,' Conan said, 'pouring this wine Rosela fetched on your wound. Rosela: you leave me now and I'll find you

171

and slit your throat! Hurt, Shubal? Good. Now we borrow part of the cloak of this killer and tie that arm up.'

'Here,' Rosela said, 'take a strip of my tunic. That cloak's filthy.'

'Crom's beard, girl, you almost aren't wearing it already! Be still, Shubal. Let the wine soak in. Good for wounds, wine is.'

'Frightful . . . waste,' Shubal gasped.

Rosela stayed; her tunic remained intact to be removed later by the Cimmerian; a strip of city Watch-man's sash, no less, bound up Shubal's arm; neither he nor anyone in the tavern recognised the unmasked bandits. The second to fall might have lived to be questioned, for all his bearing two wounds, had not Shubal sheathed his sword in the fellow's intestines to avoid dropping it or returning it un-wiped to its proper sheath. The sub-prefect handed Hilides a shiny Queenhead to cover 'whatever these two men have had this night' and gave Cimmerian and Shemite a hopeful look. The silver coin erased both their tabs altogether, but no one was of a mind to tell the sub-prefect so. When a man had made a mistake and wanted to expiate: let him! Conan and Shubal were asked, not told, to stop at the magistrate's any time on the morrow, to leave a statement. Murder had obviously been done, and justice in the form of self-defence. Still, this was not lawless Shadizar or the Mall of Arenjun, and the magistrate had his records to keep and reports to file with City Governor Acrallidus.

'Shubal,' Conan said, while the Watch moved away up the street, dragging corpses.

'Aye.'

'Feel up to walking?'

'Whither?'

'We are to escort you to the house of Sfalana, and then to . . . go our way. Think how the dear sweet melon-lady will want to nurse her wounded hero. On the morrow I will tell Noble Khashtris and darling Spartus of your wounding, so there will be no objection to your absence. Peradventure Khashtris will want to go and see the magistrate, herself.'

'Hm! But Sfalana may be abed by now . . .'

'How could she not rouse herself happily to take in a poor wounded man?'

'Ah-hmm. And you . . .'

'I am going to show Rosela the gardens behind our little home, Shubal.'

'Co-nan . . .'

'Hush, Rosela darling; say me nay and I'll search the city for that weasel who chased you into my arms – and give you back!'

'No no, dear boy, it's just that you're holding my hand and every time you emphasise a word you nigh squeeze it in twain!'

Shubal laughed and took up his place on her other side. 'To Sfalana's!'

'To Sfalana's and then to the garden!'

And so Conan and Rosela of Khauran escorted the wounded Shubal to the home of Sfalana, seller of fruits, and Conan took Rosela into the gardens of the Noble Khashtris, and showed her many things. And with his soul returned to him, and Rosela to hand, Conan let slip from his mind his nervousness and suspicions of the lord Sergianus of Nemedia – or of Koth? – and a week passed, and to the Cimmerian one afternoon fell a strange duty.

CHAPTER 8

Plot and Counterplot

It came about in this wise:

Rosela gained employment in the palace; Shubal's arm began healing nicely. Next, the queen honoured an agreement made months before; she rode down to some Khaurani town or other to join the priests in dedicating a new temple to Ishtar. With her went both Sergianus and Acrallidus. Khashtris would look after Princess Taramis.

At the last moment it was agreed that the child would remain in her own chambers rather than visit her cousin. Conan and Shubal accompanied Khashtris to the palace, with the Cimmerian feeling more dissatisfied than ever. The prospect of seeing Rosela did not help; he'd be with Khashtris and Shubal, guarding a six-year-old!

He only just saw Taramis, whom he'd never met — *if one 'meets' six-year-old pre-girls*, he thought sourly. Nor of course did she take any note of him; she had been surrounded by uniformed sword-wearers all her life and took less note of their faces than she did of individual spoons at meals. Shortly after her midday snack, Taramis became drowsy and Khashtris took her up for a nap.

The princess was provided with a suite of two rooms. While she slept, Conan was made no happier by having to sit with Shubal and Khashtris in the anteroom: the large chamber was all silk and satin and fluff, in white, pale yellow and green, the colours of Khauran. The Cimmerian proved no good student of the game with cards the two tried to teach him.

When Khashtris said she had business and departed, the men assumed it was to answer a call of nature. Shubal decided to go and see about a bit of wine; Conan enthusistically agreed and grimly remained. At least, the big morose youth thought, reduced to being nursemaid, the brat slept!

It was then that rescue arrived: into the room swayed

Rosela, smiling. She bore a man-sized goblet.

'Here, get that vast hand off me, lunk – this wine is from the queen's own supply! Drink before someone comes and I am punished for stealing. Ouch! I'm still tender there from the night before last!'

Wrinkling his features into a ridiculous expression, Conan sipped daintily. 'Hmm. Not a bad vintage,' he said, in an assumed voice that was supposed to mimic an effete esthete of the court. And then with a grin – while one hand remained intimately busy with Rosela – he drank it off. He lowered the emptied silver goblet and her upper garment, with a long sigh of satisfaction.

'And now, my dear girl, do taste this good wine from my lips!'

'Oh, Co-nan, you're such a –'

He was still kissing her when he collapsed.

Next Conan knew, Khashtris and Shubal were shaking and slapping him, bidding him wake. Foggily he saw that tears glistened on Khashtris's face. *What happened?* Suddenly he was lunging to his feet, staggering, and reaching for his sword. It was gone. Conan shot Shubal a confused look.

It was then that the dizzied Cimmerian saw the man who lay sprawled in blood on a fine green rug edged with cloth-of-gold. The fellow lay still – and his dead hand was fisted around Conan's sword! The Cimmerian reeled, glanced again at his employer and fellow guard, and sat down as suddenly as he'd risen.

'You've saved my life several times, Conan,' Shubal said. 'It is my pleasure to have saved yours.'

Conan stared. His head was far from clear.

'Shubal saved both you and the princess from that man,' Khashtris told him.

'You must have been drugged,' Shubal said, 'as the princess must have been, earlier. I came in to find this fellow on the point of skulking into her bedchamber, with your sword in his hand.'

Conan shook his head. *Drugged? Rosela?* 'Wh-y?'

'I'd say this wight meant to murder the princess and make it look as if you did it, my Cimmerian friend. See if you knew him.'

For several moments longer Conan stared dully at Shubal. Then he slid down to one knee beside the man whose blood ruined a royal carpet. Without care or that ridiculous 'respect for the dead' he had first heard of here in 'civilised' Khauran, Conan twisted the fellow's head around. A corpse stared glassily.

'He . . . he is famil . . . I have seen him befo – Shubal! This is the man who followed Rosela that night she came fleeing into the tavern!'

'Ah. Well, it wasn't Rosela he was after today!'

Conan extricated his sword from the man's hand, which had not yet constricted in that final stony grip. He stood and sheathed the weapon. 'Rosela came in just after you left,' he said. 'She brought me wine – in a silver cup.'

'It isn't here now, Conan,' Shubal said quietly. 'And she wasn't here when I entered.' Shubal shook his head. 'It looks as if your meeting with her was no accident. She and this man arranged it. You were – we were both taken in.'

'The same night someone murdered that Nemedian and tried to kill you.'

'And today, Taramis,' Khashtris said, actually wringing her hands. 'Why?'

Conan was grinding his teeth. He thought on Rosela, realising how he had been duped; how she had hurled herself into his arms, most literally, and had since trysted with him again and again. *All the while only gaining my confidence, to use me!* And she had. Because of her, Taramis should be dead and Conan accused; the big *barbarian* no one really knew anything about!

'She was someone's tool, as was this.' Conan's foot thumped the man Shubal had slain. 'And those two who murdered the Nemedian . . . Nebinio . . . *who knew there is no Duke of Tor in Nemedia!*'

'Aye,' Shubal said, nodding grim-faced. 'Aye, my friend. Remember our "writing lesson". You were noticed staring at *him* – who must somehow be Sabaninus . . . and you are a danger to him. So, the heir to the throne is killed, giving the queen even more reason and need to seek solace, and wed again. And should she . . . *die*, she'd leave *him* or *his* heir as ruler of Khauran! While you, foreigner, are safely and legally slain for a most horrible murder!'

Khashtris was pleading: What are you TALKing about? Who is HE?'

'The deaths, then,' Conan said, 'are of equal importance to him, and to someone else . . . his Khaurani confederate!'

'But WHY!' Khashtris demanded, streaming tears. 'Who?'

Her bodyguards looked at each other. They nodded in mutual decision; they told Khashtris. They told her all of it. She sank down on the couch strewn with yellow pillows.

'Ishtar!' she hissed, barely audible. 'And when I saw Rosela hurrying so, I wondered what you had done to her, Conan!'

'Saw her? Where?'

'Going – going out into the garden.'

Grinding his teeth, the Cimmerian left them. His head was trying to swim as he stalked through the palace on tingling legs. Angrily, he pinched his forearm, again and again. Blood showed there when he emerged into the spacious garden behind the palace. He did not call out; he searched. He was several minutes finding Rosela, who was in a far corner amid a little grove of some low evergreens clipped to resemble horse-heads.

She lay on the ground. She had been stabbed more than once, low.

'Oh . . . Co-nan . . .'

He crouched beside her, without touching her. His eyes and voice were intense. 'Tell me all of it, Rosela. You'll not recover from those stomach wounds. Tell me, or I'll see that you die in worse pain than you know now.'

'K-kill me-e, Conan . . .'

'Who, Rosela?'

'Ark . . . Arkhaurus. He hired my brother and me . . . that night. I was to . . . gain your confi . . . dence . . .'

'You did, bitch. The very Adviser to the Queen, is it? And today?'

'He knew of the queen's trip. He had me employed here. It was he . . . oh! Hurts, Conan . . . he who arranged that th-the princess would stay here, so you would come with N-Noble Khashtris. Taramis's . . . snack was . . . drugged.

177

And the wine I . . . fetched you. Sorry, Conan, sorry . . .'

'Of course you are. The rest of it. Arkhaurus stabbed you?'

'My brother Nardius was to . . . kill the princess, with your . . . sword.' She was having more difficulty talking. 'We were to be *rich*,' Arkhaurus said. He met me here. Instead . . . in . . . stead . . .'

'Instead he met you where you were to be congratulated and paid, and paid you with sharp steel, did he? The dog didn't even do a clean job, but belly-stabbed you and left you to die slowly. You weren't a confederate to be made rich, Rosela. You were hired help, and you know more than you should. So – he disposed of you.'

She lay staring up at him, and tears slid down towards her ears. And then her mouth and eyes went wide and she was rigid, all over. That spasm ended only with the sighing release of her last long breath.

Conan rose from the fifteen-year-old temptress and monster he had told himself was his woman, and he vowed not to love again, to be wary and but use girls where he found them, and he left her there, dead, without closing her eyes.

The three decided to say nothing of the attempt. Who knew aside from Arkhaurus?

'Let me just spit him,' Conan said, looking ugly, 'and we can put Rosela's brother there, as if he killed Arkhaurus, and we came too late, but slew him. Before he died, he implicated Sergianus . . .'

'Conan, no!' Khashtris strode about, gnawing her lips, wringing her hands until they were red. 'No! This is the palace of Khauran! My cousin is involved – I think the poor dear girl loves Sergianus!'

'Suppose you invite him to dinner,' the Cimmerian gritted, 'and I will "go berserk" and kill him! The queen will be spared knowing what we know – and saved, along with Khauran. All you need do is give me a little time to be far from here.'

'You – you'd take it all on yourself?'

'Why not? I am a foreigner, and what holds me here? I want away from this accured queendom, Khashtris. I do owe a debt to Queen Ialamis . . . you think I mind the blood of Arkhaurus and Sergianus on these hands?' He held them up and stared ferally over his fingertips. 'I want their blood there!'

But no, and Khashtris convinced them. They removed the body of Rosela's brother, in cloaks. Khashtris, after mopping and mopping the rug with her own hands, at last sliced her forearm; she'd say the remaining bloodstains were hers, after she'd accidentally cut herself. And she would talk with her cousin. Conan would not remain in the palace, saying that if he saw Arkhaurus, he'd surely kill him.

He drank much that night.

Two days later, Khashtris talked with the queen, alone. She returned unhappily to report to her two fellow conspirators.

'She wanted only to talk of Sergianus, dear Sergianus,' Khashtris told them. 'I tried to tell her. I tried. I could not. She has agreed to see you two, though she does not know why.'

Conan and Shubal looked at each other, and nodded. An overwrought Khashtris wanted Conan that night, and he refused her.

CHAPTER 9

A Wolf is Loose in Khauran

Conan and Shubal had audience with the queen, and tried to tell her what they knew and thought they knew. She would not believe. She was horrified at the very thought; she would not listen; she ordered them from her and told them they were no longer welcome in the palace. For tomorrow night's dinner, she would send her own guards to escort her cousin to her.

The two men stalked from the palace. 'We must confide in Acrallidus,' Shubal said. 'Gods! Will no one *believe*!'

'Easier if I just go and shove steel through that damned charmer Sergianus or Sabaninus or whatever his treacherous name is . . . she *loves* that demon!'

'How did you feel about Rosela?'

'Shut up, Shubal!'

Shubal sighed and faced his friend, there in the square betwixt lofting palace and imposing temple. 'No, Conan. Don't think of it. You would never escape the palace. We are suspect, now. The queen will never let us near him! Come, listen; stop staring at walls and thinking foolishly of scaling them! We must sit down with Acrallidus, who is wise, and with Khashtris. We four must plan. He will believe. He must; he is our only hope.'

'Our best hope lies in our sheaths, Shubal.'

'Damn it, *barbarian* – must you think only of leaving trails of blood wherever you go?'

Conan stared at him, and after a while Shubal apologised, and Conan agreed to share their knowledge and suspicions with City Governor Acrallidus.

'But how?' the queen's governor of her capital city wondered aloud, once he'd heard their story. He looked around Khashtris's most private chamber as though tapestried walls might provide the answer. 'How can this Baron Sabaninus make himself younger, or look younger, or –'

'– steal a younger man's body?' Conan suggested. His eyes were beginning to blaze. Talk, talk, and talk. He was tired of talk. His patience was like a wolf on a leash.

'And the way he came here, afoot, tattered, bloodied –'

'None of the blood was his own. He rode up from Koth. Koth, Acrallidus, with two retainers – and he killed them! As he smote, their blood splashed him. Then he drove off his own horses, and tore his own clothing and rolled in the filth. Thus he was a pitiful object to be taken to the queen, helped, sympathised with – damn!' Conan slapped the table around which they sat, and silver-chased goblets of bronze danced and sloshed mulled wine. 'You people, you so-civilised people, have you no power to suspect? Have you no ability to believe? It is SORCERY! By Ishtar and Crom and Bel and . . . Erlik, do you who are victims of a demon's curse on your very queen . . do you not see? Believe! It is *sorcery*!'

Conan pounced to his feet and paced from them. He wheeled. He had become a great impatient wolf, eyes aflame, every muscle poised to pounce and fight.

'Listen! You three smugly civilised people with your walls and marble halls and magistrates and your clack-clack shoes and swirly robes and ridiculous coiffures – listen! Give listen to one you call *barbarian*, who was born on a battle-field and has been warrior and thief and has lost and regained his very soul, of sorcery . . . and who has sent off to join the Lord of Death enough men to staff your very palace!'

And he told them of the battle of Venarium in which he'd fought at fifteen, and how he had fought and defeated a dead thing in a crypt because he wanted its sword; he told them of Yara of Arenjun and the elephant-creature in his Tower of Sorcery, creature from the starry gulf beyond the world; and of the dark wizard Hisarr Zul, and his brother who lived on, as sand – '*Sand!*' – even ten years after his death, and how he had bested them both. He showed them the clay amulet he wore pendent on his chest, and he told them what it was. And they listened.

'Now we know what we know. We cannot be wrong! Arkhaurus and Sergianus plot together, and they know I know, and Shubal – and now they must assume you know too, Khashtris! Sergianus does not know this amulet, or what it is. He does not know but that I am a sorcerer – we have twice escaped his snares, Shubal and I! I, Conan, foreigner and *barbarian* as you civilised folk say – I see now how to make that demon expose himself. You have only to aid me. *Do it!*'

Three staring products of the civilisation of the west, almost in shock, as if under the Cimmerian's spell, agreed.

'Shubal and I are banned from the palace. We'll not be permitted to enter with you at tomorrow night's dinner – at which we all assume that *your* queen assuredly intends to announce her betrothal to a trickster determined to hand *your* land over to Koth. Khashtris: Shubal and I need your help in getting into the palace. We may have to down a royal guardsman or two, but that is small price for Khauran itself!'

She looked about at the robed man with brown hair and grey beard, and at the Shemite mercenary from a warrior clan; they sat as if enthralled, gazing at the youthful Cimmerian – a warrior and the manager of a city waiting to be instructed; told, led. Khashtris swallowed.

If only I'd had such a son . . . if only he were my son . . . if only I could bear his . . . if only I were younger!

Ishtar! Acrallidus was thinking. *A wolf is loose in Khauran – and he fights for Khauran!*

This man will lead armies some day, Shubal was thinking. *I hope I am there to see and to participate!*

Khashtris spoke. 'We will be in the Ashkaurian Room,' she said. 'It is used as a smaller dining-room, and Ialamis loves it. It is also your means of entry. A secret palace escape route leads off it, through the pantry. You two will enter that way.' She thought a moment. 'Shubal: you must make straight for the dragon-carved door and secure it against the royal guards. Conan –'

'Conan,' Conan said low, almost snarling, 'will see to the rest.'

CHAPTER 10

Conan Magus

All present at the queen's dinner party remarked how she was dressed as a girl, and looked younger. Almost shockingly, her hair was down and bound by a fillet of silver that held a flashing sapphire on her forehead. Pearl-sewn bands of gold encircled both forearms and each wrist was braceleted in silver set with amethysts. Otherwise, she wore above the hips only a pearl-sewn bandeau of white silk imported from afar, supported by a neck-strap of woven cloth-of-gold. Her lowslung skirt was side-slit nearly to the hipband, from which depended plackets of black cloth that were scintillantly alive with rubies and garnets, sapphires and carnelians, topazes and emeralds, and a single great piece of amethyst.

Her happiness and brightness infectiously carried to most of her guests: Arkhaurus and his so-thin wife, once of Koth; Sergianus the Nemedian dukeson whose tunic and overtunic were both sleeveless to display his youthful arms; the two lord cousins of the queen, and the wife of one. Present too, though less festive, were Noble Khashtris and Governor Acrallidus and his wife.

Servants passed to and from the pantry bearing dish after savoury dish to set before the diners, whose goblets of gold were kept filled with several wines of fine vintage and bouquet.

Khashtris waited nervously. No untoward sound emerged from the pantry; Conan and Shubal did not come. She had taken leave of them at her home, after forcing upon each a little figurine of Ishtar, for Khashtris was a believer. Her heart thudded and she was hot and prickly. Already she had drunk too much wine to assuage her thirst; it was exerting the opposite effect now, drying her mouth already dry with apprehension.

At last the fruit was brought, and the queen arose.

Khashtris gripped the table's edge, awaiting the terrible announcement of betrothal. It did not come. Telling them happily that she had as unique entertainment the illusionist Crispis from down in Kandala, Ialamis clapped her hands. The tall door of carven wood, edged with filigree in bronze, was opened from without.

The diners gaped at the advent of the illusionist. Crispis was an uncommon tall man, and apparently a burly one as well, though he was swallowed within a great black robe like a tent. Its hood was up and within could be seen only shadows, darkness and the tip of a nose – and the great dark brown beard that flowed forth. He wore a single black glove; the left sleeve of his robe dangled loose and empty.

'I smell . . . horse,' Arkhaurus's wife whispered, and was shushed by her husband.

The only break in the darkness of Crispis's appearance drew every gaze. The amulet lay on his chest just below the beard, a small golden sword-shape set with a topaz at the end of each bar of its guard; they were like eyes.

'Welcome,' the queen said, seating herself, 'O Master Crispis! Though I have not seen you before now, I have heard naught but praise of your skills.'

The tall robe bowed, straightened. A gloved hand rose to finger the amulet. When the voice emerged from the cowl, it was so deep as to be obviously artificial, and one or two of Ialamis's guests smiled.

'Crispis will amaze you with his knowledge of yourselves, Lady Queen and noble guests, with the aid of the twin all-seeing eyes of the magic amulet: the Eye of Erlik! Ah! Already I perceive that the glorious Queen of Khauran contemplates the making of an important announcement! Fear not; Crispis will say no more of it, for the revelation is yours to make.'

While he bowed, Ialamis and Sergianus exchanged a look, and smiled.

Again the gloved hand fingered the amulet. 'Oho . . . Noble K – Noble Khashtris, is it not? A woman of softness and sentiment and religious beliefs! I see that you wear concealed an image of Ishtar . . . though far from Crispis to name the place wherein you have it tucked. It belonged to your mother.'

184

Though she blushed and tried to smile, the importunities of the others coaxed Khashtris to confirm the seer's words: she produced from between her breasts the little figurine Conan and Shubal had seen her tuck there. Now she wondered: in what dark closet was poor Crispis of Kandala bound and gagged, and what horse had given up much of its mane to provide the beard that flowed from the cowl of the black robe?

'How now!' Arkhaurus called, smiling, and lifted his goblet to Crispis. 'We have with us a seer indeed – and well upbrought, too!'

While others chuckled, Crispis spoke: 'Aye, O lord, for with the aid of this amulet from the mages of far Iranistan, Crispis sees all. I see you, great adviser to a queen enthroned, riding a high-stepping horse. It is a Kothic horse and bears Koth's arms, I see . . . and why is my lord's table dagger dripping with blood?'

All were silent. Arkhaurus had gone red as Khashtris had been, save for his knuckles. They were white around his goblet. He stared down at the jewelled eating utensil on his plate. Its blade was unsmeared.

'Cryptic seer,' Acrallidus said. 'Plan you a trip to Koth, Lord Arkhaurus?'

'I do *not!*'

'Ah,' Crispis said, drawing it out until he had regained their attention. 'Perhaps I see awrong. Yet beside you on another horse, a royal palfrey of Koth, I see riding an old, old man. Dry as dust he is, thin, shaky of hands, bald of crown yet with strings of hair hanging down like a fringe of yellowish white. A man two of whose lower foreteeth are missing. A man wearing a medallion . . . ah. Your pardon my good lord. I'd not seen you sitting there next the queen, in the blaze of her glory. The congratulations of Crispis on how well you bear the weight of your many, many years, and even the baronial weight of that medallion of Korveka.'

'What means he? You, Lord Sergianus?'

'Korveka?'

'Speaks he to young *Sergianus?*'

'See here, Crispis . . . '

'Ah! Now I see the source of the blood on your dagger, Lord Adviser to the Queen . . . it is that of a girl . . . a tool,

185

helpless and young . . . wait, do not speak, her name comes
—Ah! Rosela!'

Arkhaurus half rose; amid deadly silence, Crispis's voice
asked a question. 'My good lord Baron Sabaninus of Koth
. . . why call you yourself "Sergianus", and pretend to be
young? Behold – when I cover all my amulet and even the
eyes, all here see you as you really are!'

Gone pale, Sergianus could only sit stiffly, looking back
at staring eyes; the eyes of everyone at table, their gazes
fixed on him . . .

Then the queen rose. 'What means this?'

She spoke to Crispis. Poor Sergianus, already believing
that his true form had somehow been made visible to all,
made the logical error; he assumed that she spoke to him.

'It means this Crispis must be a – a – some sort of spy!'
Sergianus cried desperately, while he rose. From a side slit
in the long-skirted overtunic he drew a sword, and rushed
down-table on its left, towards the black-robed magus. 'I'll
have that amulet, dog!'

The pantry door swept open. 'No, Sabaninus of Koth,'
Shubal said, 'you'll have what you deserve, Kothic plotter
against Khauran!'

Perhaps the game was not quite up until then; Sergianus
of course remained Sergianus. Arkhaurus's hand snatched
up his dagger, and he swung, and drove it into Shubal's
thigh. 'Meddling Shemite!' Shubal groaned aloud; the
blade caught in muscle and while Arkhaurus strove to free
it, Shubal twitched his sword so that it touched the neck
of my lord Arkhaurus.

'Release the blade, traitor,' the Shemite said. 'It can
remain where it is. Others will remain still, else I slit the
throat of this mis-adviser!'

All in the room froze; Sergianus already had, at the
sudden bursting of Shubal among them. Now he returned
his attention to Crispis – who, having slit his robe up the
front with the dagger he held within, left-handed, threw
back his cowl. He dropped the robe to reveal a huge young
man in a mail corselet.

'It's – that barbarian!'

'Conan!'

'You!'

'Khashtris!' the queen cried. What means thi – guards!'

Conan kicked violently backward. The door slammed and his dagger-hand swung back to drop the heavy bar into its brace. A moment later the door was struck by a shoulder on its other side; it did not yield. This room was haven and means of escape in the event of siege, and the bar was of iron.

Sergianus drove at the Cimmerian. Pouncing away, Conan whipped up his own sword and struck hard. Sergianus was able to dodge the stroke, and a moment later Crispis's 'beard' was thrown at his face.

'Here, my lord of Korveka – a gift from a horse!'

While Sergianus fought away the mass of hair, Conan pounced far to his right, and sent his blade skimming over the head of a woman who shrieked and fainted. Had he intended his point for her, she's have been bloody rather than with her face in her gravy; the first inch of Conan's blade drove just where he had aimed: into the throat of Arkhaurus.

'For Rosela, murdering traitor – I feared Shubal would steal you from me!'

Arkhaurus's wife shrieked. Sergianus, recovered, swung high his blade and began his swing as he pounced at Conan. The Cimmerian's sword clanged off the Kothian's; both men staggered and Conan went to one knee – and his left hand flashed up to embed a foot of his dagger's blade in Sergianus's belly.

Every breath was held while Sergianus stood very still, so rigid that he quivered all over.

'He's DEAD!' Arkhaurus's wife screamed into the silence. 'O Ishtar, no, NO, my love! It was not WORTH it! I BEGGED you not to ally yourself with that Korvekan impostor! O Ishtar help me – why did I not tell the queen when first you and he plotted? My lord is dead,' she wailed, hugging a seated corpse, 'dead . . . a traitor!'

Sergianus remained standing, shaking as though caught in an icy wind. Conan's left arm twisted viciously and he withdrew his dagger. A splash of blood followed, and continued freely flowing.

'Not – enough,' Shubal gritted, and dropped his sword. With a grunt he plucked the dagger from his leg, swiftly dragged its bloody tip across the front of his tunic, reversed it, and slammed it at Sergianus with all his strength. His leg scarlet to the ankle, Shubal begin sliding down, his back against the pantry door.

The slippery knife did not fly true. Not its point but its pommel struck Sergianus, in the temple. The sound of impact was loud, and followed by the queen's scream. She came rushing down the aisle formed between wall and table, opposite Shubal. New cries and a scream rose, for as Sergianus began to fall – he changed.

The weeping, moaning queen reached the fallen man just in time to look down upon . . . not Sergianus, but the old, old man described by 'Crispis'. Who had slain him, whether Conan or Shubal, was unknown and unimportant; the fact was that he was dead, and in death Sabaninus resumed his own form. He stared up from rheumy old eyes at the queen he had duped, but he did not see her.

Slowly Ialamis looked up at Conan.

'He is the Baron of Korveka in Koth, my lady Queen,' he told her. 'Through some sorcery he took on younger appearance, and assumed a title and name; Tor of Nemedia is not even a duchy. I saw him as he was my first day here, at the instant of my soul's returning to my body. He and Arkhaurus plotted together; your treacherous adviser's *Kothic* wife will tell you the story. Only Shubal prevented their agents, Rosela and her brother Nardius, from killing the princess while you were away. You restored to me my soul, Queen of Khauran; I return to Khauran its soul!'

'I wish I'd never seen you. Get away from that door.'

In mute surprise, Conan did so. She seized the bar. When he sought to aid her, she threw her weight against him, wrenched free, and unbarred the door herself. Poised guards nearly fell, finding their swords-drawn rush blocked by their liege-lady.

'Sergianus was a Kothic impostor and Arkhaurus a traitor in league with him,' she told the uniformed men, in a flat, dull voice that might have emerged from a sarcophagus. 'Conan and Shubal have saved the realm. Call my physician to attend Shubal at once. Take your orders from Noble Khashtris.'

And she was gone in a rush of sideslit skirts and flashing legs.

Thus was Khashtris occupied for a time, ere she could hurry from the others and rush to her cousin's apartment. A leech hurried in to bend over Shubal; guardsmen removed corpses with Arkhaurus's widow still clinging to him, weeping.

'You've saved us all, Conan,' Acrallidus said. 'Ye gods – and our poor accursed queen thought she had found happiness at last – with that!'

Conan glanced at the soles of Sergianus/Sabaninus's boots as he was carried from the chamber. 'You must counsel her close and be as her father, Acrallidus.'

Acrallidus sighed. 'And you, Conan. You must remain with us, close to us, protecting the queen so that she knows she is secure . . . and her daughter, our future queen. Were Khauran to fall into dispute or a queen to die heirless . . . Kothic troops would be here within weeks!'

'But,' Conan began, 'I –'

He was interrupted by the sound of a shriek of horror and sorrow. Both men rushed, trailed by confused palace guards, to the apartment of the queen. They discovered that it was Khashtris they'd heard; she sat on the floor with her royal cousin's head in her lap. Just under her pearl-glistening bandeau of soft white silk, Queen Ialamis had stabbed herself.

'Only Sergianus,' Ialamis said in a tiny voice, 'gave me reason to live. I end this . . . miserable life. Ac-Acrallidus . . .' She shuddered. 'Good Acrallidus, counsel a-and guide Tar-amis for – uh! – for she will need you sorely. I . . . regret only tha-at I l-eave her . . . alone. Perhaps she . . . she and your K-rallides . . .' She broke off again, coughing blood. 'Co-Conan . . . I suppose you saved Khaurannn. But . . . but I – *I'd* have been ha . . . hap-peee . . .' Again she shuddered, and her head fell aside in death.

The smoke from a score of censers eddied from the temple of Ishtar, mingling with the mournful sound of the priests. Beneath the temple, in the Royal Mausoleum, Ialamis had joined her husband and unhappy ancestors. Down the broad steps paced Conan, towering over the woman at his side. Her hair was down, but covered in the white homespun veil of Khaurani mourning.

She spoke. 'Nothing will change your mind, will it?'

'No.'

She looked up at his face. 'Oh, damn you! How I wish you were older or I younger!'

'I am glad we are as we are, Khashtris, for I would love you, and I have much of the world to see ere I and a woman say words before some priest.'

'Thank your gods for that. You have re-covered that amulet with clay.'

'Yes. The Eye of Erlik has no power for me, but only for a ruler I'll not tell you of. It was I deluded Sabaninus, not the amulet. Even Crispis has forgiven me, once I remembered to go and free him and you gave him that nicely clinking bag. This amulet has served its purpose for Khauran. Now I leave Khauran, and I must have the Eye of Erlik thus again: disguised.'

At the foot of the steps, she halted. 'Take this.' Into his hand she placed a half-circle of silver: a Queenhead cut in half. 'The other half of this will be worn around the neck of her you may have made a *happy* queen of Khauran – eventually: Taramis. I will see to it. She will know of you. You will ever be able to find employment here, though I – I –' She closed his hand over the bit of metal. 'Though I am gone.'

Funeral or no, Noble Lady Khashtris or no, Conan was about to embrace her when he heard the voice of Acrallidus: 'Conan! I need to talk with you!'

Conan turned to face the man, green-robed and white-veiled. 'No need, Acrallidus. I will not remain in this shadowed kingdom . . . queendom. Shadizar may be called the City of Wickedness, but I am no saint, and my horses are ready. I ride west and north – now.' He affected not to notice the ring Khashtris was sliding on to his finger.

'But –'

'He will not be convinced, Acrallidus,' Khashtris said. 'I understand. And Shubal, too, understands; I think he would leave me to go with you were he hale, Conan. He lost much blood and must rest for a week at least.'

'Oh — he and I have a terrible bill at the tavern of one Hilides, Khashtris. Fifty Queenheads, I think.'

She looked at him, knowing he lied. 'I will give Shubal the money to pay it, Conan. I hope it doesn't end in the hands of a certain pedlar of fruits! As for you — hold on to that coin, Conan — that half-coin.'

'I will keep it,' Conan said, and thought, *or try to.* 'I will keep it, and remember. Mayhap some day I will return to Khauran, to see how fares Queen Taramis. I know you and Acrallidus will guide her well; for now, Khauran is your responsibility. I am for Shadizar, home of cults and wine and women . . . two of which are more to my liking than poor curse-haunted Khauran and service to a child enthroned.'

The Cimmerian turned and walked away towards the bored boy who's minded his horses these past several hours. Conan was a little bit older, and a little bit wiser, and he had his soul. As for his ever returning to Khauran of the Unhappy Queens . . . who could know?'

A SELECTION OF TITLES FROM SPHERE

FICTION

STILL MISSING	Beth Gutcheon	£1.75 □
INHERITORS OF THE STORM	Victor Sondheim	£4.95 □
NIGHT PROBE!	Clive Cussler	£1.95 □
CHIMERA	Stephen Gallagher	£1.75 □
PALOMINO	Danielle Steel	£1.75 □

FILM & TV TIE-INS

ON THE LINE	Anthony Minghella	£1.25 □
FAME	Leonore Fleischer	£1.50 □
FIREFOX	Craig Thomas	£1.75 □
GREASE II	William Rotsler	£1.25 □
CONAN THE BARBARIAN	L. Sprague de Camp & Lin Carter	£1.25 □

NON-FICTION

BEFORE I FORGET	James Mason	£2.25 □
TOM PILGRIM: AUTOBIOGRAPHY OF A SPIRITUALIST HEALER	Tom Pilgrim	£1.50 □
YOUR CHILD AND THE ZODIAC	Teri King	£1.50 □
THE SURVIVOR	Jack Eisner	£1.75 □

All Sphere books are available at your local bookshop or newsagent, or can be ordered direct from the publisher. Just tick the titles you want and fill in the form below.

Name _____

Address _____

_____

Write to Sphere Books, Cash Sales Department, P.O. Box 11, Falmouth, Cornwall TR10 9EN

Please enclose a cheque or postal order to the value of the cover price plus:

UK: 45p for the first book, 20p for the second book and 14p for each additional book ordered to a maximum charge of £1.63.

OVERSEAS: 75p for the first book plus 21p per copy for each additional book.

BFPO & EIRE: 45p for the first book, 20p for the second book plus 14p per copy for the next 7 books, thereafter 8p per book.

Sphere Books reserve the right to show new retail prices on covers which may differ from those previously advertised in the text or elsewhere, and to increase postal rates in accordance with the PO.